"CLAY, THERE'S NO GIVING IN. YOU DISAPPEARED FOR ALMOST SEVEN YEARS!"

"I have a different life now. I like my life. I don't intend to let you destroy it," Cat said.

"You little witch," he muttered, reaching for her arm again. "I'm trying to keep *you* from destroying your own life."

"Really?" Cat murmured sarcastically. "You seem to have a funny way of going about it. And please take your hand off me."

Clay's scowl deepened. Cat felt herself being pulled forward. He was sliding his arms around her waist, pressing her close, bringing his lips down on hers. Her senses took flight when his mouth touched hers. An inferno seemed to erupt as if from an explosion within. She wanted nothing more than to part her lips to the searing persuasion of his. . . .

CANDLELIGHT ECSTASY ROMANCES ®

HOURS TO CHERISH

Heather Graham

A CANDLELIGHT ECSTASY ROMANCE ®

Published by
Dell Publishing Co., Inc.
1 Dag Hammarskjold Plaza
New York, New York 10017

Dell ® TM 681510, Dell Publishing Co., Inc.
Candlelight Ecstasy Romance®, 1,203,540, is a registered
trademark of Dell Publishing Co., Inc., New York, New
York.

ISBN: 0-440-13780-2

Printed in the United States of America
First printing—May 1984

For sea escapes, the Caribbean, Piña coladas,
and old friends: Robert A., Bob R., Beth,
and, of course, Dennis

To Our Readers:

We have been delighted with your enthusiastic response to Candlelight Ecstasy Romances®, and we thank you for the interest you have shown in this exciting series.

In the upcoming months we will continue to present the distinctive sensuous love stories you have come to expect only from Ecstasy. We look forward to bringing you many more books from your favorite authors and also the very finest work from new authors of contemporary romantic fiction.

As always, we are striving to present the unique, absorbing love stories that you enjoy most—books that are more than ordinary romance.

Your suggestions and comments are always welcome. Please write to us at the address below.

Sincerely,

The Editors
Candlelight Romances
1 Dag Hammarskjold Plaza
New York, New York 10017

PROLOGUE

In the heat of the night he was running, running.

A low-lying ground fog shielded him, putting him on another plane of reality, as if he were racing on a treadmill through endless clouds. The sound of his breathing was heavy, an agonized rasping that ripped from his body in heaving gasps. It was all that he heard except for the ceaseless fall of his own feet, rhythmic slaps that were each a spiked rod of pain creeping upward through abused muscles that refused to grow numb. A new sound permeated his mind. Although distant, the raucous clamor was unmistakable—the frenzied barks and yelps and bays of the hounds.

Suddenly, blessed numbness seemed to come. He was lifted into the clouds of the mist, the world became silent. He was still running, but his movement was effortless. . . . And ahead of him, he saw her.

She too seemed to be clothed in the mist, an ethereal figure; the long sable hair that had long haunted his dreams fluttered around her like rich sea waves, a luxurious enticement. And as he had often dreamed, she beckoned to him . . . she knew him, she smiled in sweet, seductive greeting. . . .

He ran faster toward her, remembering the liquid beguilement and the spirited rages that could glimmer in her sea-emerald eyes. When he reached her, he would be home. . . .

He lifted his arms in the mist; he was close, so close. But suddenly he was moving in slow motion in the dead silence of the mist. He reached, and reached, but she was slipping away. . . .

Sound returned to his world with the chaotic shrieking, shouting, and fevered baying of the dogs, pierced by maddening growls. And just as sound returned, so did pain. He could run no more; his legs buckled to the spiked agony that assailed his every footfall.

The dogs were upon him. He could feel the bloodlust in the hot, fetid breath that was an inferno against his skin. He waited for the tear of their jagged teeth. But it was Lopez who had found him tonight. Even as he clenched his eyes, braced himself against the onslaught, the shouts continued; the dogs were called off. He stiffened against the inevitable as he was dragged to his feet, closed off his mind to the furious spate of reproach and abuse. He could do nothing else but tolerate with a numb silence the brutality that followed. . . . Thank God Lopez was half human.

But it still meant a return to the pit. A four-by-four space of eternal darkness. Pitch darkness, and sizzling, incredible heat. When the noonday sun rose, sweat would race in rivulets down his entire body, his blood seeming to boil. Even the strongest man could be broken after a few days of such torture. And the break would come all at once. He would open his mouth and scream and scream and scream. . . .

He awoke in a cold sweat, and it took him several seconds to assimilate his actual surroundings.

And then he realized that although his body was drenched, he hadn't screamed. Not this time. The nightmare, which he hadn't had in some time now, was ebbing, slowly, slowly, releasing its tenacious hold.

He rose from the bed and left his cabin, seeking a cleansing from the sea air. On deck he stepped past the tools and rewards of his trade: scuba gear, air blowers, ropes, chains, and sealed cases. They had finished up out here today, he thought, perhaps that was why the dream had come.

The night was black velvet on the choppy open sea. A brisk wind had picked up from the west, but he barely noticed. He breathed deeply as his hair was furiously whipped across his forehead and savored the feeling of the cooling wind on his heated flesh.

Quit fooling yourself, he thought wryly. He knew why the dream had come. They had been talking about her today; Luke had been reporting everything he knew about the situation at the cay.

10

He had waited and watched for so long, a tentative phantom in the shadows, almost a child who trembled with indecision. He could wait no longer. Not with things moving the way they were; not when she continued to haunt his dreams, his sleeping moments . . . his waking moments. He could merely close his eyes and see her . . . working, standing, sitting, breathing . . . that mystical cloak of sleek dark hair, those eyes that were the enigma of the sea, so often raised to his in glimmering challenge, yet never failing to beguile.

Rather than return to his sweat-drenched sheets, he lay down upon the deck, lacing his hands behind his head as he stared up at the few stars dotting the eternity of black-velvet dark. He felt the night wind with every pore, just as he felt the sea move beneath him. The cool rolling action was soothing.

It was time to go home. Very soon it would be summer. He smiled for a moment, his memories dry with a sad and strange amusement. They had been so young, and although many human factors didn't change, their follies had been those follies of youth.

Summer.

It was only fitting.

It was the season of the sea witch.

CHAPTER ONE

The islanders called her Cat.

A tall woman, she was lithe and beautiful in a way that endeared her to those who knew her. Laughing as she stood upon the dock, her deeply bronzed legs sturdy and shapely—sailor's legs—and sneaker-clad feet set firmly apart, she was the epitome of radiant health. Her hair, long and deep sable and touched by the gold of the sun, was swept into a simple ponytail that reached almost to her waist. She wore no makeup, for she would be facing the salt spray of the ocean and the whipping wind of the breeze at full sail. Although she wasn't consciously aware of it, she was one of the rare women who needed no complement to her natural coloring. Her cheeks wore the rose blush of perfect health and tone. Her eyes were a brilliant emerald green, fringed by thick lashes as dark and lustrous as her hair.

Her name was Catherine Miller—*Mrs.* Catherine Miller, although the islanders had little memory of Mr. Miller. Cat had always been part of the island. She had been born there and raised there, and although she had gone away to school in the States, she had always returned, loving the simple, carefree ways of the islands, loving the quiet life of easy dignity she lived with her father—a historian and scholar. Her father was long dead now, and Mr. Miller—a handsome youth who had swept in one summer and disappeared soon after—was also an entity of the past. The wedding had been a beautiful affair, the young bride a picture of loveliness in white, the groom all that could be admired in a man. Tall, much taller than his Cat, broad of shoulder, trim of waist, still young but well on the way to maturity. His face held promise of a jaw turning firmer with age, a physique that would develop into powerful muscles rather than flab.

Two such beautiful people . . .

Yet the summer was filled with strife. They were both headstrong, determined. He had the flair of a reckless devil to him; women eyed him and it was in his nature to return their stares boldly. His wife was a beauty, built to equal the classic forms of the sculptures of ancient Greece, but he was, perhaps, a man not ready for a wife. Not that he was cruel, or that his bold stares at other women were anything other than speculative—he was simply preoccupied with his salvage-diving business. He was, in a way, a modern-day pirate, seeking the lost treasures of the sea.

Cat had been in love—madly, obsessively in love. She had trusted the handsome young man with the aloof and dominating manner, and she had given her all. It was unfortunate that happenstance taught her a sad lesson—Clay Miller had wooed and married her upon her father's request. Nobel-prize-winning historian Jason Windemere knew his health was weak. To Clay, with the promise of vast strength as well as daring in his dark eyes, Dr. Windemere meant to entrust not only his daughter but his vast charts of the Bahamian waters and limitless knowledge of ancient wrecks. Jason held only one chart back, that of a dream he would cherish in fantasy until his dying breath. The resolution of that dream he would leave to chance and to Catherine's wits. Perhaps in the back of his mind he had always thought of it as a safeguard for his daughter, who would surely be the one to go through his personal possessions.

Jason Windemere had, however, made the severe mistake of underestimating his daughter as a woman. Cat was not a woman to be manipulated. She adored her husband, but she turned from him, and he was not a man who tolerated rejection. Despite the fact that his head was filled with his business and he considered his wife little more than an obligation to be cared for considerately, she was his wife. And although he hadn't been aware of it, he discovered, with a fair amount of surprise, that he was a very possessive man. He was also determined to rule his own roost.

13

She was equally determined not to be ruled and the beautiful marriage became a battleground.

And so matters stood until the end of summer. And at that time, already establishing a name for himself in salvage circles, Clayton Miller sailed away. He was after the wreck of the *Princess Leana*, a clipper of the Dutch West India Company said to have sunk a hundred miles southeast of Bermuda in a fearful storm in 1646.

And then, while scouting the waters alone before bringing in his crew, Clayton Miller disappeared. His high-powered cruiser, the *Lady Luck*, seemed to have vanished off the face of the earth.

Clayton Miller was proclaimed by the superstitious to be a victim of the infamous Devil's Triangle. Whatever the truth, he was assumed dead.

Cat, upon hearing the news, retired to her room and, despite the best efforts of her father, had refused to see anyone, speak to anyone, or open the door for three days. Long into the night, Jason Windemere had heard her sobs.

For a year she waited. She appeared serene; it was apparent that she believed Clayton Miller would come back to her. But at the end of that year Jason Windemere's failing heart gave way. Cat again cried, for her father. In time her grieving ended—all her grieving. She had given up her father, she had given up her memories. Clayton Miller was as dead and gone as Jason Windemere.

To accept the pain, Cat convinced herself that Jason had been old and sick. Death had brought relief from the tortures of his illness, and surely, if there was a heaven, Jason Windemere basked among the angels.

Rationalizing Clayton's death was a slower agony. And so, to endure, Cat continually reminded herself that their marriage had been a disaster. He had never loved her; he had used her to receive the unique gifts only her father could leave behind.

As time passed, the serenity that had begun as a shell became fact. She was free, the ruler of her own destiny. The strength and will that had been hers in her youth had doubled. She loved the island; she loved life. She owned the well-renowned Heaven's Harbour and she loved all that her work of maintaining the docks and the quaint lodge entailed. She was almost the historian her father had been; the

14

prestigious and the wealthy sailed from the mainland and the States seeking not only the secluded pleasure of the lodge but its vivacious, beautiful, and intellectual mistress. Cat was a spirit who compelled those who loved the sea to the island. She could best any man in a catamaran, and yet few could resent her prowess. She could challenge the wind in any vessel, dare the ocean with free dives to forty feet, but she was, first and foremost in any venture, uniquely, regally, enticingly feminine.

As she stood on the dock this particular afternoon, her past was the furthest thing from her mind. It had been almost seven years since Clay Miller had disappeared, and in the last four Cat had been enjoying herself. She was the reigning queen of her island, and she knew it. It was fun to date the fascinating men who sailed the waters of the Bahamas, and it was easy now to remain aloof. Cat had no intention of being reined in again. Any man in her life would have to recognize her independence. Only recently had she considered marriage again, and that only because she believed she was actually beginning to care deeply for a man again.

Jules DeVante was a Frenchman who, it seemed, owned half the Caribbean as well as half of the Bahamas. They had met when Jules attempted to purchase Tiger Cay. Although Cat had no intention of ever selling the cay, she was captivated by the Old World charm of the Frenchman. Their relationship had flourished charmingly. Although secretly amused by his somewhat outdated moral principles (she was wife material—one only had *affairs* with loose women), she was also relieved that Jules put no pressure upon their physical relationship. She did love Jules—he was handsome, courteous, and totally endearing—but she had long ago decided that passion had little to do with love, and her experience with passion had left her quite sure it was something one was better off living without. Jules' kisses were tender and caring. They stirred within her feelings of contentment. That and compatibility were the important ingredients for marriage.

Cat knew Jules considered them to be engaged and the prospect of marriage with him was pleasing. So far he had made no protests about her managing her own property. He—like the one-time hus-

15

band who was now but a vague memory—was in the business of salvage diving. His vast fortune had come from the treasures he had recovered from the sea, and consequently, despite his determined wooing, he was frequently away from Tiger Cay. But he showed no signs of ridiculous jealousy. Long before he had actually met Cat, he had heard about the gracious beauty who ruled Tiger Cay. Those who had dated her spoke of her with a certain misty-eyed reverence and remorse. Her laughter was a melody, the raging spirit of the sea played in her eyes—but like the white-foamed surf of that same azure sea, she was untouchable.

There was only one problem with Jules and that was a problem that ironically went along with the Old World charm she loved. It seemed that he humored her as far as Tiger Cay went, having little faith in her productive abilities because she was a woman. And that infuriating reality had stunned her when she had told him of her new plans.

Just recently, while going through her father's papers and charts, the excitement of her discovery had hit her with the force of a brick. She was sure, completely and positively sure, that she had the only true knowledge of a certain coveted galleon, one that had carried vast treasures from Peru in the heydey of the Spanish Main.

Cat had tentatively broached to Jules the subject of launching her own salvage expedition. And for the first time in their relationship, she had found herself furious. Jules had point-blank—and laughingly—refused to fund any such expedition. He would be happy, of course, to listen to her ideas and pursue them himself.

Cat had stubbornly refused. Ownership of the island, Tiger Cay, was hers; it was the independence she craved. She also felt responsible for the community of eight hundred–odd islanders. The lodge, Heaven's Harbour, did well—but Cat also dealt with a tremendous overhead. The one flaw in her carefree existence was the fear that she could lose Tiger Cay. Of course, when she married Jules, she would never need to fear any financial threat. But his money would make Tiger Cay his island.

Even for a man she loved, Cat would not give up Tiger Cay.

And so she determined that she alone would find the treasure of the *Santa Anita*. The *Santa Anita* also touched other stirrings in her

16

heart. If the ship was discovered, it would be one of the greatest historical finds of the century. A dedication to the quiet but great man who had been her father.

Funding, Cat knew, would be a touchy subject. Jules would be crushed if she approached another salvage company. And even if she did decide Jules deserved to be crushed for scorning her abilities, she would have to face being turned down by others. Or worse. Someone, becoming suspicious of just what documentation she was holding that gave clues to the actual whereabouts of the mysteriously disappeared galleon, might try to follow her and beat her to the claim.

How many thousands of dollars would she need to search for the *Santa Anita*? Hundreds. . . .

If all else failed, Cat knew, she would have to turn back to Jules, to place her faith in him. After all, Jules would always care for her, and care for all that was hers.

But why couldn't she give up that strand of independence? It was a dilemma she had been pondering for some months.

But now, as she stood on the dock, her heart was racing. She was nervous, yet exhilarated. An answer—an answer that might not be considered quite legitimate, but an answer nevertheless—was suddenly facing her.

She had often accepted challenges from seasoned sailors to race her Hobie Cat from the channel marker to the Leewood reef and back.

She had never lost. Before, it had always been a game. But today, she was gambling for high stakes.

She wasn't nervous because she feared she would lose. She knew the winds, the currents, and the tides. She had also judiciously studied the sailors she was up against. Jim McCay was good but too reckless. He was likely to spill upon the shoal. Clancy Barker from West Palm Beach was just the opposite—an excellent man on a yacht, but overly cautious when it came to smaller sails. Three other contenders weren't even worth her worry.

It was the thought of what she was doing that made her nervous. She was a bit of a gambler at heart, but this was different. The bet on each race was fifteen thousand dollars and the amounts made her feel a bit ill.

It was actually high-seas robbery on her part, almost akin to piracy. But although the money wouldn't be all that she needed, it would be a damned good start. Enough for her to search out the *Santa Anita* and stake her claim.

Cat firmly squelched all her feelings of guilt. She was betting against grown men—men who could easily afford to lose the money. Like little children, they were determined to best her. She shrugged, and decided that if they chose to throw their money away, it was their own folly.

A smile flitted across her features. She tilted her face to the fresh Bahamian breeze and the her pony-tailed sable hair lifted in glorious strands to the wind. She faced her contenders. "Okay, gentlemen," she murmured sweetly. "Who's first?"

Jim McCay stepped up. "I guess you start with me, Cat." He shook her hand. "Gentleman's agreement with a lady, ma'am."

Cat chuckled in return. He was brash, but she liked Jim. He was a young lawyer from Maine, and she often wondered how he could manage to keep a practice when he spent most his time in the Bahamas.

"It's agreed that Sam stands as final judge?" Cat asked.

McCay nodded. Sam was Cat's dockman—a Bahamian with a black-satin body the size and strength of a brick wall. Sam was ageless; he had taught Cat the island when she was a child, and now he was more friend and mentor than employee.

He was frowning now, his dark eyes highly disapproving.

"Sam is final judge," McCay agreed. The other men nodded silent approval. The honesty of the gentle giant would never be questioned.

"Let's get to it then, shall we?" McCay grinned.

"You're on!" Cat laughed.

Jim moved down the dock, joined by the others who would watch the action. On the shore Cat could see that half her island had turned out for the races. Anne Blackstone, the beautiful Eurasian who taught the children of Tiger Cay's single grammar school, had even let the children out of classes for the event. Cat's nervousness

18

made her queasy. Was what she was doing right? She doubted Jules would think so. But after the fact, she could surely cajole Jules from anger.

"I don't like this, Cat Miller, not one bit!"

Sam's broad hand caught her arm right before she could jump to her Hobie Cat. She lightly tugged at her arm to pull away.

"Sam—I know what I'm doing."

"The Frenchie isn't gonna like it," Sam scowled, but Cat knew that concern prompted his harsh warning.

"Sam," Cat said softly. "Jules doesn't ever have to hear about this."

"Ummph! News travels fast on the grapevine, Cat."

Cat listened to Sam's beautiful patois uneasily. He was right. Her races would hardly be kept secret, although she knew the islanders would never give her away.

"Jules will understand when I explain," Cat insisted.

"You haven't got seventy-five thousand dollars."

Cat lowered her eyes and shrugged. "I'm not going to lose these races, Sam."

Muttering his disapproval beneath his breath, Sam left her, powerful arms crossed over his chest. Cat raised her sail and easily followed McCay out to the marker, automatically testing the feel of the breeze. Calculation was the factor that would give her the race.

Positions were taken by the marker. From the shore, Sam fired a single shot. The race was on.

Cat let out her sheet line, hiking out for balance as the sail caught. Her entire attention turned to the task at hand. She didn't notice that another man had joined those on the dock.

He was about the same size as Sam, younger, though, and trimmer. He stood barefoot in faded blue cutoff jeans. His skin was very, very bronze, as if he seldom left the sun. His hair was a tawny color, coarse, and bleached almost white in streaks from constant exposure. His handsome physique was visible even in a crowd of healthy sun worshipers, but that was about all. His chin was covered with a thick beard, not fussily clipped but evenly trimmed. His full, sensual lips were hidden by a mustache. His eyes were guarded beneath a pair of very dark sunglasses.

He stood near the beach, in the background, but though his eyes were hidden, they were sharp and shrewdly assessing.

He watched the race and studied Cat as she had previously studied her contenders. He watched as she won race after race. An eyebrow lifted as she graciously consoled the losers, assuring them that the wind had been with her and that they were fine sailors.

Still, the victory was in her eyes.

He shrugged inwardly. She had always needed a bit of taming.

His vision flickered briefly over her lean, lithe body, her firmly shaped legs, long and silky to the eyes, her breasts straining slightly against the cotton of her shirt. He smiled slightly and felt a stirring within him. Then he lifted his head slightly and closed his eyes. He turned his concentration to the breeze, feeling it with his entire body. And then, his hands casually on his hips, he moved down the dock to issue his challenge.

CHAPTER TWO

Exhilaration was taking Cat for a very high ride. Her guilt was buried deep beneath her triumph as she tried to control her exuberance and slip an arm through that of Clancy Barker. The crusty old seadog was looking so crestfallen she felt she had to cheer him up.

"Come on, Clance, I'll buy you a Bahama Smash up at the lodge," Cat said. "That will take the sting away!"

"Hmmph!" Clancy sniffed dejectedly. "I don't know, Cat. I thought I had you for sure on the turn."

Cat lowered her eyes to hide her smile. Clancy hadn't even been close at the turn. "The turn did almost do me in, Clance," she said aloud. "Next time, maybe . . ." Cat paused with her eyes brilliantly shining and turned around to hail the other sailors. They were still staring at the crystal-clear water of the harbor, apparently shell-shocked. It was impossible that a woman had beaten them all.

"Come on, guys!" Cat laughed. "I'm picking up the tab!"

Jim turned to her with a sheepish grin. "This is one time, Cat, when I will let you pick up the tab!"

Cat had been walking backward as she spoke. She pivoted again just in time to avoid colliding with the man walking toward her.

"Excuse me," she murmured, frowning and automatically assessing the stranger. Hers were the only docks on the island, and the tiny airstrip was seldom used. She hadn't seen this man before, she was sure, but there was something about him that made her think she *should* know him. His sun-sleeked torso was the deep brown acquired only after continuous exposure to the elements; his body was that of a man who lived and breathed a physical life. Even next to Jim, who was superbly toned, this newcomer was awesome. At five eight, Cat seldom found herself looking up as she was now. A little flutter of nerves tickled her stomach, and it was a disturbing feeling because she couldn't quite pinpoint the cause. She was dimly aware that a certain vitality emanated from the man; something about him permeated the air with an almost primitive masculinity.

Cat recovered from her peculiar initial sensations and took a step back, trying not to be overly obvious as she further scrutinized the man. His broad chest was thickly covered with golden brown hair that trailed to a narrow line before it disappeared into the waistband of his cutoffs, where his frame became attractively trim. The frayed edges of the cutoffs, his only garment, displayed his strong, sinewy legs.

Cat flicked her eyes to the stranger's face, although there was little to be read there. Dense sunglasses hid the color of his eyes and their expression; a full beard didn't exactly hide the rugged strength of his jaw, but it did leave one wondering. His nose was long and straight, a bit prominent but handsomely so, even if it did hint at arrogance.

Cat blinked suddenly, and her frown deepened. There was something about him . . . No, it had to be her imagination. But her instincts told her that she knew this man.

* * *

21

He hadn't moved after her quick "Excuse me" and now stood returning her stare, a slow grin creeping devilishly into his features.

"Mrs. Miller," he said, and Cat raised a brow at the sound of his voice, the eerie sensation of recognition creeping through her. Obviously this man knew who she was.

"Yes?" She hadn't really meant to, but she grinned in return. She recognized immediately that this was a man who had a way with women, but that didn't particularly bother her. She carried her own streak of flirtatious femininity. She fully understood the pleasant but meaningless appreciation that could pass between a man and a woman.

"Congratulations, you handle your sail quite nicely."

"Thank you," Cat murmured, still smiling but feeling her brow begin to furrow again. His low, husky voice was like a ripple of velvet. It seemed to strike at something within her, that strange nagging sense of familiarity again. She gave herself a mental shake. She didn't know the man with the rather long and wild sun-streaked hair and radiating masculinity. This had to be nothing more than a case of déjà vu. Or perhaps it was the type of man she recognized. Those who combed the out islands on their own were a hearty, assured breed. Seafarers with self-confidence.

His devilish grin deepened. "Are you up to another challenge?"

Cat lifted a single brow higher with a bit of skepticism. Surely this man had been watching. He must have realized that it was not only her skill but her thorough knowledge of the harbor that had given her the victory. It was not a matter of conceit that gave Cat her confidence, she had simply lived and breathed sea and sky and sails for twenty-nine years. If she hadn't acquired a certain talent, she thought wryly now, she would have had to be totally inept.

"Sir," Cat said hesitantly, not at all sure it would be ethical to take this stranger's money. She had known her other challengers: knew well that any pain from their loss would be that of pride—not finances. She had no intention of leaving anyone in monetary straits. She paused for a moment, lowering her voice so that she could not be heard by the others—now interested observers—on the dock. "I know this harbor and area better than my own face. I'm very hard to beat."

It was the stranger's turn to lift a cryptic brow. "Are you afraid to take on a contestant you haven't bested before?"

Cat flushed slightly and sighed with exasperation. "I'm not afraid. I'm merely trying to warn you—this is *my* harbor."

The man's grin deepened and he quietly replied, "I appreciate the warning. I'm still willing to take my chances."

Cat was no longer feeling disturbed in the least; her exasperation was fast turning to irritation. The man seemed determined to hang himself, and then she would have his fiasco on her conscience! She winced inwardly, then took another step backward and allowed her eyes to rest tellingly upon his faded and tattered cutoffs. "Sir," she repeated, purposely setting a hint of disdain to her tone, "these gentlemen and I were gambling for rather high stakes."

"Yes, I know," the stranger returned, switching his balance from muscled leg to muscled leg as he crossed brawny arms over his chest. "Fifteen thousand a race, I believe. I'd like to raise the stakes."

"Raise the stakes!" Cat exclaimed incredulously.

"Yes . . . Raise the stakes. . . . Five hundred thousand," he replied with amusement, repeating himself with the slightest pause between his words as if she were slightly deaf and uncomprehending.

Cat couldn't suppress a shocked gasp.

The stranger kept grinning. "Cat got your tongue, Mrs. Miller?" he queried, his voice an irresistible dare. "Or are you not quite as capable as you believe you are?"

She should have walked on by the man and his ridiculous proposal, but his husky, insinuating query had sparked a boiling fury deep inside her. The man was preposterously arrogant—definitely the type who deserved the lesson of falling flat on his face.

Cat contained the sudden, turmoil of hostile emotions that had zapped her like a lightning bolt and coolly planted her hands on her hips. "Forgive me," she said dryly, "but how do I know you're good for five hundred thousand dollars? That is quite a sum, you know." At that particular moment it didn't occur to Cat that she was worth nowhere near that sum herself.

The stranger shifted and pointed off the horizon, toward the shimmering jewels of the sea that were the lower Exumas. Riding about a half mile offshore was a very impressive yacht—a vessel a good sixty feet in length. Cat shielded her eyes with a hand and stared across the water. Even at this distance it was apparent that the boat was one of the newest models by one of the most prestigious companies. Her paint was dazzling in the sunlight, so clean and white that she sat like a diamond in the azure sea.

The yacht itself could easily be worth five hundred thousand, Cat thought dryly. She dropped her hand and turned, tilting her chin back and looking inquiringly at the curious newcomer.

"Yes, she is worth quite a sum," the man told her, his velvet voice still low with amusement. "And yes"—his voice lowered again—"she is mine."

Cat stood silent for a moment, thoughts whirling through her mind. Five hundred thousand . . . the amount was dizzying. She couldn't even begin to imagine that much money. But it meant total freedom, total independence to pursue her own dreams. Jules would surely be annoyed when he heard how she had aquired the sum, but Cat was equally sure she could handle Jules. She loved him; he loved her. He had refused to help her, and God help the man, but he should know her by now! In time, she could get him to laugh with her . . . She would explain that she had had to do it, that her challenger had been this macho tough who seemed to think himself the right hand of Neptune.

"Well, Mrs. Miller?" The stranger shifted his weight again, clearly portraying a humoring patience. His voice turned to a nerve-wracklingly thin silken whisper. "You seem willing to take on old men and boys. Shall we see how you fare against a man in his prime?"

"Modesty," Cat snapped, "does not seem to be one of the virtues you have acquired in this prime of yours."

The stranger shrugged. "I'm a gambler, Mrs. Miller. You appear to be one yourself."

He was goading her and Cat was also aware that he had done an excellent job of pricking her beneath her skin. Although none of their audience had heard the preposterous sum proposed for the bet, Cat was well aware that everyone present knew she had been challenged. This man and his infuriating arrogance had placed her in

24

a precarious position. She maintained the power to rule her realm with no sexual harassment from either the rugged salts who were her customers or the other owners of nearby islands and docks because she had earned the men's complete respect. It had taken her years to build that complete respect. Refusing a challenge from this man could cost her heavily. And damn! He deserved to have the pants beaten off him!

What if she lost? The thought hit her sinkingly for a moment, but she forced herself to brush it aside. She couldn't allow herself a moment's hesitation—or a measure of fear. She couldn't allow him to chew away at her self-confidence; she couldn't afford a case of nerves. She blinked, and in that time her mind whirled. She had to answer his challenge, and she couldn't afford to lose.

She stared at the stranger, shook her head slightly, as if driven by pure exasperation to humor him. "Sir," she said wearily, "if you must, you're on."

His lips now were a compressed line, but Cat could sense that behind the dark glasses his eyes still registered his amusement. "The Hobie Cats belong to the lodge, I assume?"

Cat nodded. "Take your pick."

The man turned down the dock, inclining his head to ask, "Same markers?"

"Yes," Cat called back, returning to her own small craft with a springing leap.

"Good luck, Cat!" she heard Jim McCabe call. She compressed her lips, nodding to Jim but not at all sure he wished her luck at all. She highly resented the looks she saw upon the faces of her immediate audience. They were her friends, but in certain corners of their hearts they were hoping she would lose. For the same reason she was determined to best the domineering newcomer. She was a woman; she had bested them. Just as she thought the stranger deserved a comedown, it would salvage the pride of the men she had taken to see her finally succumb to one of their own sex.

Cat clenched her teeth together, then shrugged. There were certain things about human nature that couldn't be changed.

"Cat!"

Cat paused as she heard her name hissed admonishingly. Even

before she met his scolding dark eyes, she knew it was Sam who had called her. He balanced his weight expertly between the dock planking and fiberglass boat.

"What, Sam?" Cat asked, annoyed with the lecture she knew she was about to receive.

"What do you think you're doing, missy?" Sam charged, with the familiarity of long affection and acquaintance. "You tell me what you bet that man. I saw your face, missy, and I know you, so don't feed me none of your lies."

"Sam—I've never lied to you," Cat protested.

"That's right, so don't start now. What's the bet?"

Cat tried to slough off "Five hundred thousand" and sound casual, but it was a little ridiculous even to attempt to make such an amount sound anything but absurd.

"Five hundred thousand!"

"Shhhhhh," Cat implored; she didn't want the amount known to the entire island.

"You ain't got no five hundred thousand!"

"And I didn't have any seventy-five thousand, either!" Cat hissed back, relenting immediately as she saw Sam's brow furrow with worry. "Sam," she implored, "what was I going to do? I was trapped!"

"And what are you going to do if you lose?"

Cat hesitated. No papers had passed—none were necessary. A gentleman's agreement such as this was honored by all parties.

"I'm not going to lose, Sam. You know I'm the best there is in a Hobie Cat—"

"I know you're the best I've ever seen," Sam agreed sagely, "but, missy, I ain't ever seen the likes of this man. . . ." Sam paused in midsentence, frowning as Cat had earlier.

"What is it?" Cat asked quickly. "Do you know him?"

Sam brought a gnarled black hand to his forehead. "I'm not sure, but . . ."

"Mrs. Miller!"

The call came from the stranger, an imperious reminder.

"I've got to get out there, Sam."

"You could lose Tiger Cay."

26

"And if I don't get out there, it won't matter if I lose it or not. Sam, I have security and freedom in the islands because of two things. I'm rumored to be as tough as nails, and I have you. Besides," Cat added, lowering her lashes to hide the misery underlying her words, "I can always turn to Jules—"

"And the Frenchie will own Tiger Cay."

"Mrs. Miller! Are we racing, or pausing for tea?"

"I'm not going to lose, Sam," Cat said firmly, reaching for her sheet line.

Sam stepped back off the Hobie Cat. Noticing that he was no longer watching her but had switched his attention to the stranger, Cat frowned, perplexed. Sam was studying the man and Cat could swear she saw a glimmer of recognition in her dockman's eyes. But she was already moving away from shore and she had to forget all else and turn her concentration to her opponent.

He smiled and tipped an imaginary hat to her as they reached the marker point that signified the beginning of the race. Cat tilted her head and returned his smile dryly, wondering what lurked in the eyes beneath the dark shade of the glasses. Stop wondering, she warned herself, twisting her vision from his to signal she was ready to Sam. She tensed, feeling and holding the fiberglass beneath her with her feet, hands held to go on the sheet line.

A single shot—Sam's "Go"—sounded from the shore.

Cat eased out her line, her sail billowing into the northeasterly breeze. Cat let her sail grow fuller and fuller for wind speed, hiking her slender frame far out to achieve the balance necessary for a smooth cut through the water. For several seconds of pure thrill, Cat forgot that she was engaged in a high-stakes gamble. She exalted in the fresh salt air pounding her face, in the foaming rush of water—so clear as to be translucent, "liquid light," as the Bahamians called it, beneath her feet, gushing, spilling high, spraying her with its temperate quicksilver touch.

A Hobie Cat, like nothing else, was an extension of the sailor, to Cat's mind at least. Each slightest point to the wind, each angle, was powered by her body, calculated by her mind.

She took the time to check out her competition; they were running neck and neck. His proximity spurred her spirit to greater effort. Cat let out another half inch of line, automatically adjusting her body hike.

She would never know what might have happened, although in her heart she had to admit that the stranger had pulled to an edge of several feet. It didn't really matter. Still shy of the finish, the race was rudely interrupted. A speedboat, a Cigarette obviously manned by a landlubber with no right to the sea, speared across the route of the Hobies. It was amazing that no collision occurred, but nevertheless the wake created in the water was disastrous.

Cat's Hobie took a flat starboard dive and despite the respectable strength in her slender arms, she was hurled from her craft.

The water—clear, beautiful, peaceful, tranquil—could become a formidable, raging foe, as all who loved it knew. The swirling suction created grabbed at Cat, hanging to her, holding her like the tenacious fingers of quicksand. Trying not to panic as pressure pounded her lungs with the speedy descent, Cat closed her eyes, praying desperately to remain calm. If only she went with the power that assailed her, it would shortly release her.

She was in no more than forty feet of water, but she had never before descended to such a depth without her lungs being filled with air. Don't! her mind screamed in warning, don't fight, don't flail.

It felt like hours that the sea gripped her, interminable hours in which the blood began to pound viciously in her head, the "liquid light" of the water became a swimming black. But it wasn't hours. It was doubtful that it was more than a minute. Cat felt the water release its hold. The pressure in her lungs was becoming unbearable, but she still fought against panic. She had neared the bottom of the harbor, she couldn't just rush upward. She could cause herself inestimable damage. Cat forced herself to begin a smooth ascent.

She was startled, as her vision began to clear, to find the stranger streaking toward her. He was so strange-looking, hair whipping away from his temples, features so tense, the tiny lines around his eyes emphasized in the distortion of the water. His eyes, she thought, seeing them for the first time. She was growing giddy with lack of air. A less experienced swimmer would have drowned. She was still near panic and might open her mouth to fill her lungs with

28

the sea and she was noticing a man's eyes.... But they were familiar ... disturbingly so.

His arm slipped around her and she didn't protest. She couldn't have. Besides being so dizzy, she was fast losing her reserves of strength.

It was a powerful kick of his legs that brought them to the surface. His arms stayed around her until they reached her Hobie Cat, listing ever so slightly after having righted itself. His hands came around her rib cage beneath her breasts and she was hoisted high out of the water. Her mouth opened; her lungs, starved for oxygen, sucked in. She coughed. A thunderous slap hit her back—one she was vaguely sure would hurtle her again into the water. But her cough desisted— she was gulping for air again, and this time it filled her lungs smoothly. Hung over the fiberglass with the man behind her, Cat let her head go limp and rested her chin, thinking of nothing else but filling her lungs until the mad heave of her chest slowly gave way to a quiet, easy sound. She became aware of the lap of the sea around her, of his flesh against hers....

"Are you all right?"

Cat nodded to the anxious question and tried to twist to see the face of the stranger. His position would allow no such thing, and rather than accommodating her by moving back, the stranger pressed closer. She glanced at the arms that came around over hers. Well-built arms, she thought, lightly freckled, tufted with dark hair, so sinewed, she doubted if the skin could be pinched.

Familiar.

Just as the eyes, so strange in the sea, had been familiar.

"You are all right," he ascertained. Cat felt a little quiver race oddly down her spine. She couldn't see the man's face, but she had felt the touch of his lips, the velvet whisper of his voice against her ear.... God! She could feel him! Wrung out as she was, she could feel him ... quiver at that brush of his lips....

He was suddenly gone. She sensed him move out, inhale and hold a deep breath, and then smoothly jackknife his sleek form back into the crystal-clear water. He repeated the gesture several times. Cat kept breathing, vaguely wondering what the hell the idiot was doing.

He reappeared by her side—dark glasses beaded and dripping with water but firmly back in place. "Lost them when I plunged in after you," he explained briefly, adding, "My eyes are sensitive to light."

It was a lie. Cat knew it was a lie. An obvious lie! But she still didn't have the strength to tell him he was a liar and demand that he remove the glasses. He was unlikely to do so at her command, and she was in no position to remove them herself.

She just kept breathing and hanging on to the fiberglass, watching him with eyes that clearly accused him of being a liar.

The man hoisted himself onto the Hobie Cat and gripped her wrists to pull her up. "I'll take us back in," he murmured. "Seems a couple of your friends are already on their way out for the other Hobie."

Cat remained silent, watching the tall man steer their craft. She was fascinated by his well-shaped legs, which stretched dripping and glistening not a foot from her face. They were legs like many she had seen, powerful from swimming, from striding a deck. . . . Nicely covered with that golden brown hair, tanned, deeply, deeply tanned. . . .

He glanced down to where she leaned over the craft. "Seems like I won, Mrs. Miller."

It was amazing how the spurt of pure rage could instantly return strength to her body. "What?" Cat shrieked. She almost bolted to her feet but controlled the motion when the craft took a hard keel.

"I won," the stranger repeated firmly.

"You did not! The race was interrupted!"

"Un-unh," the stranger said firmly. "The sea is not a predictable critter, Mrs. Miller. You have to be prepared for her idiosyncrasies —even when caused by man. I held my craft."

"You must be twice my weight!" Cat snapped.

She saw a brow lift in a high arch above the rim of the glasses. "Mrs. Miller—we all enter the game with no handicaps decreed. You have the advantage of harbor knowledge. I didn't see you give your previous contenders any quarter because of that point in your favor."

"I freely acknowledge that I know the harbor!"

30

He tilted back his head and laughed. "I'll be happy to freely acknowledge my weight." His tone suddenly grew hard and serious. "You wanted to play the game, Mrs. Miller. Well, you've lost. I'm sure Sam will assure you that I shot the finish line. You owe me five hundred thousand dollars."

"You're crazy!" Cat protested hotly. "I spilled."

"That's your misfortune. According to the rules, I won."

"You're all heart and sportsmanship," Cat said scornfully, determined that she shame him into a rematch. But could she win a rematch?

It didn't seem to matter if there was a possibility of her winning another race or not. "I'm not interested in sportsmanship at the moment, Mrs. Miller. Like you, I played to win."

"Tremendous," Cat muttered with hostility. "Well—sir—" she continued, placing as much disdain as she could manage upon the title, "I'm afraid you're out of luck. My sportsmanship is as poor as yours. I haven't got five hundred thousand dollars."

"I know that."

Cat's eyes shot to his, trying to fathom his expression beneath the glasses.

"If you know it," she demanded with high irritation, "then what the hell are you getting at?"

"We'll work something out," he told her complacently, laughing as he saw the firm tightening of her jaw. "In private, of course. I promise no one will know that Cat Miller has to bargain to pay her debts."

Damn, did she hate this man, Cat thought viciously. Still, she returned his stare, a spark of hope rising within her. Perhaps those on the shore would proclaim the race aborted. They would demand that she be given a rematch.

He laughed again, and Cat had to clench her jaw tightly to keep from jumping up and attempting to strangle him. "Cool down, Mrs. Miller," he warned lightly. "I was laughing simply because the wheels turning in your head were visible. You think someone is going to rush nobly to your cause. You're wrong. Every man up there is going to leap to your side—to make sure you're okay. But

31

I'm willing to bet another half a million that all of them—even your Sam—will proclaim me the winner."

They were nearing the dock. Heedless of the Hobie's balance, Cat came to her feet, ready to spring to the planking. "We'll see about that," she muttered ominously before leaving him.

But a half hour later she was having to bitterly accept defeat. Just as he had said, her friends and customers had swarmed around her, assuring themselves that she had survived her spill in full health. But after she had cheerfully assured them all she was fine, those same fickle friends turned enthusiastically to the mystery man to offer admiration and heartiest congratulations. Even Sam, damn him! Cat thought. Why couldn't he be just a little partial when it came to her? But Sam's honor meant more to him than even Tiger Cay. And he would expect Cat's honor to be the same.

Sighing as she viewed her sodden reflection in the beveled mirror of her dressing table in the large master suite of the main house, Cat began to nibble at a nail. What the hell was she going to do now? She decided she was as shell-shocked as her first, planned contenders had been with their losses. If she wasn't in shell shock, she would be standing here screaming in panic.

She turned from the mirror and stared blankly at the nail she had just torn ragged. Legally, she decided, she didn't owe the man a dime. In fact, their gambling had been *il*legal. But legalities weren't the point. Here in the out islands, one's word and honesty meant everything. The man—wasn't it ridiculous, she owed him more than she owned and she didn't know his name—apparently didn't have a moral qualm in the world. And for a man engaging in a "gentleman's agreement," he sure as hell wasn't any gentleman. If he were the least courteous, he would have claimed a mismatch.

The discomfort of still being soaked finally permeated through her mental dilemma. Sighing her frustration and turmoil, Cat moved into the old but elegant Victorian bathroom and stripped off her soggy clothes. For many moments she stood perfectly still, almost incapable of action, as hot water poured over her chilled body.

What the hell had she done? Too late, the question seemed to scream in her mind. She had known all along he had been goading her and she had fallen into the trap. Pride, she thought remorsefully, does goeth before a fall. *He* was supposed to be flat on his face. Instead, she was up to her neck in quicksand, floundering worse than she had been in the water.

This can't really be happening; I couldn't possibly have done anything so stupid! But she had. And so now, as she mechanically worked shampoo through the heavy length of her hair, she desperately pondered the stranger. What did he want? He had known she didn't have the money; in fact, it was if he planned on her not being able to pay up. Bargain to pay her debts, he had said. Bargain what? And when would she get to discover just what he did have up his sleeve? When they had come up to the lodge from the dock, he had cheerily informed her they'd talk later. When was later? Later had best be soon. Forgetting all about her hair, Cat was tearing away at another nail.

Lord, things weren't half as bad as they were going to be. Jules was due to return to Tiger Cay tomorrow. Maybe that was good. If he irritated her any further, Cat could just tell the stranger to go to hell. She began to laugh, imagining herself calmly asking Jules for five hundred thousand dollars. She'd have to endure a two-hour lecture on the idiocies of her sex.

But Jules had let her down before. She wouldn't have been gambling in the first place if he had put a little faith in her abilities. Maybe, she thought a little desperately, she could push the wedding. Jules couldn't possibly refuse to pay his wife's debts and the five hundred thousand dollars couldn't be that much of a hardship to him.

Cat sighed and stuck her head beneath the shower spray. She couldn't do that. Not to Jules. She loved him, even if he did have his quirks. Honor, she told herself bitterly. Sam would be glad if he were to know that she did have a certain sense of honor.

Only if she were desperate would she think of not stalling her upcoming marriage. What do I mean, desperate? her mind shouted. I am desperate!

And waterlogged.

Cat stepped from the shower and vigorously dried herself, toweling her hair so that it wouldn't drip. Calm down, talk to this man before going berserk. He planned to beat you—by fair means or foul. Maybe he wants something simple.

Like what? Cat frowned suddenly, thinking of Sam's strange behavior after the race. He hadn't appeared half as perturbed as he should have been. Cat had demanded to know if he—by any chance —had any idea of who the stranger was. "Maybe, maybe not," Sam had replied enigmatically. With the crowd heading for the lounge within hearing distance, Cat hadn't pressed him. "If he's who I think he is," Sam had said smugly just before she had left him disgustedly to shower and change, "you'll figure it out soon enough. You should have figured it out by now."

"I'm not exactly in the mood for riddles!" Cat had snapped. Sam had only turned away and smiled.

Now I have to wonder what's the matter with him, too, Cat thought peevishly. Tiger Cay might be slipping from my hands and he's smiling and talking in puzzles.

I'm going to face that damned cheat right now, she decided firmly. He had played enough games. He wasn't going to tear apart what was left of her nervous system with any more procrastination.

With determination giving her every movement extra vehemence, Cat wrapped her towel around herself and threw open the bath door—only to stop dead still, incredulity and rage burning her from head to toe.

She had no need to seek out the arrogant stranger who had just made a catastrophe of a life of peace and tranquillity. He sat comfortably, a bare ankle crossed over a bare knee, in the wicker rocker that flanked her bed, casually reading her copy of a *Smithsonian*, his eyes, still hidden by the dark glasses, rising as she froze in the doorway.

To top off his disgusting arrogance, he had the audacity to give her that devilish grin she was coming to loathe.

34

CHAPTER THREE

"You may have won a bet," Cat enunciated crisply, "but as of this moment, you have no rights to Tiger Cay. And if you did own Heaven's Harbour and the lodge, you would still have no rights to my room. What are you? A lockpick as well as a cheat?"

He tossed the magazine on the bed, and smiled as he laced his fingers behind his head and nonchalantly crossed his ankles with his feet propped on her bed—an indication of a long and comfortable stay? Cat wondered.

"Relax, Mrs. Miller," he told her, "I have no designs upon Tiger Cay."

Cat carefully hid her surprise beneath another demand. "How did you get in here?"

"No lock-picking needed. You left your door open."

"How did you know this door was my room?"

"That's no great mystery."

Cat stood silent for a moment, wishing she could either hurl something at him or kick a hole in the bathroom door. He'd love that, she thought, he wants to see me lose my temper.

She remained in the doorway, afraid to sit lest she lose her towel, yet also determined not to rush around like an idiot to grab her clothing—and further display the discomfort he was causing her.

"All right," she snapped. "Just what do you want?"

"Let's see," he murmured. "You owe me five hundred thousand, correct?"

"Even that is debatable."

"Not debatable," he argued firmly. "You owe me five hundred thousand." Feigning mock sympathy, he added, "Really, Mrs. Mill-

35

er, instead of outrage you should be displaying appreciation for my discretion. I came here to avoid any of our conversation being overheard."

"That was magnanimous," Cat said sarcastically. "Get to the point. What do you want?"

He still didn't answer. Deserting his relaxed pose, he stood and began idly prowling her room. Heaven's Harbour Lodge had been built in the late eighteen hundreds by the head of a small colony of British subjects. Everything about the place was airy and spacious with a touch of island ease combined with basic Victorian principles. Cat's room was huge, yet warm and inviting. Her bed and the wicker rocker sat far across from the modernized bath, a wardrobe sat in the far corner from the bed, her dressing table and a second dresser stood sentinel at either side of the bathroom door. Dead center in the room was a charming and light circular teakwood table, displayed beautifully by a burst of sunlight from the floor-length window that opposed it.

Cat watched suspiciously as her strange intruder walked to the dresser—uncannily as if he knew where he was going—and picked up a piece of scrimshaw. Upon the piece of ivory was delicately etched the fine lines of an old clipper ship. The stranger began to prowl again, palming the ivory and moving it in his hand with his fingers. He approached the window and stared out. Cat was about to lose her cool when he spoke again.

"I hear you're about to marry Jules DeVante. Is that true?"

Cat bit her lip but couldn't keep the impatience from her voice. "Listen, I'm getting tired of this. I don't know who you are, or what you want, but if you don't get out of here I'm going to scream and get Sam in to throw you out." And, she added silently, in two seconds I'll rip off those glasses. . . .

He turned back to her—that constant, annoying, amused smile still clearly etched into his unperturbed features. "Really?" He chuckled. "I wouldn't bother if I were you—Sam is nowhere around, and if he were, he wouldn't throw me out. Oh—don't touch the glasses. Remember? Curiosity killed the cat."

"Go to hell," Cat snapped, irritated that he could so easily read her and chagrined with his certainty concerning *her* employee. So

Sam did know him! And whoever this thorn in her life was, Sam respected the man.

"Don't count on that," Cat snapped out. "Sam may like you, sir, but this is my bedroom—" She broke off, suddenly furious with his mystery and games. "Who the hell are you?"

"Answer my question first."

"If you're writing a book on the islands," Cat drawled, her eyes sparkling with venom, "I don't care to be a chapter."

"If you want answers from me, Mrs. Miller, you should give some."

"All right," Cat replied dryly. "Jules is no secret either. Yes, I intend to marry him. You've got your answer. Now, who are you and what do you want? You say you don't want the cay—quite bluntly, it's the only thing I've got that comes near that sum in value. Unless, of course, you're willing to give me some time to raise the money—"

"Until you marry Jules?"

Cat hesitated. "Yes."

He paused for a minute. "No, I'm not willing to wait."

"Then what do you want?" Cat didn't exactly break, but her cool was gone. Her question was much more of a semihysterical hiss than she had intended.

"Oh, Mrs. Miller, for all your apparent savvy, you are naive. What am I after? You—of course."

She was sure her jaw dropped. It felt as if it fell all the way to the floor. Lord, she was naive. But then the whole thing was so ridiculous. Incredulously, she began to laugh, recovering a modicum of brittle composure.

"Surely you must be joking," she managed. "I value my self-esteem, but really, I can't imagine your considering having me for one night to be worth five hundred thousand dollars!" Cat sobered uneasily as she realized the man was still smiling.

"You're right," he said, not unpleasantly. "You do look rather tempting in that towel—but one night, definitely no. I was thinking more along the lines of two months—maybe three." He paused a second. "Really, Mrs. Miller, I do think you should sit down. You're whiter than the sand."

Was she white? she wondered vaguely. Quite possibly. The realization that he was serious seemed to have drained her blood . . . her strength. A chill reverberated down her spine, then she blinked, mentally stiffening.

"I don't want to sit down. Your proposal is absurd—out of the question."

"Oh?" He moved a few steps toward her from the window, and she was fully aware, despite the darkness of the glasses, that his eyes were searing into hers. "You were willing to sell out for a night, but not for two months?"

"I never said any such thing," Cat grated. She suddenly realized that she was close to tears; she was finding it difficult to breathe. Belated remorse filled her. How did I get myself into this? she wondered desperately. She knew how to handle herself, but he was corroding the self-confidence of a lifetime. Nothing she said daunted him. He was like a cat playing with an unwary mouse, fully aware that the mouse was trapped while the mouse still believed in an escape hole.

"Will you please get out of my bedroom!" she demanded, not caring that her voice held a note of beseechment.

Something about her plea seemed to touch him. His voice gentled. "Soon," he promised. He began to stalk the room again, the scrimshaw still in his hand, still being idly massaged by his fingers.

"What about Mr. Miller?" he suddenly queried, fingers tense around the ivory.

Cat was too overwrought at the moment to sense the depth of the question. "What about him?" she asked through clenched teeth. The stranger said nothing and she uneasily blurted, "Mr. Miller is ancient history."

"Oh," the stranger said lightly. He finally returned the scrimshaw to the dresser. "Think it over, Mrs. Miller. You have until tonight. All I want is two months."

"There's nothing to think over," Cat told him. "I'm not for sale. I'll think of something."

"Well," he warned, his deceptively low tone carrying a husk of danger, "I wouldn't go to Monsieur DeVante if I were you."

38

"Oh, and why not?" She shouldn't have asked him, Cat realized, she should have just let him go.

"Because you won't be marrying him."

"I certainly will."

The stranger shook his head. "Correction," he said firmly, and a tone that was low, carrying a strange combination of bitter sadness and mockery, suddenly sent eerie shivers through her. Even before he slowly slipped the glasses from his eyes, a part of her *knew*. As Sam had said, *she should have known all along!*

Pinwheels in black exploded in her mind; her limbs grew as weak as liquid. How could she have known? Clay Miller was a ghost, a ghost of the long-forgotten past. Almost seven years had passed since she had seen him, almost six since she had accepted his death. If he really were before her now, he had to be a ghost.

He had changed. Drastically. He was a good twenty pounds heavier. The years had changed his frame from that of pliant youth to that of well-defined maturity. She had never seen him with a beard, never seen his hair long enough to curl over his nape, wave past his forehead, the color changed by the bleach of the sun. The mustache had hidden his mouth, the glasses, his eyes. . . .

But now that she could see those fathomless eyes, she knew there could be no mistake. No one had eyes quite like Clay. Their brown so dark . . . so incredibly dark. When he was angry, they seemed as black as jet. They could pierce the soul, sizzle and burn the heart. And sometimes, sometimes touch upon one with such tenderness that the entire earth might have been swept into an ocean-blue hole, leaving only the delight of that strange mesmerization.

But, oh, God! She had been married to him, how had she failed to recognize him?

Because he is a ghost . . . a ghost . . . a ghost. . . .

Cat's hand moved to her throat; it jerked before her, fell back to her side. Quicksand. Drowning hadn't been in the water. This was drowning, in a quagmire of emotions that crippled and stunned. What was she feeling? Everything was whirling. This man had used her; their lives had been hell. When he had disappeared, she had wanted to die. She hated him; she loved him. She didn't feel anything because it had been so long. . . .

39

He was alive!

"I think you'd best sit, Catherine," he said softly. "I assure you, I'm not a ghost."

He reached out to touch her and the spell of the shock was broken and the emotion that prevailed was rage. Once, long ago, a girl had wanted to die because she thought he no longer existed. She had cried until her eyes had run dry remembering their stormy parting, spent years, *years,* learning to live again, convincing herself she could love again.

And now here he was, obviously in the peak of health, waltzing in to hand her further torture, further humiliation . . . But, oh, dear God, yes, he was alive. For a second, years slipped away. She wanted to fly across the room, hurl herself into his arms, touch him, feel him, cry and hold him.

He is alive, her mind murmured over and over again. Thank you, God, thank you, God, thank you, God. . . .

Cat closed her eyes for a moment, silently hearing a mental screech of agony that shouted out, *"No!"*

Yes, he was alive. In her prayers and dreams she would never stop being grateful, happy that he walked the earth. But he was her past. She didn't, couldn't, love him anymore because she loved Jules, because her life was back together. She had her own strength and she couldn't lose it because she couldn't bear a repeat of what had happened before.

And he was very obviously in excellent health, in excellent financial shape. She was shaking with joy that he was alive, but also with rage because this meant that he had simply deserted her. She had spent a year in tears over a man who had walked out on her cold . . . nights in agony, longing, praying . . . burning, tossing . . .

A man who was still reaching for her.

He could never, never know what he had done to her, how it had taken her years to want to breathe again, how just seeing him now brought back the ecstasy they had shared with a deafening torment that almost obliterated the hell he had put her through.

"Don't!" Cat rasped out. "Whatever you do, don't touch me." She took a deep breath.

He stared at her a long moment; the strong, sun-browned hand he had extended dropped to his hip and he shrugged. "Sorry—I thought you were going to keel over."

"For you?" She couldn't keep the bitter venom from her voice. "Hardly. As I told you, Mr. Miller, ghost or real, you're my ancient past."

His brows, high-arched over the hellfire eyes, rose slightly. "I'll admit, Cat, I wasn't expecting you to shower me with kisses. But out of normal human decency I hadn't expected you to resent the fact that I was alive. You might have had a question or two about what happened."

"I don't care what happened. You didn't come home. That shouldn't have been a tremendous shock to me. It was probably foolish for me to assume you dead. I was certainly never the driving force in your life."

"Cat—"

"Clay, I'm serious. I don't want to know what happened, or where you've been. You're not dead. Fine. I mean wonderful, really. I'm very happy for you. But don't expect me to feel much of anything else. I'm a very different person now. And I'm in love with another man—one I still intend to marry—"

"Cat!" The slash of his voice cut across her full-speed monologue. "You can't marry that damned Frenchman. You're still married to me."

"The hell I am!" Cat protested.

Clay sighed and patiently scratched his bearded chin. "You can't have declared me legally dead—you have a few more months before that could have been done. And you haven't divorced me."

"How do you know?" Cat demanded, stalling for time. Why hadn't she divorced him? Because she had thought him dead! And though engaged, she hadn't applied for a marriage license and therefore hadn't thought of declaring him legally dead. She couldn't grasp the fact that she was still legally tied to a man she hadn't seen in years.

"I know everything about you at the moment, Cat," he told her, his tone now a little weary, a little harsh. "You're still my wife and indebted to me as well. I want my two months, Cat. If you want a divorce after that time, I'll see to it that it's quick and easy for you. And in the meantime, I'll keep my identity secret—your fiancé won't know a thing."

"No! I don't need to bargain with you! I can get a divorce right now with no deals," Cat interrupted. "Desertion," she added, "is considered excellent grounds."

"Not, Mrs. Miller, if the judge is willing—where you are not—to hear what did happen and where I've been."

Icicles suddenly seemed to form in Cat's bloodstream. He was so certain. For a moment her heart lurched heavily against her chest. Some secret part of her was crying out, a part that had never forgotten how she loved him. Where had he been? Dear God, what had happened? Was there a legitimate excuse for disappearing for almost seven years?

No. She clenched her eyes tightly closed. She *had* made a new life. She *was* strong, she felt a comfortable love for a man who gave her everything so gallantly . . . a man with whom she had only ever had one argument . . . a man with whom she could reason.

"Clay," she said coldly. "I'm in love with Jules."

"Are you?" He appeared only mildly interested. "Then I suggest you agree to humor me. Two months. Then I'll disappear quietly, if that's what you wish, DeVante none the wiser."

"Don't be ridiculous," Cat protested, lifting her chin. "I'll tell Jules you've made an appearance—"

"Will you?" Clay asked, his incredulity lacing the two softly spoken words. "I think not. *Mrs.* Miller." He took a step toward her on a lynx-light tread. "I told you, dear wife, I know everything about you at the moment—that includes a tremendous amount of information about Monsieur Devante. The man has no backbone—"

"How dare you judge Jules!"

"—and when I saunter up to introduce myself as your husband, he'll be long gone with the wind."

"You're wrong!"

"No." Clay shook his head, almost sadly. "You're too much of a woman for him, Cat," he added softly. "I'm not wrong, but take

42

your chances, if you choose. You're my wife, and you owe me. The next step is yours. One way or the other, I'll get my two months."

Cat stared at him, and then the sound of his voice permeated her system. A wave of heat assailed her, striking from deep within her, spreading furiously throughout. Memory of her marriage had become a distant blur, shrouded with the misery of tears. But suddenly she could remember lying in his arms, responding to the fever of his wild demands . . . touching him . . . feeling his lips, hot, fervent, moist, seeking all her pleasure centers. She could remember that more recent feeling in the water simply because he breathed . . . because his lips touched her ear.

"No!" she said again, aware that the flame of her feelings had crimsoned her face. "You can't force me—"

"Into my bed?" He chuckled lightly.

She couldn't prevent herself from blushing, but she could will her chin to remain high, her eyes to lock with his. "I really can't see the need. I'm sure you must have tremendous success elsewhere. To the unwary, those eyes must be magnets and you know damned well you're built like a brick wall."

"Glad you approve." He laughed, the jet light in his eyes taking on a rakish twinkle, "even if the approval is totally objective!" He turned from her, heading for the door, and his voice changed again, losing amusement, becoming harsh. "I don't remember saying anything about forcing you into bed, Cat. I simply want your time. However, if memory serves me, I wouldn't even need to be persuasive . . . for long."

"Get out of here!" Cat gasped.

He paused, turned around, and smiled. "That *is* what I was doing."

She stood silent, her eyes glittering emerald antagonism.

"I will see you later, Cat. And tomorrow. DeVante comes in sometime in the afternoon, doesn't he? We'll see where we go from there."

He turned to leave again, but not knowing exactly why, Cat was compelled to stop him.

"Clay?"

He turned again, brows lifted in query.

43

"Just suppose I listened to this ridiculous bribe of yours. What in hell would I tell Jules anyway. How could I disappear or whatever for two months?"

"That, Cat," he told her, "would be your problem." He spun on a heel and placed his hand on the doorknob.

"Why?" Cat exploded. "Why are you doing this to me?"

"Why?" He returned the question, and then paused. Emotions raced swiftly through his dark brown eyes that Cat could neither pinpoint or fathom. He shrugged suddenly. "Treasure, Cat, why else. We're actually going to give to one another. We're going after the *Santa Anita.*"

The door opened and closed. He was gone, and Cat was left staring after him, her heart and mind torn asunder, scars of old wounds ripped and raw.

The *Santa Anita.* He had come back for treasure.

The *Santa Anita,* the coveted mystery galleon, the one great secret that her father had kept and she had unraveled. . . .

Clay hadn't changed. Not at all. And not enough. . . .

The pain of memory suddenly came cascading down upon her.

She had been racing down the beach when she met him, laughing with the sheer joy of being home after obtaining her Master's that her father insisted she needed. Not that she hadn't loved school, or the fascination of Boston, and except for the short summer vacations and holiday breaks, she had been away from the island for five years. In the last year, she had strenuously crammed to complete her courses in half the allotted time, and now there was sheer joy in the damp grains of pink sand beneath her feet, in the breeze, so clean, so fresh, stinging her face. She was sure there was no one near on the secluded beach near the north end; most of the islanders would be busy with their day-to-day lives, any tourists would be hovering closer to the lodge. Only the sun and endless blue sky were there to watch as she ran, laughing delightedly, pausing occasionally to spin beneath the sun and then take flight again.

Hands and face uplifted to the striking teal of a cloudless day, arms outstretched, Cat again felt laughter bubble through her, erupting like the northern streams when winter lifted her tenacious

44

icy hold. And then her laughter abruptly ceased; she had the uncanny feeling that she was being watched.

Cat paused, turning slowly, warily, toward the surf.

There he stood, rising from the water with mask and flippers in his hands. Apparently he had watched her in silence for some time. A grin of amusement, a little bit yearning, a little bit admiring, touched his full sensual lips and sparkled in the depths of eyes that were amazingly dark, amazingly compelling. His face was fascinating, utterly fascinating, his brows cast high over the wide-set eyes in a thick, slightly imperious flyaway arch. His nose was straight, long and arrogant, perfectly set between high, strong cheekbones. His chin was squared, decidedly squared, decidedly firm . . . obviously stubborn. And as he grinned, hard, pearl-white teeth flashed handsomely against the bronze of his rugged complexion.

She was staring at him, Cat realized, but she didn't halt in her assessment. He was young, but older than the boys she had occasionally dated in college. Finding much time for a social life had been difficult while also trying to obtain her Master's before her twenty-second birthday. And she hadn't felt that she'd missed too terribly much. The boys who had surrounded her had seemed terribly immature, even the supposedly "seasoned" Casanovas of the crowd did little to stir her imagination. She had, in fact, found many a passionate overture disappointingly sloppy and fumbling.

But just looking at this spectre in the surf touched something in her, something as yet undiscovered. He was very tall, and although lean, the expanse of his chest, the cords of his muscles strong in his arms, the trimness of his hips—all cast a peculiar spell upon her, one that frightened, one that excited.

"Sorry," he apologized, finally speaking. "I'm intruding upon a special moment, it seems. But you'll have to forgive me for being a silent spectator. I've enjoyed watching you. I know the feeling. Salt, sea and breeze and wide-open spaces under the sun."

Cat returned his grin. She was feeling a little breathless, but a little bold. She was young and toned and slender but fully formed, and she knew she wore her emerald bikini with attractive grace. She also knew that look in his eyes. He found her more than just attractive; he found her sensually appealing as a woman.

45

And for the first time, acknowledging that look sent a whiplash of excitement racing down her spine. It was a pleasant sensation . . . dizzying. It played upon her nerves, it seemed to steal her breath . . . but it was wonderful. She wanted to feel his fingers brush her flesh, to explore the sinewed contours of his shoulders with her hands, touch the short, crisp lion-colored hair that capped his head, that tufted over his chest. She had never seen a physique such as his.

He chuckled suddenly, and the husky sound touched upon her as surely as caressing fingers.

"Do you talk?" he murmured, "or are you just an ocean mirage, a mermaid who's sprouted legs, a sea witch?"

"No," Cat replied, wanting to say something, wanting to do something to keep him near but feeling ridiculously tongue-tied. How strange, she had always led such encounters. "I'm Catherine Windemere." She introduced herself, finally drawing away from his spell enough to speak. And she laughed at herself, reviving a spurt of cool self-confidence. "Who are you? You must be the spectre from the sea! My dad owns Heaven's Harbour Lodge—and the docks. I'm usually aware of everyone on the island, and I know I haven't met you."

His eyes narrowed slightly. "So you're a Windemere! And your father must be Dr. Jason Windemere."

"Yes," Cat replied with no surprise. Her father was known well beyond the realm of the Bahamas. Every other winter he toured for the more prestigious colleges and appeared on numerous academic talk shows.

"Well . . ." the young man murmured, "I'm here to meet him. It's been a pleasure to meet his daughter first." He advanced toward her, extending a hand. "Clay Miller, Miss Windemere. And I did come from the sea. That ratty-looking cruiser out there is mine."

Cat touched his hand. The electricity that had hummed within her took a heated jolt. She was loath to let him go. Her mind was so attuned to his physical aura, to his blatant masculinity, that she barely remembered she had heard his name. Clay Miller . . . hadn't he been making big waves in the salvage world? Yes, far, far away. He had brought up a World War II sub from the depths of the Pacific in almost perfect condition.

46

He laughed again, a sound that was another caress. "Well, sea witch," he murmured. "Are you willing to take me to your leader?"

He slipped an arm around her waist. And where he touched, there was a fire.

She would have led him anywhere.

In the next two weeks Cat was to learn about another sensation— one not so pleasant.

Jealousy was, in actuality, searingly painful.

Clay Miller spent long hours with her father. The two men never tired of speaking about ancient wrecks, about the hazards of the ocean, the art of diving. It had been a long time since Jason Windemere had donned mask and tanks to explore the undersea world he could chart like a city block, but Clay's fascination with his knowledge of history and shipping spurred him on with fresh life. Clay shared Jason's belief; only thorough research of all pertinent history could lead a diver to any victim of the sea's mysterious hold. Locating a treasure trove was half the battle.

Sometimes Cat was able to join their discussions. And at those times she would be fervently grateful that her father had insisted upon the years at college. Her knowledge of the once vast Spanish Main was astounding, and when she spoke of the great galleons, she did have Clay's undivided attention. But although he was courteous to her, polite and caring, he made no advances. His touch was only to lead, to assist, to perfectly, platonically, escort her. Where he disappeared at night, she didn't know . . . until the lodge hosted a "Midsummer's Fest," and Clay appeared, rakishly handsome in a jacket and tie, tawny hair sleek, freshly shaven, rugged cheeks seductively scented with a clean male cologne—with a voluptuous, platinum-blond tourist in tow.

Cat wasn't quite sure how she made it through the evening.

The pain that lashed her was physical. She was aware that she should ignore him, yet she felt compelled to follow his movements all night. And when she saw his golden-brown head, high above the crowd, disappear out to the terrace and hibiscus-ringed pool, she had to follow. . . .

The blonde was coquettishly teasing him, long-nailed fingers raking lightly over his jacket . . . down, slipping around the waistband of his pants tauntingly. Cat lingered in the shadows, frozen, holding her breath to halt the stabbing agony her torturous voyeurism was creating. Still, she couldn't draw herself away. She watched as he jerked the blonde to him, caressing her breasts, his eyes a jet sparkle before they closed as his lips descended over the woman's mouth.

Cat heard soft moans and wanted to scream. The blonde kept whimpering, pressing closer and closer. Clay's hands were touching her, touching her. . . .

The kiss ended, but the two didn't draw away. The blonde stood on tiptoe and moistened his ear with her tongue, then moved away to look at him. "I think we should go to my room. . . ." she offered seductively.

No! Cat thought absurdly. No! And at that instant she knew she had fallen in love with Clay Miller and that somehow she had to stop him from going with the blonde. She wanted him, and in her life so far, she hadn't confronted rejection.

At that moment, no morals stood in her way. She rustled the bushes as if just appearing, calling a cheerful "Clay!"

The two split apart as Cat approached them. "Oh—good evening, Miss Lanier," she excused herself to the blonde. "Clay, I'm sorry. My father has been looking for you. Would you mind . . . ?" She cast them both an apologetic glance.

"Jason is looking for me?" Clay seemed puzzled, but he frowned and addressed his date. "Trisha, will you excuse me, please? I'm sure it must be important."

"Of course, darling," Trisha drawled, running slender fingers over his chin and ignoring Cat. "I'll be in my room."

Cat smiled politely. He won't be, she thought. She hoped. What was she going to do?

"Where is Jason?" Clay asked.

"Oh—ah, in the den, I believe."

Cat led him to the den, fully aware that her father had long since retired, leaving a capable staff to run the party.

Why had she lied? she wondered desperately as she led Clay up the stairs and down the hallway. Clay would know in the morning Jason had never looked for him. All he would have to do was ask.

And now, now that she had him alone in the den, what was she going to do, how was she going to keep him?

Memory of the searing kiss she had just witnessed flamed across her mind. She tried to think back to those few times she had dated, the forays her escorts had attempted to solicit a response.

"I don't know where he's gone," Cat said nervously as they entered the empty den. "I imagine he'll be right back." Her eyes lit upon a seafarer's ancient map on her father's desk. "Oh, Clay!" she exclaimed. "Come look! It records one of Drake's expeditions. . . ."

She felt him behind her. Instinct made her lean, innocently pressing her back against his chest. "Look how they've marked Cartagena," she murmured, and then she turned, managing to twist herself into his embrace with her eyes, sparkling emerald, staring into his.

The heat between them became combustible.

It was all that she planned, and yet the shock of his kiss was staggering . . . frightening . . . all-consuming fire. She felt his tongue plundering her mouth, his mouth bruising hers, his hands splaying on her back, her ribs, her hips, her breasts, his thumbs working against her nipples, creating peaks that stood against the thin fabric of her halter dress.

It was wonderful, it was terrifying. She could do little but hold on to his shoulders, shivering, wanting it to go on, wanting it to stop so that she could breathe, trying to understand the ache that burned where his hips pressed against hers, teaching her that desire was real, alive, insistent.

A moment's panic engulfed her and she tried to draw away. He held tight, crushing her, then apparently found control. And when he pulled away, he was angry. With himself. With her. "You're playing games you don't know how to play, Catherine. And I don't want any part of them. I think too much of your father."

"My father?" Cat murmured stupidly, and then a flood of humiliation washed over her like a tidal wave. She had attempted to seduce him, like a tart, and then failed miserably. Her nervous withdrawal had clearly alerted him to her inexperience, and he had found her sadly lacking.

"Cat," he said quietly, his anger abating. "You're a very beautiful girl. But I don't think you really know what you want."

"Don't be absurd," Cat declared. "I'm a college graduate, Mr. Miller. Not a naive teen-ager."

Clay sighed. "Honey, you've definitely got all the right stuff, you just don't know what to do with it."

She was going to burst into tears, but she couldn't. She really didn't know what she was doing, she just had to hurt him. She brought her hand across his cheek with all the strength she could muster, savoring the sound of the sharp retort. "You cocky bastard!" she hissed. And then what she had done shamed her, but it was too late. She saw the brown eyes darken to that incredible jet, his left cheek swell, the welt on his tense face red.

Praying she wouldn't panic and run hysterically, Cat spun around to flee. She didn't return to the party but discarded her heels in the sand and ran to the docks, her chest heaving. She reached the end, where the tranquil azure of the harbor had become as dark as the jet of his eyes in the moonless night. Exhausted, she fell to her knees, staring sightlessly into the black water.

If she'd had any breath, her scream would have rent the night as she felt herself plucked from the dock and into strong arms. As it was, the sound was no more than a gasp.

She was staring into liquid black again. It wasn't the ocean. It was Clay's eyes. Dazzling, dazzling jet. He was angry again, an icy anger that was partly reckless revenge, partly cold control.

"If you want to play games, Miss Windemere, I think you should learn how. I suppose I can be as good a teacher as any. Any protests? This was your idea."

Protests? She couldn't even speak. She could feel his raw, unleashed power. It was a surge, a relentless tide. She said nothing, but continued to stare into his eyes.

His looked away and walked swiftly down the dock and without pause for balance leapt into his cruiser with her in his arms. She was set down unceremoniously within the ragtag cabin. With dry, semi-controlled rage, he stuffed a paper cup of wine into her hand. "Relax, Miss Windemere," he told her. "We won't go far."

He left her. She felt the hum of the engines; they were under way. And all she could do was sit and stare at the cup.

As he had said, they didn't go far. The sound of the anchor hitting the water made her jump. She came from her dazed state to survey her surroundings. There was scuba gear everywhere, and shelves of books lining all available space. The cabin was clean but rampantly unorganized. . . . Even on the blue-sheeted bed where she sat, maps and charts spilled over the foot.

What was she doing here? she wondered. This wasn't at all what she had intended. She loved this man. Everything should be beautiful. A gentle fog should drift from the heavens . . . it should be bright and soft and splendid. . . . Except that he didn't love her, and he had been right all along. She had chosen to play a game she didn't know how to play and she had taken one turn too many.

"You're not drinking your wine," he observed, entering the cabin with his jacket slung over his shoulder. He walked to a tiny closet, extracted a hanger, and hung up his jacket. Yanking his tie from his neck, he slipped that over the hanger, too, and unbuttoned his shirt.

Cat took a sip of her wine. She noticed her hands were trembling and she clenched them tightly around her cup. He no longer seemed so terribly angry. Maybe the cool Bahamian sea breeze had soothed the heat of his temper.

He sat across from her, an ankle crossed over his knee as he observed her, searching her face for something, his own impassive.

"What do you want, Cat?" he queried softly

Why was he questioning her? How could she put into words what she did want anyway, when it wasn't clear in her own mind. Him, of course, but with all the flowery phrases, his eyes answering the light in her own, soft breezes and gentle decor, down pillows and silk.

"Come on, Miss Windemere," he prodded, "let's talk."

Cat took another sip of wine, and returned his glacial stare. "I don't want anything," she said coolly, hating him for making her feel so ridiculous.

"Stop lying," he snapped. "Why did you tell me your father wanted to see me?"

"He did—"

"Bull."

"Really, I'm not going to sit here and argue with you."

"That's nice to hear," he said wryly. "But it seems as if you went through a fair amount of trouble to interrupt what I was doing. Why?"

Cat remained stubbornly—and miserably—silent, her eyes meeting his only through great willpower.

"Okay," he said quietly, "I'll help you. Actually, it's rather flattering. You've decided you want to make love to me—or vice versa. But it's turning out not to be quite what you imagined. A kiss doesn't stop at the lips. It's not a hazy dream out of a fairy tale where you ride sweetly off into the sunset. I'm afraid it all boils down to something rather basic and simple, and I fear 'love' seldom has much to do with it." He fell silent for a moment, watching her. "Am I right, Cat?"

"No—you're being absurd," she lied sickly. "You really do underestimate me, Clay. I'm not a sheltered islander. I lived in the big bad city for a long time."

"Oh." His lips pursed slightly as he mulled over her statement. She didn't really know him well enough to recognize the amusement glimmering in the jet of his eyes, which had completely replaced anger. "Okay," he said finally. "Take off your clothes."

"What?"

"Take off your clothes. It's possible to make love half dressed, but much more satisfactory with both parties naked."

A flush of surging blood rushed to Cat's face. He was laughing at her. He had dragged her all the way out here to laugh at her.

She had never been especially good in controlling her temper. She was on her feet in a split second, splashing the barely tasted remainder of her wine in his face. "You are the ultimate bastard!" she hissed, whirling for the deck steps.

This time she didn't even irritate him; she heard his laughter follow her trail. "What do you think you're going to do, swim back?"

He heard her determined steps upon the deck. "Damn," she heard him swear, "that little witch does think she's going to swim back!"

He was after her in a flash, but he had underestimated his adversary. She was in the water, disappearing like a streak of gold.

"Get back here, you little fool!" he shouted after her, swearing a mile a minute beneath his breath. "Damn it, we're in a good sixty feet of water, almost a mile offshore!"

Cat paused long enough for an answer, ironically glad she had chosen the light halter-dress for the evening. The weight wouldn't drag her down. "I've taken every scuba and lifesaving course offered, Mr. Miller," she shouted at him. "A mile, you say? I'll be just fine."

He was a silhouette in the light of the cruiser against the pitch-darkness of the night as Cat began to swim. She heard him laugh suddenly. "Okay, you want to swim—swim."

Cat was relieved by his quick agreement. She could make the mile, and she could probably outdistance him if he came after her, but she could better utilize her strength by moving slowly and fluidly. But she was a fool, and she knew it. Even an excellent swimmer faced dangers at night. Lemon sharks and makos chose the evening hours as preferred feeding times and one never knew when one might encounter the trailing tentacles of a man-of-war.

Don't think about it, she warned herself, utilizing a steady Australian crawl. It wasn't really hard to face such hazards. She would rather see a man-of-war at the moment than Clay.

Cat paused for a moment treading water, startled as she found herself captured in a spotlight.

He was letting her swim, all right—but he was following just far enough behind for safety.

"You can come back up!" he advised her. He looked nice and rested, sipping a beer as he manned the small tiller.

"I hope you split up on a coral or hit a sandbar," she replied sweetly.

Cat frowned as she saw his grinning expression suddenly change. The smile was radically erased from his face. "Get out of the water," he yelled.

"No, you think this is a joke—all highly amusing. Well I haven't been amused and you can follow all you like, but I'd rather swim than accept a second of your brand of hospital—"

53

Her words were drowned out by the splash of his body cutting cleanly into the water. She hadn't been prepared for his jumping in after her and was caught off guard when the strength of his dive brought him beside her.

"Let me go—" she gasped.

"God damn it, this is no joke, and I'm not playing!"

She was propelled to the cruiser's starboard side and hoisted high into the air. Her shoulder, derriere, and head hit the deck hard, but before she could rage her protest, he hurtled over her. And then before she could even stutter, she was ignominiously dragged to her feet and swirled to stare into the spotlight.

Her words caught and died in her throat. In the shaft of yellow that had bounced upon their heads just moments ago, two large fins speared the surface, cruising stealthily, turning in figure eights. She could feel his anger, intensified by fear, in the harsh grip he maintained over her shoulders. She tried to twist in his arms, to apologize, to thank him.

He turned her himself, shaking her. "All this over making love. "Okay, Cat. You want to make love, we'll make love. I had thought to protect the vestal virgin, but I suppose deflowering beats death by shark bite."

Cat opened her mouth. She wanted to tell him that she was really very sorry about the whole evening, that she had acted like an idiot, made a total fool out of herself. She was even ready to explain that she had fallen in love with him and hadn't known how to handle the situation maturely. Could he possibly understand such a thing? She really wasn't usually so incompetent.

She didn't have a chance. Her mouth was nothing more than an open invitation as his lips burned hers. His tongue was hotly seductive, plunging deeply one moment, withdrawing with his lips a whisper away the next so that he might trace the line of hers, weave his moist trail along her cheek, to her lower earlobes, to her throat. She was hanging on to him again, her fingers splaying into the damp hair on his chest, working beneath the dripping sides of his opened shirt.

She felt his fingers at her nape, struggling to untie the wet knot of the halter. Apparently he had a certain expertise, for the knot gave. His hands pursued a course over her body, peeling down the wet fabric until it gave and fell to her feet. Cat was stunned, but also filled with a raging fire, an exhilaration like nothing she had ever known. His hands teased the small of her back, cradled her buttocks, lifting her, pulling her, pressing her against him, and then she could feel the lean masculinity of his chest against her breasts, the nipples crushed and teased by his hair.

His kisses ceased as he stepped back, dark eyes heavily upon her as he stared at her revealed before him. He had seen her before in a bikini, so the lush perfection of her body was no surprise. Slender, slender waist, full firm breasts, a tantalizing curve to the flare of her hips, and seductive emerald eyes that stared into his unblinkingly.

She was clad in only a wisp of white lace over her hips. Clay shed his damp shirt, dropping it to the deck. He unbuckled his sodden and ruined belt, and stepped from his pants and briefs.

Still she watched him, eyes holding his, dropping, widening just a hair, returning to his.

He took her back into his arms. Her hands began to move this time, running across his shoulders, threading into his hair. He was startled, jolted, and then inflamed as she returned his kiss, her tongue moving with subtle seduction, her lips sweetly inviting, her delectable body moving against his, writhing, adjusting.

He broke away again, only to sear a kiss into her shoulder, slide against her, to find and tease and hold her breasts with his mouth and his hands. He was a little crazy. The blood was pounding in his head and he lost all thought . . . all awareness of time. Somehow they had gotten to the bed below, and he was still tasting the nectar of her body, his fingers slipping beneath the band of elastic to remove that last wisp of lace, his lips tracing the beautiful line of her hips.

Cat moaned as his hand moved between her thighs. She was past apology, past speech, past reason. Fear still hovered over her, but it was mainly obliterated by the fever of anticipation, the culmination of something that would ease the agonizing ache that was also so good.

She felt his withdrawal from her, his hesitation. There was a rumbling anger and agony to his voice when he spoke. "Damn it, Cat, I never meant this to get this far. . . ."

She reached out to touch him. Her hand slid down his chest; he caught it. "Cat . . ." She closed her eyes in an instant of misery. He couldn't have led her so far without wanting her.

A little cry escaped her and she twisted to burrow into his chest. He gripped the sides of her hair, pulling her back. "Cat," he murmured again.

Her hands were freed again. She touched him with a tentative assurance, sliding supple fingers low over his stomach, hesitating only fractionally, taking the step from which there would be no return.

She felt him shudder, heard him groan, saw the intensity of his eyes as he moved over her. Instinct caused her to tense, but it made no difference. He was as gentle as his desire would allow, but there would be no pulling back.

There was a moment of acute pain. Cat felt a scream of protest tear her throat. Suddenly she wanted nothing more than to rip away from him. But his lips stilled her scream, his arms held her secure. She lay still beneath him, braced against the demand of his passion, actually wondering how this could be considered such a rapturous act.

But slowly the pain became just a throb and miraculously the fever of deliciousness returned. She wasn't sure when, but suddenly she was undulating to his rhythm, writhing against him, her lips answering his, her fingers splaying, clutching his shoulders.

Suddenly he drew away from her, taking his wonderful pulsing life away. "Please," Cat gasped with confusion, but she felt his hands and lips covering her again, finding, seeking intimate spots that were now easy access. She hadn't the power to protest, not that he would have allowed her quarter anyway. And then she was begging, and wondering how she had ever thought this anything but rapture.

He filled her again, a passionate drive that was but an answer to her mad twists and pleas. Her need had become voracious, his hunger something she could appease. She learned what it was to float, to soar, to forget everything but the moment of wild magic.

56

A moment that culminated in staggering ecstasy held her spellbound even as the feelings sweetly ebbed to contentment. It left her feeling exhausted but shiveringly pleased with the dual explosions that shook her body and yet suddenly unable to face the man beside her.

He was watching her. She forced her eyes to his. He was studying her, his dark eyes intently enigmatic.

"I'd better get you home" was all he said. But his hand touched her cheek once more, lightly tracing her body from throat to abdomen.

Then he was gone, striding from the cabin, oblivious to his nakedness. Why should he worry, Cat wondered, he must know he has the body of a Greek god.

She bit her lip then. Was this it? This feeling so intense it eradicated all others, and then the absolute misery of feeling bereft? She shivered, closed her eyes. God, how she adored him. . . .

She finally managed to stand, swaying dizzily for a moment as she realized how achy she was. She kept her eyes from the sheet, and winced slightly as she returned to the deck, feeling naked and awkward.

He stopped her as she reached for her sea-soaked dress, pulling her back into his arms for a brief moment. "You are beautiful, Cat. Simply stunning." He smiled at her for a moment, brushing damp tendrils of hair from her face. "I wanted to make it good for you," he said softly.

She blushed. Surely he was well aware from her shameless moans and whimperings that it had become wonderful beyond description.

He kissed her lips, gently, then both her breasts. "I've never met anyone quite like you, Cat," he murmured, and then he was helping her replace her clothing.

Alone in her room that night she had tossed and turned, burning with the memory her body wouldn't allow her to forget. She alternated between joy and fear. She would die, surely die, if she didn't see him again, and again. . . . And he hadn't really wanted her. He had tried to stay away from her.

But the next morning her fears were dissolved. Her father informed her that Clay had been in at the break of dawn to ask Jason's

57

approval for an immediate wedding. No bride was ever more ecstatic, more beautiful, more passionately in love.

But although the ardor of the physical side of their relationship increased—and Cat rapturously learned that her husband was as enamored of her sensuality as she was of his—the very temperaments that had brought them together drove them apart.

Clay wanted no interference in his life. He spent hours with Cat's father; he spent hours pursuing the sea himself. And he was, as always, appealing to other women. . . .

And then came the day when Cat overheard a conversation between two women of the lodge staff.

"The girl's beautiful . . . surely he couldn't have married her only because of Windemere's wishes—and sea charts."

"Well if he did," came the other woman's chuckle, "he'll wind up sorry. He's in for a lot more than he bargained for. She's known as the Temptress of the Isles throughout half the Caribbean and Gulf. An independent and feisty lady, our Miss Cat."

It was that same night that Clay told her he would be leaving on a salvage trip. And unfortunately, he happened to be leaving with his two financiers—a brother-and-sister team—and the sister, it seemed, had little respect for the sanctity of marriage.

They had been married less than a month. Cat told Clay she didn't want him to go.

"Don't be ridiculous," he informed her. "Salvage is my job."

"I mean it, Clay, I don't want you to go."

She had seen the hard twist to his jaw. "You're my wife, Cat, not my keeper. I'll be damned if I'll be dictated to by you."

The nights that he was gone were torture. And then she decided that neither was Clay her keeper. Despite her father's rigid disapproval, she took to scouring the seas herself, leading the lodge's dive parties, actively participating in all social events.

One night found her on the terrace with a handsome young diver from California. Cat was missing Clay, and resenting him, too. She intended to ease her hurt with a mild flirtation, just friendly words to try and convince herself that she was appealing, that Clay hadn't married her because he knew her father wished it, because Jason held keys to the sea.

58

Cat pushed her luck a little too far. Just as she was attempting to disengage herself from the arms that had crept around her, Clay appeared. She would never forget his eyes that night.

He cut in, claiming her, just as the young Californian grew insistent. "I can understand where you might want to throttle this lady, friend, but sorry, I'd have to stand in the way. I'm her husband." As he led her away, he muttered something about throttling her himself.

She was frightened of his anger; more frightened that he had spent his time away with other women. He didn't really love her. Only her forcing his hand and her father's promise had given him to her.

The argument that followed was terrible, but it ended passionately in bed. Yet when the storm had passed, the seas had not been calm. Clay curtly informed Cat she was his wife, his property, and that was that. If she wasn't careful, she'd find herself left under lock and key.

Cat's pride wouldn't allow her to tell him that all she wanted was not to be left.

He was gone again in a few days. This time, his success was heralded across the world. He had recovered a treasure chest of Jose Gaspar the pirate off Cudjoe Key.

Before he returned, Cat cornered her father. She insisted to know the truth of what she had overheard. Jason had admitted that he had expressed an opinion to Clay about wishing to see her married and that he had also demanded immediately that Clay consider nothing less than marriage.

"You always needed a strong man," Jason tried to tell her. "I knew what you were feeling, I know you love him. And he does love you, Cat. And with me in poor health, you'll need someone to help you."

"Oh, Dad," Cat murmured, "you know no matter what happens, I'll be able to take care of myself."

"I know, Cat. But aren't you happy with him?"

"Of course I'm happy," Cat assured him. "Very happy."

And she was, at times, when the strange truces would come between them. But Cat learned then how it hurt to love too deeply.

59

If she ever learned to lose this feeling, she would never allow it to come again.

And yet, if she had known at that time that she stood a chance of losing him, she would have forgotten her pride and all else. She would have welcomed him home with open arms, admitting all that frightened her, begging that they spend more time together.

But as it was, she didn't know how to handle her hurt when he returned. And so she greeted him as cold as ice.

Clay, in turn, was grim and brusque. He refused to allow Cat to remain cold; his devilish laughter, touched with bitterness, rang dryly to her ears when he managed with pathetic ease to seduce her in their bed.

And too soon he was leaving again, and he was holding her close, and she was clinging to him.

"What's wrong between us, Cat?" he asked softly.

A pain had torn at her and she had answered honestly. "What can be right, Clay, when you don't love me?"

"What?"

"I know why you married me, Clay. I've talked to my father. Don't lie to me, please."

"Oh, Lord, Cat," he mumbled, his fingers threading through the magnificent fall of her hair. "I won't lie to you, certain things did happen, but Cat, we really need to talk. When I come back, we'll clear the air of everything."

He had kissed her long and hard, and while he was gone, Cat had belatedly realized all the mistakes she had made in her marriage. Childish mistakes. Granted, Clay could be hard. He had flaunted many things in her face. But if she had been older, a little more secure in her love, a little more mature, he might have understood her tempestuous nature, gentled his handling of her, opened himself to her.

None of the lessons of belated wisdom she gave herself were ever to do any good. Clay never returned. And in time, Cat knew she would never, never love that way again.

CHAPTER FOUR

Cat would have liked to stay in her room, nursing old wounds, for the remainder of the day and night. She did manage to spend hours, just staring at the beamed roof overhead, thinking, trying not to think, alternately shivering and freezing, and growing so warm that tiny beads of perspiration broke out on her forehead only to turn to pinpricks of ice and she would feel the shivering chills again.

When she dragged herself up, the room was beginning to grow dim. She took a look at her reflection and winced, touching a finger to her damp cheeks. I've been crying over him, again, she thought miserably. Damn him! I get him out of my life and he walks back in.

But I was wrong so many times, she told herself. I simply wasn't old or mature enough to handle love or marriage.

Cat stiffened. I was jealous, yes, but not without provocation. It was easy to remember Clay's charming smiles, the debonair look of the rakish pirate he bestowed so easily on other women. The trip he took, arm in arm with another woman, just after their marriage . . . well, not arm in arm, maybe, but the blonde on the salvage operation had made no attempt to hide her desire for Clay, and Clay certainly hadn't appeared to mind her attentions.

And where the hell had he been for all those years, appearing now just in time to wreck her life? Pity she had been caught so off guard. She should have queried him, just to save herself this torment.

There were shadows beneath her eyes already. She appeared taut and strained, as if she had aged years in the last few hours. Damn him, damn him, damn him! Cat closed her eyes, fervently wishing she could crawl back into bed and pretend the entire day had been a bad nightmare. She could just sleep and sleep. . . .

No. She always made an appearance in the dining room, casually exchanging a few words with her guests, assuring herself that all was well. Clay Miller was not going to return and intimidate her. Heaven's Harbour Lodge was hers, she was going to run it as she always did, and ignore him if he was rude enough to make an appearance.

Cat dressed with very great care, winding her hair in a chignon and choosing a black halter dress with a swaying hemline. The neckline came high, forming a collar around her slender throat, but leaving her shoulders and back, other than three decorative straps, bare. The material was a simple polyester, but it clung to her shape nicely. Simple and casual Bahamian elegance. With a pair of heels and her hair piled high, she would almost match Clay in height, and for some reason—although she was determined to avoid him—that seemed important.

Coral drop earrings and a matching bracelet completed her ensemble. Taking a step back from the mirror, Cat sighed and turned to leave the room. But her eyes lit upon the scrimshaw and she too picked it up, feeling the cool ivory with the palm of her hand. She had given Clay the scrimshaw. It had been a wedding present. Her fingers tightened around the ivory, and she felt tears forming in her eyes again. She quickly closed her eyes, stuffed the scrimshaw into a drawer, and fled the room.

The dining room was bustling when Cat made her way to the front of the main house and the breezy setting where rustic tables overlooked pleasure boats listing at berth. The restaurant catered to many yachtsmen passing through as well as those staying at Heaven's Harbour or the nearby lower Exumas.

Cat paused to say a few words to Clancy and his peppery silver-haired wife as they enjoyed their dessert, forcing a smile as Martha congratulated her on her winnings and commiserated her loss. "Clancy said a Cigarette cut right across," Martha sniffed, patting her husband's arm. "If these buffoons weren't such spoilsports, they would have had the match recalled!"

Cat felt her smile grow strained. "It wasn't your husband's fault,

Mrs. Barker. Sam called the race. We were both up against the same wake. My, uh, contender held to his craft."

"Yes, well," Martha Barker muttered, disgruntled. "It just seems a little strange to me. That Cigarette appearing out of nowhere."

Cat stood suddenly, anxious to move away. It had been a little strange . . . a speedboat suddenly crashing through their path. . . .

"Umm, well, will you two excuse me? I haven't been to the kitchen yet. . . ."

"Yes, dear, you go right on!" Martha said. "And tell Swen the seafood creole was simply superb!"

"I'll do that, thank you." Cat grimaced. Even as she moved away, Cat could hear Clancy whispering that Cat really hadn't faced any great loss since she had won five races before losing one. Poor Clancy, Cat thought, he didn't know what the stakes were for that one race.

She merely smiled and said hello as she passed several tables, keeping her smile serene, although she couldn't help but hear pieces of conversation—all about the race—and about the mystery man who had been the winner. She had almost reached the swinging kitchen doors when she heard herself hailed and turned to greet Jim McCay's table of young men.

"Hey, gorgeous!" Jim called, whistling low as she approached his group. "Cat, you look dynamite! Takes the sting out of being beaten!" Cat smiled and thanked him and nodded to the others. Jim spoke to his three friends. "But you should have been there. Some guy looking like a long-haired and bearded Conan the Barbarian suddenly appeared and took Cat! Hey, honey, who was that fellow anyway?"

"Ah . . . Jim, I really have to get into the kitchen," Cat excused herself. "Enjoy your meal . . ."

As Cat moved on into the kitchen, her head was pounding. She kept thinking of Martha Barker's words. *That Cigarette appearing out of nowhere* . . . Would Clay have gone so far as to plan such a thing? Especially when he might have won anyway? But then again, he knew that she was good with a Hobie Cat, very good.

Sailing through the kitchen with only a vague smile for the five employees who ran the small place, Cat stared out the window to the well-lit dock area.

No Cigarette was pulled into berth. She sighed with frustration. That didn't prove anything. A speedboat like that could be anywhere by now, and if the owner were smart, he or she would be long gone anyway. Those who had witnessed the faulty seamanship would have torn the captain apart with severe tongue-lashings.

"Moon madness, Miss Cat?"

Cat was so badly startled that she jumped and cracked the top of her head against the window frame.

"Sorry!" Swen, her chef, apologized quickly. "I didn't mean to send you for a jolt!"

Cat smiled vaguely, trying to massage her bruised skull without making a disaster of her pinned hair. "That's okay, Swen, I guess I was a little preoccupied."

"What were you looking for?"

"Oh, ah, nothing. Moon madness—like you said, Swen." Cat grinned and moved to the massive stove sitting in the center of the room. "Everything smells delicious, Swen. Mrs. Barker sends her compliments on the seafood creole."

"Does she now?" Swen beamed. He was a large man, pale-skinned and florid like his Swedish ancestors, with a heart of gold and a way with seafood that was simply not to be excelled. Cat's grin deepened as she watched him blush; her cay was a little United Nations—people of all races, creeds, and colors living together harmoniously in their own little world. She really couldn't bear to lose Tiger Cay.

"You tell Mrs. Barker I'm sending her a dessert—a true specialty of my island kitchen!"

"Yes, I will," Cat murmured. "Well, I see things are well under control here. Swen, have you seen Sam?"

"Not lately, Cat. He ate early and said something about repairing some loose planking on the dock."

"Okay, thanks, Swen," Cat said, heading back for the dining room.

"Monsieur DeVante is due in tomorrow morning, right?" Swen

called after her with a cheerful smile. At her nod he added, "I'll plan some of those croissants he's so fond of for breakfast."

Cat nodded again, forcing a sick smile. "Lovely, Swen, thanks."

Cat paused only long enough in the dining room to tell Martha Barker about Swen's pleasure at her compliment and the special dessert she would be receiving. Then she hurried out and made her way across the lush lawn of the lodge to the sand spit that wedged before the dock. She walked carefully in her heels, shivering slightly as the cool night breeze swept across her bare shoulders.

Sam was nowhere in sight, but out on the water, she could see the silhouette of the sleek cabin cruiser that had brought Clay to the cay.

"Damn that traitor's hide!" Cat muttered aloud, thinking of Sam.

"Talking to yourself, huh? That isn't a good sign."

Cat spun around so quickly that she almost lost her balance in the sand. As it was, her heels sank low and she was only kept standing by the support of the powerful arm that shot out to steady her.

"Must you sneak around *my* island!" Cat hissed, wrenching her arm from Clay. Her words were definitely shaky; he was managing to catch her off guard a few times too many.

He laughed, and she was suddenly reminded of how stunning he could look in casual evening attire. He wore no tie, and his white silk shirt complemented the satin bronze of his throat and face. His light tweed suit was impeccably cut, displaying every fine feature of his somewhat barbaric build. The neatly trimmed beard added age to his thirty-three years, but she also noted at that moment that something else made him look older. A cast to his eyes; something deep within them, something that had aged him on the inside.

"I wasn't sneaking around your island, Cat. I was taking a walk along the beach. Care to join me?"

"No."

He shrugged, hefting his shoulders. "Suit yourself."

"I intend to."

He hesitated a moment. "Cat, you never did know when to give in."

Cat lifted a brow and tilted her chin. "Clay, there is no giving in.

65

You disappeared for almost seven years. I have a different life now. I like my life. I don't intend to let you destroy it."

"You little witch," he muttered, reaching for her arm again, "I'm trying to keep *you* from destroying your own life!"

"Really?" Cat murmured sarcastically. "You seem to have a funny way of going about it. And please take your hand off me."

Clay's scowl deepened and Cat felt herself being pulled forward. For a moment she didn't protest. He was sliding his arms around her waist, pressing her close, bringing his lips down on hers. She had meant to remain entirely limp, entirely passive, to prove that what had been was gone. But her senses took flight when his mouth touched hers. An inferno seemed to erupt as if from an explosion within. She froze in his arms, but she couldn't deny what she was feeling. Her limbs were weak and vitalized at the same time; her arms were willing to creep around his neck. She wanted nothing more than to part her lips to the searing persuasion of his tongue.

Wildfire . . . she had felt nothing like this in years; she had never wanted to feel this again. It was ecstasy, but it was pain, it was craving, it was needing. It was feeling that incredible burning inside that only he could create, only he could quench.

Somehow she managed not to move, not to allow her lips to part, not to slip her arms around his neck. Reminding herself that he had deserted her was a strong help. Only that painful fact helped to alleviate the agony of ignoring the pulse of his warm body against hers, the splendid vibrance, the intriguing tickle of his mustache. Why couldn't Jules kiss like this? she wondered desperately. Why didn't she feel this insane desire to forget there was a world when she was in his arms?

I don't want to feel this! she reminded herself, and with all her willpower she forced herself to remain still. Feeling like this meant wanting the earth to end when the rapture was taken away and the end of this fire meant the beginning of an age of ice.

Cat feigned an exasperated sigh and pulled from his touch. Clay didn't appear disgruntled or angry, merely speculative.

"You're not a bad actress, Cat," he murmured, "but that's not quite good enough. I feel your skin burn when I touch you . . . I can hear the thunder of your heart."

"You are an egotist!" Cat exclaimed, managing a disdainful ripple of light laughter. "I let you do that because I wanted you to know that things have changed. Clay! Listen to me. You've been gone almost seven years! Seven years! I have changed. I don't love you anymore—you have to understand that. And as soon as I can divorce you, I'm going to marry Jules. And if you won't be decent enough to forget that ridiculous bet we made today, I'll get your money somehow."

"I told you my terms today, Cat," he interrupted, his tone calm and deceptively casual. "I didn't get my five hundred thousand today. Therefore I get you for two months."

"Don't be ridiculous!" Cat snapped.

"You did want to search for the *Santa Anita,* didn't you?"

Thrown by his change of subject, Cat hesitated. "Where did you hear about the *Santa Anita?*" she demanded.

"I heard about her the same way every diver and treasure seeker has. We've all known she's been out there for centuries."

"Why this sudden interest in this particular wreck?"

He paused, hands stretched in his jacket pockets, shoulders shrugging. "I believe you might have pertinent information as to her actual whereabouts."

A very dry, bitter chuckle escaped Cat. "So that's it, Clay. Same as always. You never gave a damn about any woman really. I happened to be halfway presentable and I came complete with a headful of sea charts."

"You know, Cat," Clay enunciated slowly, his voice still disgustingly calm and casual, "you have a quality about you that really makes one long to tan your rear end."

"Well, don't get any ideas," Cat warned him sweetly. "You have been gone a long time. During one of those years of your disappearance, I happened to have taken some sound lessons in judo."

"Really?" Clay still insisted upon appearing amused. "How did that come about?"

"Easy," Cat murmured. "I had a young Chinese visitor who got a little carried away gambling on a trip to Freeport. He had to scrape the money together to return home and couldn't pay his bill for room and board. He convinced me a few lessons in self-defense would be invaluable for a woman running her own enterprise."

"How nice. Have you found your lessons invaluable?"

"*Most* men who comb the islands are gentlemen," Cat said with a sweet smile. "I've only used my lessons once—with a young man who got a little carried away in the lounge. A nice guy, really, very apologetic when sober. But yes—I discovered my lessons were invaluable. My inebriated friend was with the Notre Dame football team—twice my weight—and I was able to handle him."

Rather than appearing in the least perturbed or forewarned by her statements, to Cat's frustration, her phantom of a husband tossed back his head and laughed. "Oh, Cat, I really will be doing you a favor! You and Jules DeVante! You'd run him to the ground in a matter of weeks and despise him forever after. You need a very strong hand, my love, if you're ever going to share respect. I told you, Catherine, you're way too much woman for DeVante!"

"And I told you not to judge Jules!" Cat hissed back. "Now if you'll excuse me—"

"I'll join you for a nightcap."

"I didn't invite you to join me for a nightcap!" Cat protested as he slipped an arm through hers. "Clay, let go—"

"Or you'll throw me?" Clay chuckled. "Cat! Think of your clientele! They'll think you a terrible sportsman—sportswoman, sorry—if they see you trying to flip a man simply because you lost a race to him!"

"Clay—" Cat grated. "I wish to retire for the night. I'm going to my room."

"If you want to get technical," he warned her lightly, "it's my room, too."

"I don't want to get technical, and it isn't your room!"

"Then I suggest we have a nightcap in the lounge."

Cat took a deep breath and held it, seriously wishing she did have the nerve at present to dunk him over the dock. If only a vast hole would open in the earth and swallow him up! Tomorrow she could pretend that this whole thing *had* been a nightmare. Except she could still feel the spot on her lips where his hand touched them, and just thinking about his body next to hers sent delicious tingles of shivering anticipation.

Noooooo, she warned herself. There was a compatible chemistry between their bodies—seven years hadn't taken that away. But that was all. They were a storm and a fire—totally incompatible otherwise! She wouldn't allow him or his attraction to overwhelm her existence again.

She couldn't allow him into her room, nor did she want him in the lounge, where her friends and customers would be congratulating him and questioning him.

"I'll bring a couple of Jamaican coffees out back to the terrace."

"As you wish, Mrs. Miller."

"Don't you call me that!" Cat snapped.

Clay smiled slightly, but as Cat had noted earlier, the smile didn't touch eyes that held a touch of ancient wisdom. "It is your name."

Cat didn't contradict him. Biting her lip, she spun as gracefully as she could in the sand and turned for the lodge. She didn't hear him move, but when she had reached the intricately designed main double doors and cast her vision back to the dock, he was gone, as silently as he had come.

Cat considered ignoring her offer and locking herself into her room for the night. But Clay had done a very effective job of digging beneath her skin. She wasn't sure what he might do if she didn't appear on the terrace. What can he do? she wondered. Sighing, she realized it really didn't matter. He had made her a bundle of nerves. If she were honest with herself, she would have to admit quite frankly that she was afraid not to appear on the terrace.

Ten minutes later she was circling the aqua free-form pool and nervously looking for Clay.

"Over here!" he called pleasantly.

Her father's addition of a terrace was a magnificent piece of landscape planning. A tiny, decked island in the center of the clear water acted as a fruit juice bar in the daytime and a cocktail stop at night during the busy seasons of the year. It was reached on foot by vined bridges, and in the center was a pump that created two delightful waterfalls on either side. The pool itself was tiled and hedged by handsome Chattahoochee planters of hibiscus, blooming now in beautiful colors.

A few swimmers were enjoying the pool this evening; and the bursting bright displays of the waterfalls were all that could be seen against the black sky. Cat was glad she had thought of the terrace. There was safety in having others near. Safety! She chastised herself. She was safe. . . .

Cat carried her little tray across the tiny bridge and slapped Clay's mug down hard before him. "Your nightcap," she told him flatly.

"Thank you." He smiled. "You remembered—heavy whipped cream."

"I didn't remember anything," Cat mumbled. "My bartender happens to have a heavy hand." But she had remembered, she thought, sliding onto the stool next to his and pretending an interest in her own swizzle stick. She had automatically requested extra whipped cream.

And then she was remembering their wedding night, how they had flown to New Providence, and ordered Jamaican coffees in their room. As if it were yesterday, she could remember how he had licked a drop of whipped cream from the corner of her mouth and how they had laughed, and how somehow they had begun a teasing fight and she had discovered just how erotic whipped cream could be. . . .

"You do have a memory," he told her huskily. "I can see that becoming shade of red you're wearing beneath your tan, even in this light."

"Clay—" Cat brought her fingers to her throbbing temple, praying he would quit reading her every movement and thought. It wouldn't be so terribly bad if *she* could quit *feeling* him, but she couldn't. As if every cell in her body had been ripped open and left raw to the greatest sensitivity, she could literally feel him, although he wasn't touching her. He exuded a warmth and a strange heat and an indefinable aura that made her want to reach out and touch him, burrow against him, cling to his chest with exploring fingers.

I can't be feeling this, her mind raged, it's been so long.

She was thankful that Clay seemed willing to forgo further reference to their intimate past. Even as Cat was admitting to herself that Clay had always had and definitely still remained basically intriguing simply because he was so very male, Clay was patting his jacket pockets. "Have you got a light, Cat?"

"For what?" she inquired automatically. "You don't smoke."

He grinned, and although she was aggravated and confused and barely hanging on without screaming, Cat found herself responding in turn to his rakish smile. He would have made a hell of a pirate, she thought, riding the high seas with Drake.

He was a pirate. A modern-day pirate, claiming and ruling the treasures of the seas. . . .

"You changed—or so you tell me," he said. "How do you know I haven't picked up the smoking habit?"

"Because you wouldn't do anything to inhibit your ability as a diver," Cat said dryly.

"You're right there," he agreed. "But I did start smoking now and then. A pipe. I don't inhale."

"Well, I don't smoke and you know it. Why would I carry around matches? I don't even have a purse on me."

"Come on, Cat, humor me," Clay said, proving his point by pulling a small meerschaum pipe from his pocket. "There must be matches in the back of the bar somewhere."

Sighing, Cat slipped from her stool and lifted the hinge on the counter. It was almost pitch-black in the unlit service area, and she had to feel along the shelves, searching blindly with her fingers.

Clay waited until her sable head disappeared as she stopped on the other side, then slipped a tiny packet of white powder into her steaming coffee, swirling it quickly with her swizzle stick, wincing, feeling a physical pain at what he was doing.

I have to, Cat, he thought, because I can't let you marry that man. I have no right in your life, but I have to use every means, fair or foul, to keep you from DeVante. I wish so badly I could just explain it to you, Cat, but you would never believe me. You would defend him until the earth stopped spinning and I love you, Cat, you were all I thought about, when I knew, and when I didn't know, and I can't let you be used, I can't let you be hurt. . . .

"Here!" He saw her slender fingers—the nails not long but evenly filed, buffed to a shine as she seldom used polish because of the ravages of salt water—deposit a book of matches before him. Then her sable head appeared, the curled coils of her upsweep reflecting the dim light that filtered to them in a sheen of moon silver. She stayed on the other side of the counter, standing.

Clay watched her as he filled his pipe with tobacco from a leather pouch. She had always been beautiful. She was more so now, wearing her maturity like a regal cloak, and yet she still carried that essence of reckless spirit that was more tantalizing than the light hint of French perfume.

"That's a beautiful outfit, Cat," he said, cupping his hands around the bowl of the pipe as he struck a match. "Stunning." He raised a brow cryptically. "Might your exceptionally lovely appearance be in my honor?"

"No," Cat lied evenly. "I wasn't even sure I was going to see you." She frowned suddenly, and then laughed, a sound that was as light as the breeze, finally entirely natural. "Aren't you ever afraid you're going to set that beard on fire when you light your pipe?"

Clay laughed in return, lowering his head suddenly as he felt the sound choking in his throat. Damn, how he wanted to crush her into his arms. She had been a dream all those years, and now he could reach out and touch her skin that was satin, her hair that was silk. His hands could remember the lithe curves beneath the black outfit. His body could remember the perfect fit of hers beneath it, moving with overpowering sensuality, driving him insane, taking him to heaven on earth. "No." He raised his head and laughed easily again. "I've never thought about lighting my beard, but then I don't smoke this thing that much. By the way—what do you think of the beard?"

"I—uh—"

"Do you like it?"

"Yes, oh, I don't know. It's not bad. But no, I don't think that I do like it. It's strange, Clay. I do know you, and I don't know you. Maybe if you didn't have the beard, you wouldn't be quite so strange. I mean, you've really changed, Clay."

"Yes," he said abruptly, "I have changed." Oh, Cat, you don't know how I've changed, but you don't care to hear, he thought

72

bitterly. I understand, it's been so long, but I wish—yeah, I was praying—that you would have cared. . . . You think that I left you.

"Clay," she was saying, her voice soft and serious. "I have to tell you now, I'm simply going to tell Jules all about you tomorrow. I want what I have with Jules. I don't know why you've suddenly decided to make an appearance now, but it doesn't change anything for me. You'll get your money, Clay, but you won't get me. You're going to have to go right back to wherever it was that you were."

"So you're going to hand Tiger Cay over to DeVante? I'm not so sure you can, Cat. The island is half mine."

"Don't be absurd."

Clay smiled, biting down on his pipe. "Bring your tale of righteousness to court, Cat. If we ever get that far."

"All right, Clay," Cat hissed, losing patience. "You're right—we will settle all this in court, and Jules will be beside me! Now, I am going to bed—"

A hand came down over hers, a hand that pressed just enough to hint at the raw strength behind it. "We were having a nightcap, Cat. You haven't finished your coffee."

Cat picked up her mug and drained the warm liquid in quick swallows, ignoring the burning sensation of heat and liquor. "I hope you're not staying in my lodge, Clay."

"My boat is out in the harbor," he replied evenly, crossing his arms over his chest.

"Good," Cat said, depositing her empty cup on the counter. "Enjoy the view on the terrace as long as you like. I am going to bed."

"Good night."

It surprised Cat that he let her go so easily, but she wasn't about to ask him why. "I'm not sure if any of my nights are going to be good for a while," she murmured, lifting the counter hatch and striding by him.

She didn't pause as she walked across the tiny bridge, nor did she dare look back until she had entered the rear doors of the lodge. She could just make out his form, seemingly magnified by the mist of spray from the tinkling waterfalls.

Oh, God, why did he come back? she wondered desperately.

73

At that moment she turned and ran, hoping she would encounter no guests. In that respect she was lucky. She didn't encounter a single soul as she raced through the main house to the left wing and her own door. She closed it behind her, as if barricading herself against an attack, her heart thundering. But no one was behind her; Clay hadn't chased her. Still, she was careful to bolt her lock.

When she felt her breathing return to normal, she moved away from the door. She automatically began to pull the pins from her hair, scattering them haphazardly as she did so. Things will work out, she tried to assure herself. I do love Jules, and Clay is wrong, Jules will stand beside me. Oh, God, I'll never sleep, he has made me feel like a volcano about to explode and I can't stand thinking about him but I can't forget him and when I think about him I think that I want him again.

No, she reprimanded herself, a lifetime isn't worth a few minutes of pleasure, a marriage has to exist outside of the bedroom, but oh, lord, would I love to be with him again and why am I such a fool to feel this way. I can't help what I'm feeling; my body won't let me. I will never be able to sleep.

But as she paced, she dragged a nightgown from her closet and carelessly shed her black halter-dress to drag the thin peignoir over her head, and out of habit her pacing took her to the bathroom, where she almost made her gums bleed by viciously scrubbing her teeth and then turned her face pink by attacking it with her washcloth.

She paced the huge bedroom again with her thoughts running rampant, thinking she should have perhaps dressed in a bathing suit and returned to the pool—surely Clay would be gone by now—to work off steam in a series of energetic laps.

But she found herself yawning instead, and then curling into her bed. It's stupid to try, she thought, plumping her pillow, all I'll do is lie here—and think back all those years to the days when I was a wife, sleeping beside him.

But she didn't suffer the torment of memory anymore, because surprisingly her head had barely hit the pillow before she was deeply, soundly, out, her sleep undisturbed by dreams or sounds.

* * *

74

Cat was dreaming and the dream was pleasant. It was a vague dream, undefined, but she could feel the warmth of the sun and hear the delightful cascade of the waterfall bubbling. The dream slowly faded with the irritation of a persistent rapping sound. Cat fought the sound for a while, but it drove away the pleasant, relaxed sensations of the dream. Her eyes flickered and opened, and then she realized someone was knocking at her door.

"Yes?" she murmured sleepily, blinking to clear her vision.

"It's me, *chérie*, Jules. May I come in?"

"Oh! Jules!" Cat brushed her disheveled hair from her face and rubbed her eyes. Was it that late? She had slept so soundly.

"Just a second!" she called, about to leap from bed and grab her robe.

She never made it off the bed. She froze in shock and disbelief as the bathroom door suddenly flew open and Clay—sans beard and with little white flecks of shaving cream still specking his face—strode quickly toward the door, clad only in a large white towel knotted low over his hips. "Don't bother, darling," he said cheerfully, "I'll get it."

And before her benumbed senses could respond, the door opened. A half-naked Clay was facing a dumbfounded Jules.

"Oh," Clay said, his tone deeply laced with regretful sorrow, "you must be DeVante. I'm Miller. Cat's husband. Sorry we had to meet this way. Cat should have had a chance to tell you. . . ."

Cat wasn't really hearing him. She knew she had gone parchment-white beneath her tan, as white as the man staring over Clay's shoulder at her. Jules' thin, sensitive brows had flown high, his hazel eyes were so dilated they appeared to be a solid sheet of empty pupil. His slender patrician nose was pinched and the line of his lips had all but disappeared, as chalk-white as his face.

Jules was ignoring the hand extended by Clay. He snapped out a single epithet in French that totally expressed his opinion of her.

Cat flinched, but his stinging word broke the freeze of incredulous horror that had held her immobile. "Jules, wait!" she shrieked, fingers clenched tightly in her sheets. Oh, God, what was she going to say? How on earth was she going to explain the half-naked man

75

in the towel, her own rumpled appearance, the state of the bed. More than anything in the world she wanted to kill Clay, tear him limb from limb as he stood before Jules with his expression of pained discomfort.

"Jules, this isn't what it appears to be! This man has set me up, he's trying to destroy you and me."

Jules' voice sounded as if it were coming from deep within the ocean. "*Is* this your husband, Cat? Your *deceased* husband?"

"No! Well, yes, but—"

"Cat!" Clay interrupted in mock agony.

Jules turned smartly on his heel.

"Jules, wait! *Attend-moi!*"

But Cat's semihysterical pleas were ignored. Jules kept going. She sprang furiously from the bed to race after him, but Clay slammed the door before she reached it. Cat slammed into the wood, screaming at Clay every label she could think of from her not-too-limited seafaring vocabulary. "You bastard! You set me up—"

And then she lost all reason, so infuriated that she simply went berserk, flying at him.

If she had been calm, she might have stood a small chance. Her mind instinctively turned to weight, counterweight, and balance. A foot wedged correctly behind his ankle and a subtle shift and she was able to bring Clay down. But Clay had obviously had a few lessons along the way she had known nothing about. She had the deep satisfaction of hearing him grunt with pain, but then she was sailing herself, landing hard beside him. Then he rolled, and his weight was secured over hers; she was pinned, but still half crazed with outrage and fighting like a wild woman.

"Calm down, Cat, I don't want to hurt you."

But she couldn't calm down, she attacked him with furiously pounding arms, trying to strike, scratch, bite—anything—hissing a spate of oaths at him all the while. But despite her half insane and staunch efforts, he managed to secure her wrists and pull them high over her head, subduing her wild clawing.

Their eyes met. Both were breathing heavily; the air around them seemed heavy with explosive tension.

"Catherine," Clay said slowly, shaking his head slightly and concealing a wry grin. She was like no other woman alive, determined, capable, totally oblivious to odds. Willpower kept her from knowing the meaning of the word *lose*. Powered by sheer fury as she was now, she could tax even his strength. "Cat," he repeated quietly, breathing more normally. "I know you can't believe this now, but I did what I did because I care . . . because I don't want your life ruined."

He winced slightly as his words brought about another explosion of fighting energy and whole new line of epithets. He tensed and waited, tightening his grip around her wrists. She stopped in shock when her struggles served only to disengage the towel from his hips. Her eyes riveted back to his as she lay still, eyes wide and then narrowing. "Damn you," she hissed, but he couldn't help a small smile then as he saw her blush despite herself. "You were taking a shower in *my* bathroom!"

"Technically—our bathroom," he corrected. As well as robbing him of his towel, the struggle had hiked Cat's gown high to her hips. The material was thin anyway, but now the flesh of their thighs touched; the coarse curled hair of his crushed to the smooth softness of hers. Clay could feel his own heat rising, and he was aware from the erotic electricity racing beneath him that she too could feel it. Her features were suddenly white, chiseled stone, as if she were afraid to breathe and give away more. A satanic urge gripped him. "What's the matter, Cat?" he queried, brows raising in a sardonic tease. "Can't you handle it?"

Her emerald eyes touched his, glittering like a million facets. "Hell will freeze over before I can't handle you, Clay."

Knowing he was infuriating her further—if possible—Clay still could not prevent another deep chuckle. "Come to think of it, Cat, you always did handle things remarkably well. . . ."

"You son of a—"

"Okay, stop it!" Clay interrupted her, his voice a whiplash, his mind turning to the seriousness of the situation and the maneuvering he had yet to manage. "I'm really sorry—"

"Sorry!" Cat raged. "You purposely set me up, you destroyed my life, you dragged me down to the floor—"

"Self-defense," Clay interrupted curtly. "Sorry I was so rude as to learn a few countermeasures myself. I know you're currently wishing that I had disappeared eternally into the Atlantic, and you're probably envisioning various means to return me to the devil. For your own sake, Cat, settle down."

"Settle down! Do you know what you've done?" Cat shrieked, testing his grip on her wrists again. It was impossible to break his vise of steel and she was worn out. "Clay—you're crazy. A sane man doesn't do the things you're doing. Now, I'll try to forget everything that's happened if you just get up and let me go."

Clay tilted back his head and laughed. "You'll forget! Cat, you've never forgotten a wrong in your life. Hell will freeze over before I ever believe a comment like that from you. And—" His voice deepened, his spurt of humor gone. "I guarantee you, hell will be a place of dangling icicles before I let you run after that Frenchman."

"I'm going to marry that Frenchman!" Cat exploded.

"No, I doubt it," Clay reiterated calmly. "I told you he had no backbone. He left here like a jellyfish."

"Oh?" Cat narrowed her eyes to emerald slits. "What did you expect of him after that farce you pulled?"

"If it were me, Cat," he said heatedly, his face leaning dangerously close to hers so that she was treated to the enticing scent of fresh shaving lotion and a too close view of the iron in the shape of his now unblurred jaw, "I wouldn't have walked out. I would have demanded my explanation then and there. You might have been throttled, but I wouldn't have walked out."

Cat clenched her teeth down hard in misery. She wanted to claw his handsome face to ribbons, while at the same time becoming more and more aware of his body pressed to hers, the heat that touched her, alive and warm, the hands that held her, hips crushing hers; his chest, riddled with hair that brushed through the fabric of her gown to tease her breasts.

"Walk out!" she suddenly hissed. "Don't you dare mention the words *walk out!* You took a cruise out of here one day that walked you out of my life. Now get off me! I am going after Jules—and I'm going to explain that you came back totally insane!"

"And he's going to believe you? You're sounding crazy, Cat. Besides, I'm sure Monsieur DeVante is long gone by now, Cat."

Cat paled. He was right. When crossed or hurt, Jules left immediately to sulk.

"God, do I hate you, Clay," she told him.

His smile twisted into something very bitter and a touch sad. "Do you, Cat? Maybe. I hope to change that, and you should try to change it yourself, for your own benefit. My two months start today."

"Your two months! What two months? I never agreed—"

"You don't have to agree. You've got no choices left. You owe me either five hundred thousand dollars—or yourself. It seems I get the latter—and I want it today. Tomorrow we're going to start preliminaries on the search for the *Santa Anita*. That means I'm going to have to hear everything you know about her whereabouts tonight."

"Oh, Clay, you really are crazy," Cat said, shaking her head. "You may have me down right now, but you can't hold me forever. And if you think I'm going to follow you anywhere once I'm up, or help you in the least, you'd better start thinking again."

He smiled, switching both her wrists to one hand—easily, to her chagrin—and lightly caressed her cheek with the knuckles of his free hand. "I don't think I need to think again, Cat. Granted, I'll be watching my back when you're around, but I seriously believe you'll see things my way shortly. You can't pay me. And besides that, you want to find the *Santa Anita*. I'm the only hope you have."

Cat suddenly started to laugh. "I don't owe you a thing, Clay! If we're still married, as you claim, then I can't owe you anything! Wives don't owe their husbands!"

"But wives do live with their husbands," he countered. "And you're going to start living with me."

"Oh, really?" Cat demanded sardonically, twisting from his touch. "Starting when?"

He released her very slowly, tensed for a spurt of action and warning her with his eyes that she not attempt one as he deftly retied his towel. "Tonight, Cat—platonically—if you wish. But we do start out tomorrow, and I can't believe that will be a hardship for you. We both know the *Santa Anita* carried Aztec crown jewels. Think of the history, Cat, think of the archeologists and historians

79

the world over, who would die for that find. And it would really be your father's. Think of what it would mean. . . ."

Clay stood and offered Cat a hand, which she ignored, rising gracefully on her own steam and still poised for a quick flight if he reached to touch her again. He smiled and walked toward the bathroom door, then paused, his back still to her. "And—when this is all over, if you still decide you want the Frenchman, I'll do the explaining. If he loves you, Cat, he'll come back."

As Cat stared after him incredulously, torn to pieces by anger and pain and a million other emotions she couldn't even begin to fathom, he calmly reentered the bathroom and closed the door behind him.

CHAPTER FIVE

Cat finally galvanized into action and slammed a clenched fist into the bathroom door. "Would you please get out of there—and out of my room!"

Clay chuckled. "Give me a minute. If you toss a naked man out your door, your situation is going to appear even worse!"

Muttering explosively, Cat decided to forgo a shower and hastily slipped into a pair of jeans and a tank top. If he wouldn't get out, she would. Raking her brush quickly through her hair, she left her room behind, grateful for the moment that she lived in the lodge and could wash in the lobby facilities.

It was early and still quiet. Cat left the lodge and hurried past the dock and sailors and fishermen, forcing a smile as she waved cheerfully. Her footsteps took her to the north beach, where she plopped down on the sand, closing her eyes and praying that the cool morning breeze would soothe her tumultuous fury so that she could *think*.

Just yesterday he had appeared and today her life was a shambles. He had come out of the blue, maneuvered her—using no scruples—and now, thanks to him, she didn't even have Jules.

I should hurt worse than this, she thought. Jules is gone, and thinks the worst of me. But she wasn't hurt. She was angry—and very, very confused. Why am I not more worried about Jules? she wondered. I do love him. No, she answered herself. Not really. You didn't want to care that way, not again, and this is the price you now pay, this emptiness. You will miss certain things, but to say that that was love . . . And yet, until yesterday, she would have sworn she was in love.

I'm not thinking straight. Everything is still such a shock. But I have to think because I have to decide what to do. Since they were still married, it was doubtful that he could hold her to a debt. But then the gambling they had engaged in wasn't legal anyway and so legal consequences weren't the problem. She didn't put it past Clay to announce to the yachtsmen who supported the cay with tourism that Cat gambled with money she didn't have, didn't pay up when she was the loser. And Clay wanted the *Santa Anita*. He wasn't scoffing at her belief in a secret theory. He wanted to know what it was, he was willing to put the salvage in her hands.

But she couldn't go with him, not after the things he had done. She didn't even know yet if he might have been purposely responsible for her spill. And how in hell did he get into her locked room without her hearing him? Cut and shave that beard without her awakening?

And where had he been all those years? Cat groaned softly, fingers clenching into the pink sand. Why hadn't she let him explain? Maybe there wasn't a reason, there couldn't be. He simply hadn't wanted to come home. Only the *Santa Anita* had brought him now. I can't still feel anything for him, Cat told herself, it's just been too long.

Too long or not, the fascination that had first drawn her to him was still there. Like a fine wine, he seemed to have improved with age.

81

"I did what I did for a reason, Cat."

Her reverie broken, Cat turned with dismay to see Clay behind her, dressed now in tan leisure slacks and a navy Izod. The navy seemed to enhance the incredibly deep color of his eyes, or maybe it was his face, clean-shaven now, so ruggedly contoured.

"I brought you some coffee," he offered, stooping to hand her a steaming mug.

Cat accepted the cup silently, and turned back to study the ocean, not particularly at ease to have him hunched so close beside her. "What do I have to do to get away from you?" she questioned tonelessly.

"You can't get away from me," he told her, sitting cross-legged a foot away. "Accept it and you might enjoy herself."

Cat took a sip of her coffee. One sugar, no cream . . . apparently there were things he remembered easily too.

"How can I accept anything?" Cat queried bitterly. "Don't you realize what you've done?"

"I told you, Cat, I have reasons, good reasons."

She spun on him. "How did you get in this morning without my hearing you?"

He smiled. "I came in last night and it was easy. I picked the lock."

"Last night!"

"Don't get huffy. I slept on the floor. And it was damned uncomfortable. And you didn't wake up because I slipped a very light sleeping potion in your coffee."

Cat stared at him, past anger. "You're incredible! Simply incredible. How can you possibly admit all that so casually?"

"Would you rather I lied?"

"I'd rather you return to wherever you've been!"

Clay shrugged, eyes steady on the turquoise surf. "Well, am I abducting you in the morning, or are you coming along willingly?"

Cat laughed suddenly. "I must say, you do have faith! How do you know we'll find the *Santa Anita*?"

Clay lifted a brow with a pleasant smile and sipped his coffee. "Rumor has been floating around that you want to search for her.

82

In fact, rumor got fairly specific. You and DeVante were at odds over the possibility of salvage. Your fiancé didn't have any faith."

Cat lowered her eyes. "But you believe I know what I'm talking about?"

"Yes." Clay stared straight at her and she found herself meeting his eyes. "The Frenchman is a fool. Anyone who knows anything about these islands would be a fool to scoff at any of your knowledge. Armchair history chasers the world over know Jason Windemere possessed the finest authentic ancient mariners' charts to be had."

"Ahhhh . . ." Cat murmured, "we're back to my father."

"Only in the same sense that Jason gave you your love for the sea and the islands, Cat."

They both fell silent for a few minutes. Cat was more bewildered than ever. He had moved in like an earthquake at sea, but now he seemed determined to find calmer waters. What was he really after? Cat wondered. And wasn't she much, much better off hating him?

"Tell me something," she said crisply. "Were you responsible for that Cigarette just happening to slash across the racecourse?"

He twisted his form in the sand, leaning slightly as he caught her chin between his thumb and forefinger, holding her eyes steady to his. "No. I would never have done anything to put your life in danger."

"All right," Cat said, trying not to flinch from his touch. "One more question. What happened all those years ago? Where have you been?"

Clay released her chin and turned back to the sea. "I don't want to talk about it now, Cat. But I promise I will tell you before the expedition ends."

"I haven't agreed to go on any expedition."

"I haven't asked for your agreement." Clay laughed. "I only gave you two choices—coming with me of your own accord, or coming by friendly persuasion."

"Miller," Cat snapped, "you just sank your own ship."

Clay laughed easily, threading sand through his fingers. "Poor Cat. You do hate to lose. That's half our problem, isn't it? I'm the one man who can beat you—no matter what your game."

"You haven't beaten me."

"But I have, Cat. In a Hobie Cat—in your room." He grinned, feigning apology and fear as he saw her fingers tighten around her mug and her teeth clench. "But only because I'm heavier, of course!"

Cat suddenly wasn't sure whether she wanted to laugh or bash the mug over his head. His next statement, quiet, serious, halted any action on her part. "But I can give you something no other man can, Cat. Real faith, real belief, and real respect. Because I'm not afraid of you, Cat. Nor do I put you on some type of unreachable pedestal, adoring from a distance. I know you, Cat. DeVante will never know you as I do."

"Don't be absurd," Cat interrupted. "You don't know me anymore."

"If I'd never known you, Cat, I'd know you. We're two of a kind. I think you know that too."

"Really?" Cat arched a brow cryptically. "If you have faith in me, Clay, it's new." She suddenly found herself fighting an absurd urge to cry. "I wanted to go with you on other salvage trips. You never let me come."

Clay stood, dusting the sand from his pants. He was silent for a minute, looking down at her. Then he spoke, softly. "I was wrong, Cat. I made a lot of mistakes—I'll never deny that."

He started walking back toward the lodge, hands in his pockets. Twenty feet from her he stopped, turning back. "If you want to find the *Santa Anita*, Cat, meet me in your father's library at eight tonight."

Cat stared at him, hesitating, then asked, "Clay, where have you been? How can you expect me to agree to assist you in making my life a disaster when you won't tell me anything?"

Clay grinned. "If I remember correctly, you didn't want to know." He shrugged. "But meet me tonight, and I'll tell you a little."

"Sounds like you're bribing me."

"Am I? Not really. I already warned you that curiosity killed the Cat."

"Maybe I'm not that curious."

84

"Maybe—but I doubt it."

Whistling, he started back toward the lodge. "Think I'll check on my docks."

"*Your* docks!"

"Sure—if we share five hundred thousand, we share the docks!"

"You're too much, Miller!"

He didn't respond. Cat stared after him until his tall form, so lithe and agile as he walked the sand, disappeared. "Damn him!" she muttered. Cat turned her eyes back to the ocean. On the horizon she could see the yacht that had brought Clay, listing gently in the calm surf. Shading her eyes with her hand and squinting, she tried to read the boat's name. Her heart took a little leap as she made out *Sea Witch II.*

There were little things that Clay hadn't forgotten. *I was wrong, Cat. I made a lot of mistakes—I'll never deny that. . . .*

His words came back to plague her. I made mistakes too, Clay, she thought, but I really can't tell you that because it's too late to matter. It has to be too late.

Sighing, Cat hugged her knees to her chest. What am I going to do, she wondered, staring out at the boat. If only she had seen the name yesterday, she would have known, she would have recognized Clay. And never fallen for his goading. But would it have made any difference? Clay said it himself, he played to win. He would have merely found another way of twisting her arm.

Why the hell am I playing these games with myself? she asked herself next. Because no matter what he had done, she knew she would meet him in the library. He was right. She wanted the *Santa Anita.*

And I want to know what happened to Clay, I want to know where he has been, even if the answers hurt. *And I want to go with him.*

No, she told herself, it will be a simple business venture. I will never give him my heart again; it's already been shattered.

"Oh, hell!" Cat muttered, rising and brushing the sand from her jeans. "Why is this happening? I had forgotten you, Clay Miller. I really had. . . ." Well, you were almost forgotten, she added silently.

She turned her steps purposefully for the lodge. The night's menu needed to be discussed with Swen. Harris Smith of Georgetown was due to arrive for lunch so that they might discuss a trade on diving trips for the guests of their respective lodges. She had a meeting with the staff at three, and with a sales rep from Star Divers at four. By eight, she would be able to meet with Clay with a certain amount of collected cool.

Where the hell was Sam? Cat wondered irritably. She stopped in her tracks and her gaze turned back to the turquoise water and the *Sea Witch II* swaying like a crystal beauty at anchor. Clay would never leave the yacht like that for an extended period of time.

Damn it! So that's where Sam was! Guarding the *Sea Witch II*. He had already gone over to the enemy. Cat could feel the temperature of her blood rising steadily, and kicked up a pile of sand to lose steam. "Oh, the hell with all of them," she muttered. "There's probably not a male in the world worth trusting! I just hope one of those two is planning on taking out the afternoon diving party!"

Clay took a long sip of beer, crooked his elbow behind his head, and lay back against the hull of the *Sea Witch II*, squinting as he stared into the brilliance of the sun at noon. He closed his eyes completely. It was comfortable here, the sun was hot but the sea breeze cool, the waves beneath him created a gentle lull. Last night hadn't given him much sleep, and now he could feel lethargy seeping into his system. He didn't really fight it.

It was funny, he thought, it had been a day just like this when his life had taken its strange detour. The boat had been another *Sea Witch*, his first, and the woman who had filled his thoughts, as she did now, was also his sea witch, Cat. He had thought of her thus from the day they had met. She combined all the elements and mysteries of the sea, passion and turbulence, gaiety and depth, crystal calm and clarity and raging storms.

He hadn't known he loved her when he married her. He did know that Jason Windemere wished to see his headstrong daughter wed, and he knew that Cat fascinated him as no other woman ever had. Never had he met a woman more innately sensual, beguiling, and innocent, yet possessing an inner peace. Once he held her, he became entranced. She was a witch—a sea witch. He couldn't sleep, because all he could do was think of her, remember her in his arms, the feel of long slim legs entwined with his. She was an obsession, he had to have her, had to keep her, his alone.

But at twenty-six, he had also been determined to seek his fortune and make his name. Somehow he had expected that marriage would tame Cat, change her into a sweet and docile creature, content to wait to greet him each time he returned, the perfect female, soft and beautiful, welcoming him with fragrant hair and silken skin.

Cat had other ideas, and why he had opposed them, he wasn't sure. He admired his wife's quick mind; he knew her knowledge of the Bahamian seas and history was comparable to that of a well-programmed computer, and that as well as being one of the most competent divers he had ever met, Cat was capable of spieling off every step taken by Jacques Cousteau in his quest to develop modern-day scuba gear. He didn't resent his wife's keen mind; it fascinated him, as did her darkly fringed emerald eyes, abundance of sable hair, her lithe form, so slender and yet so shapely, so perfectly toned.

He simply hadn't been ready to make her his partner in all things. An orphan, Clay had, by nature and inclination, become a loner. He had worked for every penny he made, seldom strengthening friendships because he was either studying or earning a dollar.

He'd grown up in the heart of Kansas, but even there the lure of the sea had reached him. The ocean granted her treasures to those with perseverance, and he had plenty of that. And the United States Navy had been quite willing to take a poor boy to sea and school him and open up the mystical world of aqua and indigo magic to him.

The Navy had enhanced Clay's talents and also had given him a certain worldliness and sophistication. He learned he held the power to charm and persuade and had very little trouble getting backers for his first expeditions. He quickly became a "name" and the basic principles of honesty and judicial dealings ruled his business from the first; there wasn't a time when he went out that his backers weren't well rewarded. By the time Clay married Cat, he was well on his way to a position of prominence—and he had become his own backer.

Had it all really been seven years ago? he wondered, feeling the hot kiss of the sun on his face. Almost. Summer would make it exactly seven years. Seven years since he had lain like this, thinking of Cat, realizing that he loved his wife, admitting to himself that he did flirt with other women in front of her to hurt her. To remind her that he was his own man, that marriage didn't give her a right to his mind, his plans. He made his decisions, he worked where he chose, when he chose, with whom he chose.

Cat had tied him into knots. Since his years in the Navy, he had enjoyed the company of women, loving variety, taking pleasure, giving pleasure, but never giving his heart, never caring much about seeing any female again. His true mistress had been the sea—until Cat, and reason and logic had gone up in flames. She drove him crazy, and he was well aware he demanded more than he gave. If he could have, he would have possessed her completely, locking her away from everyone. The night he had seen her with another man almost sent him into a murderous rage.

But on the *Sea Witch* that day so many years ago, he had admitted he really loved her, and needed her. And that all their fights were so stupid, because there was no reason on earth why he couldn't share his dreams and desires with her and have her with him always. She would make a magnificent partner. If he hadn't been such a macho jackass, he could already have had a life any man would call heaven.

And that was when the sea had begun to swell. Deep in the bowels of the earth, a plate had shifted. And as he had groggily lifted his head, the world began to spin. The water, tranquilly blue just moments before, had become a vortex of viciously spinning black.

Somewhere, miles and miles away, a tidal wave hit from the shattering of the earth deep within the sea. But only those who studied the strange and erratic workings of the *tsunami* would ever guess that the disappearance of Clayton Miller was related. He would simply be cast as another victim of the infamous Devil's Triangle. . . .

And yet it would be years before he would remember the action of the sea. It would be years before he would remember anything. His first memory would be that of opening his eyes, of seeing a strange Bahamian with a mouthful of gold teeth smiling down at him with concern. "Hey, mon, you all right? You been floating out there on that plank for a long time, mon. What's your name? You an American?"

"I don't know. . . ." Clay had said.

And so his rescuers had adopted him. They were a carefree crew, singing calypso late into the night, teaching him to play their rattrap guitars. They sang and ate and swam and fished—and carried illegal contraband between the Caribbean and the States. Clay didn't know a damned thing about himself (not even what he looked like until he saw himself in the mirror in the galley), but he did seem to remember bits and pieces of history and geography. And he didn't condemn the men with whom he sailed. The islands were famous for breeding poverty; these men had families they hoped to feed and they trafficked in nothing deadly.

But that was not the opinion of the officials who had picked them up in certain hostile waters. They had interrogated the crew, showing a special interest in Clay.

"*Qué es su nombre?* What is your name?" an officer bellowed at him.

"I don't know my name. *Yo no sé* . . . I don't know. . . ."

They asked him for hours and hours, lights blinding his eyes. If he started to fall, they prodded him up and continued hammering at him. "What is your name? Who are you . . . who are you . . . who are you. . . ."

Then he started to break, laughing until he cried. "I don't know, if I could tell you, I'd be just ecstatic. . . ."

They weren't sadistic monsters; they were merely officers in a country where rules were stringent, liberty meaningless, and duty all. Clay suffered no broken limbs, no beatings. To their credit, they tried very hard to discover his identity. They took his fingerprints, but apparently they never went to the right agencies. And so Clay worked the endless fields of sugarcane. Day after day after day, growing closer and closer to his Bahamian rescuers, who kept singing away their imprisonment.

The nights were the worst. He suffered a dream. He would be lying there and she would come to him, sleek as satin, her movements as fluid as turquoise seas. She was tall, her naked flesh a whisper of silk, her hair, a luxurious tangle of deepest mahogany, cascading over her shoulders, fanning over her breasts, touching him.

Her eyes were emerald, secretive, promising, beguiling. Her smile was as seductive as Circe's song. She would come near, he would reach out to touch her, to entwine his fingers into the night velvet of her hair, to bring her down to him, feel the length of her hair against his chest, bury himself in its richness.

And then he would waken shaking, sweating. She was so close, so real. Every time he dreamed of her he was sure he would remember. . . . But the memory didn't come. He knew he was haunted by an enchantress . . . by a witch. . . .

The days became months, the months, years. His body grew hard and strong from constant labor while his mind was honed by all that was around him. He learned that men could be bought, and that escape was possible.

On a moonless night he and his Bahamian rescuers left their prison behind them; their means, a rowboat and the cunning of desperation.

But Clay could not escape his dreams. They haunted his new life as he returned to the sea, following instincts that were also dreams.

And then there was Ariel. Ariel who loved him, but also knew he loved someone else. Ariel who knew she would give him up the day he returned with his memory intact.

It was the sea that had taken his past.

It had been only natural that in the sea he found his past returning. . . .

Cat entered the library that night as calmly and coolly as if theirs were a prearranged business meeting between casual associates.

"I do trust that whatever I have to say will be kept entirely confidential," Cat queried flatly as she sailed regally into the room to take a position matter-of-factly behind her father's old maritime desk.

Clay, comfortably seated in a well-padded recliner with his legs dangling casually over the side, arched a brow, not attempting to

90

conceal his amusement. "Of course," he murmured sardonically. "I certainly don't intend to hand the treasure over to someone else." He snapped shut the book he had been reading and rose to seat himself upon the desk, leaning his torso toward his wife. "Let's cut the Queen of Sheba act, okay, Cat?"

"Do you want the theory or not?" she asked icily.

"Oh, please!" he murmured, "by all means let's hear it."

"Why in the hell are we bothering wi—"

"Okay, okay, wait!" Clay said, interrupting her with a hand lightly clamped over her mouth. "I'm sorry. But we can't work like this. Let's start over. I have to know where we're going, of course. And it's hardly likely that I'm forcing you on a trip I want to hand over to someone else."

Cat watched him suspiciously until he removed his hand from her mouth. Then she sighed, lowering her eyes. "Okay—common knowledge. The *Santa Anita* left Cartagena with her full flotilla in the spring of 1585. She carried not only the customary silver and gold from Nombre de Dios but a special cargo of precious inlaid gems—the Aztec crown jewels, gifts from the governors to King Philip II. The flotilla was hit by a hurricane just south of Cuba and at least twenty ships in the flotilla went down, among them, *supposedly*, the galleon *Santa Anita.*" Cat really couldn't help herself, her voice was growing excited. She knew she was right, and Clay was listening.

"Key word," he murmured, "is *supposedly*. What do you think really happened—and why?"

Cat pulled out the middle drawer of the desk and triumphantly produced a document in strange English. It was a mimeograph of something else, and the old language was difficult to decipher. He strained his eyes as Cat began to talk again. "My dad bought the original from an old woman in London years ago. Oh, Clay, I know it's authentic! I had the parchment carbon dated and it was written in the early sixteen hundreds!"

Clay chuckled softly at her instant change to enthusiasm, but frowned perplexedly. "I believe you, Cat, but I don't get it! As far as I can make out, this was written by a mate from one of Drake's ships—"

"Precisely!" Cat exclaimed.

"Cat—Drake was English. Pirating for his queen."

"Right! Just listen for a minute. Drake left England in 1585 with glorious plans. He was attacking Hispaniola, Cartagena, and Panama. But everything went wrong. The cities didn't have the ransoms he demanded for pay, his plundering was-poor all the way round. Before he could even reach Panama, rumors hit that the Spaniards were flooding the area. Drake left, sailing for home. He was supposed to stop by the Roanoke colony—"

"Cat—"

Exuberance brought her to feet, reaching out to grab Clay by the shoulders, determined to shut him up so that he would listen. "According to this letter a boat from Drake's fleet broke away, sailing into the Bahamas while Drake went northward up the Florida coast. Anyway, this mate from the *Golden Hind* writes about meeting a galleon upon a reef so terrible her corals were already strewn with wrecks. They meant to seize the galleon and plunder her treasure, but they fired too hastily and the galleon went down upon the reef. It has to be the *Santa Anita*, Clay. The crew of the *Golden Hind* never reported their meeting with her, because their carelessness cost them the treasure! And the reef can only be the Mira Por Vos in the western sector of Crooked Island Passage!"

Cat suddenly realized that she had slipped her arms around his neck, that she was laughing, staring into his eyes and feeling heady with the response of his interest.

"You mean," he said, "that no one has ever been able to find the *Santa Anita* because they've all been looking in the wrong place—south of Cuba?"

"Yes! Oh, Clay, I know I'm right! I just have this feeling. . . ."

"I believe you!" Clay laughed. "First thing in the morning we head for Crooked Island Passage and Mira Por Vos."

That simple, Cat thought. She said something, and it was that simple. He believed her, he was ready to go.

A silence sprang between them suddenly. The first thrill of excitement ebbed from her, and Cat suddenly felt trapped. She became aware of the fabric of Clay's shirt beneath her fingers, aware that their breaths were mingling, aware again of that beguiling scent of his aftershave, of his sizzling jet eyes. Aware of the heat of his body, emanating to hers.

She withdrew her arms quickly and turned away, walking across the room, her heels clicking against the wood flooring. She had almost forgotten that he had walked out on her and had returned only to make a mess of her life, had manipulated her just this morning, had brought her down and proved himself the stronger.

"I've a good chart of the passage within this bookshelf," she said crisply, tensing as she suddenly felt Clay behind her. A shiver raced up her spine. He was so different, she really didn't know him at all anymore. And yet he was right. She did know him, would always know him. Adventurers, they were two of a kind.

She clenched her eyes tightly closed. No, not again, she prayed, please not again.

"Forget the map, we'll get it in the morning. Let's get some sleep now. I want to be under way by six."

Cat nodded stiffly and replaced a book she had pulled out in a random movement. "Swen will have to be in charge if Sam is coming with us," she murmured, more for something businesslike to say than to inform Clay of anything. He wasn't touching her, but she was afraid to turn around. "Well," she said, sliding past him, "I guess I'll go on down—"

Clay caught her around the waist. "*We'll* go on down."

His autocratic tone had the exact effect she needed to regain her senses. "Oh, no, *we* won't—"

"Cat!" His fingers tightened around her midriff, his voice was harsh with exasperation. "I told you we started living together as of tonight! When we go out tomorrow it's for a pleasure cruise as far as anyone else knows. Mr. and Mrs. Miller reunited at last. Do you want a pack of scavengers following us all the way?"

"I'd rather have scavengers than a vulture in my—"

"Not *your* anything, remember? Share and share alike—what a lovely couple we are! I'm too damned tired to argue anymore tonight."

"Oh! And I'm supposed to be sorry you're tired when you spent the night destroying my life?"

"Oh, shut up. Right now, Mrs. Miller, I'm planning on sleeping on the floor. But if you keep me awake any longer, I just may get a second wind and decide your claws are worth the rewards!"

Cat clenched her teeth and stared at him, wishing fervently she had kept her judo instructor around a few months longer, long enough to teach her how to handle Clay. She jerked out of his grasp. "All right," she said hoarsely. "Sleep on my damned floor. Just keep your hands off me." She turned, threw open the library door, and started for the stairway.

He was right behind her. "My hands?" he whispered, the sound tickling her ear. "Those were your hands thrown around my neck earlier. Poor Cat, you never could decide whether to seduce me or not!"

"If you don't stop, you'll be sleeping in the bathtub."

"Sounds erotic."

"Clay," Cat snapped. They started down the wing and Cat pushed her door open, sailing in and ignoring Clay as she rummaged for a heavy gown and stalked into the bathroom, slamming the door behind her. She heard him moving about the room as she brushed her teeth, then drowned out all sounds with the furious jet of the shower.

What have I let myself in for? she wondered like a broken record. The water seemed to numb her. She didn't know what she was feeling. She couldn't force herself to any more anger. She couldn't think of Jules, although she should. Just this morning, she had been waiting for him. And now her biggest worry was coming too close to this man she had sworn to herself she would hate for eternity. Her husband. A man she didn't know; a man she did know. . . .

Well wrapped in her heavy gown, she left the bathroom. The bedroom was dark. Before turning off the bathroom light, Cat scanned the room.

Clay was curled in a blanket at the foot of her bed. She glanced at the bedside chair where his clothing was draped. Then she flicked off the bathroom light as she felt a flush rising to her face. Certain things hadn't changed. Clay always slept with a cover but he always slept nude.

94

Cat walked quickly across the room in the dark and dived into her bed, pulling her covers to her chin, She didn't like to think of him at the foot of her bed . . . . unclad. Visions from this morning of his towel kept filling her head as she tried unsuccessfully to forget him and sleep. Why did he always have to be so perfect, she wondered resentfully . . . so perfect that she couldn't forget him. Broad, broad, bronze shoulders, taut, curly-haired chest, narrow hips. . . .

"Cat?"

She waited tensely for a minute, wondering if she should feign sleep.

He knew she wasn't sleeping.

"Didn't you forget to ask me something?"

A thousand little shivers seemed to take hold of her body. What was he talking about?

"Ask you what?" she finally said hoarsely.

"Where I've been."

"Oh!" She fell silent. Did she want to ask him? Yes, she did, but she didn't know if she really wanted the answer.

"Okay, Clay, where've you been for all these years?"

"Prison," he said bluntly.

Cat lay in shock for a long, long time, unable to question him further, her blood turning to ice.

"All that time?" she rasped.

He hesitated. "No."

It was the only answer she received. She heard him adjust himself, turning his body away from her in the darkness.

Prison. Dear God, what had he done? Why hadn't she been informed, why hadn't he written, why hadn't—something? And she was back in circles again. Where had he been since?

"That's all I'll tell you for now, Cat," she heard him say softly. "The next step is going to have to be yours."

Step? She couldn't take any steps. No, oh, please, Clay, she thought silently, punching her pillow; please, Clay, don't do this to me. . . .

CHAPTER SIX

It was a world that fascinated and compelled, eerie, soundless except for the effervescence of escaping air. Rainbow colors created beauty beyond the imagination, bright yellow tangs spurted about like a million tiny drops of sunlight, purple sea fans waved a welcome, anemones in all shades held a drifting sentinel.

Mira Por Vos.

In some spots the reef stretched less than ten feet beneath the surface. Then she dipped low, opening the way to depths that plunged far into the sea.

But for all her beauty, she was deadly. She hosted an eerie graveyard within the sea, having taken her toll upon unwary sailors for centuries. Her beautiful yellow tangs lived among the crevices of bows and hulls long since claimed by salt and water. Sea creatures of all kinds had taken over planking and steel; they disdainfully eroded things that had meant lives: silver table-settings, once-coveted llama wool taken from the strange creatures of the Spanish Main, fragile china, the ladies' silks and satins.

It was a haunting experience to seek the treasures tenaciously held by Mira Por Vos. As Cat floated, her flippers seeming to actually allow her to fly in this weightless world, she couldn't help but wonder about those who belonged to the shells and frames and bits and pieces of wrecks remaining upon the corals. Not much was left upon the easily accessible sections of the reef; treasure seekers had been plundering the corals for ages. And while she was sure that the *Santa Anita* did lie somewhere within the coral prisons of the reef, she was beginning to feel the enormity of their task. She was searching for a needle in a haystack so vast that it was incomprehensible.

Cat was startled as she felt a touch upon her shoulder. Twisting, she saw Clay smiling around the mouthpiece of his regulator. He signaled that they should rise, tapping his diver's watch. Cat nodded dispiritedly. Another dive was up, and they had found nothing, nothing but pathetic shells of the past.

They didn't need to stop for decompression time, they had only been in fifty feet of water and had been down only an hour. Clay believed that a number of short dives per day were more productive than elongated trips. Rested, one was more alert, more attuned to the messages the sea gave the senses.

Cat rose slowly and smoothly to the surface, lifting her mask and puffing out the mouthpiece to her regulator as she broke the water line. The *Sea Witch II* was about forty feet away, but Cat waited in position for Sam to bring the boat around. Clay worked by strict rules that always remained the same. The boat would move to pick up the divers.

As the hum of the *Sea Witch II* sounded, Cat felt Clay rise behind her, but she didn't turn or speak. She had been so sure, was still so sure, but they had been looking for two weeks now, diving steadily, and they hadn't seen a single clue to validate her theory.

Cat slipped off her flippers and tossed them over the side of the boat before accepting Sam's help out of the water. At the question in his eyes she shook her head. "Nothing, Sam," she murmured as he helped her off with her tanks. "Not a damned thing."

The slap of Clay's flippers hitting the deck preceded his growl of irritation. "Now I know why I always left you at home, Mrs. Miller. What were you expecting? The *Santa Anita* isn't going to bubble to the surface to meet you!"

Cat glared at Clay and dropped her weight belt, spinning on her heel to march into the cruiser's cabin. She might not be so impatient, she thought irritably, if the two weeks they had spent looking hadn't felt like twenty. Unless they were beneath the sea, she and Clay were constantly at one another's throats. And a cruiser—no matter how nice, and the *Sea Witch II* was nice—was not an easy place to avoid another human being. The quest so far had been as platonic as Clay had promised. During rest periods Cat read inside the cabin if Clay was busy outside. If Clay was inside, Cat would decide to improve her tan outside. Meals were awkward. Poor Sam! He was left to carry on conversations with both Clay and Cat, neither of whom addressed a remark to the other.

"Get back here, Mrs. Miller," Clay ordered in the autocratic tone that so irritated Cat. She turned and stared at him, brows lifted in coolly rebellious query. "Your gear," he said curtly. "Rinse it."

Sam cleared his throat a little nervously. "I'll take care of it, Clay."

"No, you won't," Clay said curtly. "Divers take care of their own gear. No exceptions."

Eyeing Clay with venom, Cat moved swiftly to collect her diving gear. He was right, she thought; only his comment had made her forget to care for her things. Not that it would have killed someone else to do her the favor, but she didn't want Sam in the middle of their arguments. Procuring the deck hose, she set to thoroughly spraying her mask, flippers, regulator, and tank.

Clay watched her silently, taking the hose when she finished. "Leave your tank," he said abruptly. "I'm going to refill it."

"Don't be absurd," Cat protested. "I wouldn't dream of having you do anything for me."

Clay gripped her arm. "Leave the damned tank."

Cat shook off his hold. "Whatever you wish, captain."

Sam, miserably feigning interest in a snagged fishing line during the exchange, looked up. "There's a pot of hot coffee on, Cat. And sandwiches in the refrigerator."

"Thanks, Sam," Cat murmured, escaping through the cabin doors. Seawater was dripping down her nose and she hastily grabbed a towel from the counter and blotted her face, breathing deeply and then whistling out a long sigh. She poured herself a cup of coffee and sank into the vinyl booth that served as dining table and desk. Why were things going so badly? she wondered. They had started off with a certain degree of cordiality. The first few days had been enjoyable. She had forgotten what it was like to dive with Clay, forgotten the touch of his fingers upon hers so that he might point out something special, a rare fish, an especially beautiful display of coral. She had forgotten his secure and possessive touch when he wished to warn her of danger, fire coral within a too easy touching distance, the tentacles of a man-of-war, which could float far below the surface of the water.

Face it, she told herself, the problems that had arisen between them were of her own making. She had turned to rudeness because she was afraid of his touch. Even his casual touch. They loved all the same things. It was too easy to dream that they could really have a life, and it was stupid to dream of it. Clay apparently had no intention of telling her any more about his years of absence, and, after all that time, he was, essentially, a stranger. He might comment that he had made mistakes in their marriage, but he certainly never suggested that he was interested in resuming a relationship in which he changed his ways. He had returned because of the *Santa Anita*, and nothing more.

But if that were the case, her mind taunted her, why had he returned like a whirlwind, trapping her, cornering her? Why hadn't he just come and asked her about a joint salvage venture?

Because she would have turned him down flat, Cat thought dryly, and he would have known that. Wives didn't tend to bend over backward for husbands who disappeared, leaving those who loved them thinking them dead. Clay might have suspected that she could have used his arrival for a bargaining point with Jules . . . help me, or I can turn to this other man. . . .

Why Clay did what he did made no difference. Her dreams were absurd because one thing was certain: a relationship with Clay meant nothing but pain. He was, despite the fact that he enjoyed people and could be personable and cordial, basically a loner. There was a part of him that he held back. In the best of times, Cat knew, she had never really held any influence over him. He forged his own destiny. And that destiny had landed him in prison.

For what? she wondered. And where? For how long? He refused to talk to her. Perhaps if he had, she wouldn't have been so determined to let him nowhere near her. But he had said enough to damn him if she had any sense. He had apparently been free long enough. The *Sea Witch II* was definitely a luxury craft. Clay had been free long enough to accrue much more than financial security.

A chill suddenly seized Cat and she shivered, clutching the warmth of her cup miserably. She absolutely couldn't feel anything for Clay, she kept telling herself. No one stayed in love that long, and she had been so sure about Jules.

But whether her love had actually stayed alive, or whether it was simple chemistry, Cat couldn't deny to herself that reason and logic and even memory of all that happened were doing nothing to quell the raging physical attraction that Clay held for her. Her misery had been in his nearness, in the effort not to touch.

If you touched fire, you were burned and she had already been burned by Clay Miller.

But although she had a comfortable cabin and studiously worked to avoid Clay at all times, it was impossible to live with a man on a boat and not be near him at times. In the water things were fine. In that mystical fantasyland, they both dropped the barriers that sprang between them in the normal world. But aboard the *Sea Witch II* they had to meet, and they had to clash. When this was over, Cat wanted her divorce. She wanted Clay to sail away again. She wanted to forget that there was a man who could send her senses soaring just by speaking, just by hovering near. She wanted to forget Clay Miller again, forget the crippling pain that came from loving.

"Ahoy there!"

Her thoughts were suddenly interrupted by the cheerful call from the deck. Frowning, Cat set down her coffee cup and stood, then, curious, opened the cabin door.

They were broadside of another boat, and Clay—a disgustingly virile-looking specimen in white swim shorts that contrasted with the sinewed bronze of his tall form—was cheerfully introducing Sam to the three men aboard the second vessel.

"What took you so long?" Clay demanded of a handsome Bahamian, obviously the captain of the cruiser similar to their own.

"Hey, mon, you wanted provisions!" the Bahamian smiled back, obviously very familiar with Clay. He hunched his shoulders and lifted his hands. "It takes a while to get provisions. Besides, you said not to hurry."

"Did I?" Clay queried dryly. "That was a mistake on my part!"

As if a sixth sense had suddenly alerted him to Cat's presence by the cabin door, Clay turned abruptly to her. "Cat, come here. I want you to meet the main men of my salvage crew."

Curiously, Cat stepped forward, ignoring Clay and smiling sweetly for the newcomers. But ignoring Clay was not easy to do. He slipped an arm around her shoulders, as if their relationship was a very friendly one, if not truly intimate.

"Cat, this is Luke, Billy Bo, and that blond fellow over there is Peter Gruuten. He's an amazing man with a blowtorch and underwater explosives. Gentlemen—" Clay paused only momentarily. "I'd like you to meet my wife, Catherine."

Cat's smile became a bit stiff and her shoulders tightened beneath his touch. "How do you do?" she murmured.

Luke, the Bahamian captain, allowed his grin to deepen wickedly. "Whew!" he murmured. "How do you do! We've heard a lot about you, Mrs. Miller, and apparently it's all true. . . ."

"Eh! That's enough, Luke!" Clay interrupted, his tone light but the touch of warning in his voice sincere. "I want to keep a distance of about a half mile between us," he said, becoming strictly business-like. "I don't want any other boats cruising around to know we're connected."

"How much territory have you covered so far?" the hearty-looking blond man, Peter, queried.

"About a mile," Clay responded. "South of here. We're moving northward. And it's a real hassle because there's so much down there. Finding the right wreck is the real problem."

"I don't know. . . ." Peter countered. "Finding a real galleon . . . it's going to be a real treat, really worth the effort."

"I agree," Clay said simply, once again changing his manner to smile easily. "Why don't you guys take Sam aboard for the night? He can fill you in on our dives so far. And he must be half bonkers after spending the last two weeks with us."

"Clay—" Cat began to protest. What was he up to? She didn't want Sam off the *Sea Witch II*. If Sam were gone, she would be alone with Clay.

"Cat," Clay interrupted her firmly, "Sam needs a break. Luke

101

needs to know what's going on. You and I need to decide where we're going to start tomorrow."

"What are you talking about?" Cat demanded impatiently. When had they ever decided anything? And who the hell were these crew members of his. He had never mentioned bringing anyone else in on the search, although she had assumed he had a crew in mind once the vessel was found.

"Sam?" Clay queried, ignoring Cat.

"I could go for a change of scenery, all right," Sam said, half grinning, half sighing.

"Sam!" Cat hissed. Some protector. He had been as loyal as a brother for years. Reenter Mr. Clayton Miller and suddenly she was out on a limb.

"I'll just get my gear," Sam said.

Cat watched in frustration as Luke handed supply boxes to Clay and as Sam disappeared into the cabin only to return and hop with agility from boat to boat. "Let Sam take her around for a while," Clay called to Luke, referring to the second boat, which was also apparently his. "You'll enjoy her, Sam, she has a real souped-up motor!"

Sea Enchantress. Cat noted the name of the second cruiser as it motored away. A witch and an enchantress. . . . Pity it was the first that had been named for her. . . .

Cat spun on Clay. "What was that all about? You never told me we were supposed to meet another boat. You never mentioned anything about a crew!"

"Don't start, Cat," Clay warned, suddenly sounding tired as he hefted a supply box into his arms and headed for the cabin doors. "You knew damned well we'd need a salvage crew to begin to bring anything up."

"Yes," Cat protested, "but you keep talking about secrecy! How well do you know those men? How much do you trust them?"

"I'd trust them with my life," Clay interrupted coldly. "And that's that, Cat. I don't want to hear anything more about it."

"Great," Cat said sarcastically. "We're going on my knowledge and theory, and we're pretending to be pleasure divers, watching out for every little rowboat that goes by, and you're bringing people in whom I have never met before!"

The cabin doors swung shut behind Clay, but not before she heard his "Caatttt!"

"Damn you!" Cat hissed, but not loud enough to be heard beyond the doors. Why couldn't he ever simply explain anything? He was evidently very close to the men of the *Sea Enchantress*. There seemed to be some type of bond between the lot of them. Where had they met? And how had they sealed their friendship with such allegiance that Clay trusted them completely?

Cat's eyes turned to the other vessel, moving away in a spew of foam. She squinted, frowning. On the bow now stood a woman. It was difficult to see her clearly, but she appeared to be very blond, very fragile, and very pretty. Why hadn't she presented herself for the introductions? Did Clay know she was aboard the *Sea Enchantress*?

Thoroughly irritated, Cat followed Clay into the cabin. Crossing her arms over her chest, she leaned against the closed doors. "This," she said firmly, "is getting out of hand. First of all, you and I don't have a damned thing to discuss. You know you're going to do whatever the hell you please in the morning. Second, I'm not at all pleased with your surprises. You could easily have told me you were expecting others to join us. And third, I definitely do not like being introduced as your wife!"

Clay stopped arranging the new box of supplies in the galley and stared at her, hands on hips. "You are my wife, Cat," he reminded her dryly.

"Merely because of an oversight on my part," Cat said stiffly. "And I won't be your wife once this is over."

"Oh, I see," he murmured on a note that sounded indifferent. "So you're still determined to make it up with the Frenchman."

Stung by the tone of his voice, Cat replied, "Of course. You did promise to set Jules straight on the situation."

Clay poured himself a cup of coffee and took a sip, watching Cat over the rim of his cup. "Yes, I did say that. But this isn't over. So for the moment, Mrs. Miller, you are still my wife. And in all honesty, I do find it rather difficult to believe that you really want to make anything up with DeVante. You haven't acted terribly upset, you know. The man you supposedly love walked out on you. I haven't seen a single tear, Cat. A lot of rage, yes, but only because I had the audacity to tamper with your life."

Cat lifted her brows slightly. "I don't run around crying, Clay. It's a rather unproductive thing to do."

"Oh, unproductive," Clay agreed, still studying her as he sipped his coffee. "Of course."

Cat decided to change her vein of questioning. "There was a woman aboard the *Sea Enchantress*—which I assume is your boat too. Who is she?"

Did he hesitate slightly, or did Cat imagine a slight wince, an expression of pain, before his features returned to a fathomless state.

"Ariel," he said simply, setting his cup down and returning to the task of storing food. "She's Peter's wife," he added.

She might be Peter's wife, Cat decided, but Ariel must also be more, someone special to Clay as well. Why else hadn't she appeared for the introductions? A little stab of pain caught Cat in the midriff. Jealousy, she thought. It came with the territory. After all this time, logically knowing full well that this man who couldn't reasonably still mean a thing to her, she couldn't prevent feeling the pain of jealousy.

"Why did you make Sam get off the boat?" Cat demanded sharply.

Once more Clay stopped and stared at her. Where on earth had those eyes come from, Cat wondered bitterly. So deep, so jet, bottomless bits that compelled and threatened. Nowhere on earth, she decided. His eyes, framed by the high-arched brows, were the devil's own.

"I didn't make Sam get off the boat. Whether you've noticed it or not, the man's been between the devil and the deep. He deserves a break. Living with the two of us can't be easy."

What had she been expecting him to say, Cat wondered. That they really did need to talk, that he had wanted to be alone with her?

Clay stuffed away the last of the supplies, picked up his coffee cup and refilled it, and moved toward the doors. Cat froze as he approached her, then flushed as she saw amusement riddle his eyes and quirk at the corners of his lips. "Excuse me," he murmured, indicating his desire merely to pass through the doors.

Cat moved quickly so that he could get by her. As the door closed behind him, she felt a spasm of disappointment. Why should she feel disappointed? she wondered wearily. All their conversations ended this way, neither one ever really telling the other a thing.

Cat sighed and moved down the hallway to her small private room. If Sam was gone, they were evidently done diving for the day, and the salt water that had dried upon her flesh was now giving her an uncomfortable sticky feeling. Cat peeled off her bikini and crawled into the tiny shower stall. She paused, hands in the shampoo lather on her head, as the soft sounds of a guitar filtered through the rush of the water.

Clay's accomplishments with the instrument had surprised her from the first day. He had never played before; music in general had always been something he vaguely appreciated but could live without. Cat remembered her astonishment when she had first seen the instrument leaning carefully against the booth in the salon. "Do you play?" she had inquired incredulously.

"Of course I play," he had responded impatiently. "I would hardly keep such a thing around for ornamentation."

And during their weeks at sea she had learned that he did indeed play rather well. And that his deep velvet tenor could also play soothingly upon the soul, touching the chords of the heart.

Cat rinsed out her hair and stepped from the shower, drying herself quickly with a rough white towel. She had intended to stay in her cabin, reading and resting, but she suddenly felt too agitated to do so. Clay was playing Jimmy Buffett tunes, soft, light, and inviting. Cat slipped into a knee-length terry robe, belting it securely around her waist, grabbed her hairbrush, and walked out on deck.

Clay was balanced on the bow, one leg on the deck, the other crooked so that the guitar rested on his knee. He glanced up at her appearance, lifted a brow, and with a small curious smile of surprise finished out his lightly strummed "Margaritaville." Cat sat cross-legged in a deck chair, brushing out her wet hair as she listened.

"You're not bad," she said as he finished playing and watched her with that curiously amused expression.

105

He shrugged. "Thanks. Got any requests? Don't get too carried away," he added in warning, "my repertoire isn't great."

Cat couldn't help laughing at his sheepish apology. "How will I know what I can request, then?"

Clay laughed. "Pick out about ten songs, and I'll tell you when to stop."

"Okay." Cat listed a number of songs; Clay shook his head with a rueful grimace after each.

"Hold it!" Clay interrupted her. "I can handle ballads, a little calypso, and a little reggae. Find something in there."

Suddenly, Cat couldn't answer. He had started her laughing, and now she had laughed so hard that her sides hurt.

"Forget it!" Clay groaned with mock exasperation. "I'll think of something myself—and I'll give *you* a request instead. This half-baked minstrel could really go for a glass of wine. Would you mind?"

Cat stopped laughing, a little unnerved by the enjoyment they were sharing. She paused a second, then shrugged. "Sure," she murmured, rising quickly. Dropping her brush, she slipped through the cabin doors. Why am I doing this, she asked herself. Why am I taking these chances with him? There was no answer, but as she reached for the plastic cups they normally used up on deck, she hesitated. There was a set of long-stemmed wine crystals in the cabinet above the sink. She found herself reaching for one of those rather than the plastic cup.

"Join me, won't you?"

Cat's fingers trembled slightly as she heard his voice, uncannily at the exact moment she was debating the question herself.

I shouldn't, she thought, I shouldn't even be sitting with him, listening to his music, laughing. Little prickles of danger seemed to riddle her system. But her fingers were ignoring the messages of her mind. She poured two glasses of wine.

Cat walked back out on deck and handed Clay his wine. He noted with his eyes that she had decided to join him, and merely smiled a thanks and accepted his glass. Cat returned to her deck chair, sipping her wine as she watched him. This was a new side to Clay. Still clad in his white shorts, his body very sleek and bronze beneath

106

the setting sun, his sun-bleached hair still damp, he made more than an attractive appearance. There was something very light about him, completely confident, but so comfortable and easy. At twenty-six there had been nothing light or easy about Clay. He had been perpetually tense; his mind had continually worked overtime. It was as if a little age had given him a little youth or perhaps that complete confidence he had acquired had taught him to allow himself to relax.

"I've got one I think you'll like," he said suddenly, setting his wineglass down on the bow. He ran his fingers in a light strumming motion over the strings for a moment, and then launched slowly and poignantly into the opening bars of a song.

Just these few strains of music seemed to reach out and touch Cat. She felt a warm trembling permeate her blood, as if the melody, and then Clay's voice, encompassed her in an embrace.

It was an old island song, one that she had always loved, especially those years back. Did he remember, she wondered vaguely? Or did this just happen to be a song that he knew?

What was it about the song that always touched her so? The tune was pretty, soft and melodic, but it was more than that. The lyrics managed to epitomize all that was so beautiful and usually inexplicable about loving a person. Senses filled with the essence of nature . . . the simple, humble joy of lying down together . . . of always being with one. . . .

Cat lowered her eyes, clenching the stem of her wineglass so tightly that it was amazing it didn't shatter. He was doing this on purpose to her, but suddenly it didn't matter. She was ripped apart on the inside, and before his fingers had strummed the last chords, she was staring at him, and without preplanned purpose or intent she suddenly blurted, "Why were you in prison, Clay? Why wasn't I notified? How—" Her voice finally choked. It had been naked, it had portrayed her agony. It had left her so vulnerable, letting him know how much she had cared, letting her know how much she still cared.

Clay set the guitar down carefully, his eyes on Cat. She knew he hesitated, weighed his words, and was worried about the effect his answer would have.

107

"Drugs, Cat," he said softly. "Nothing big or deadly, but it was drugs."

"I don't believe it!" Cat exclaimed. "You wouldn't . . . you wouldn't. I—" She caught herself. He wouldn't, but he had just told her that he had.

Clay moved over to her swiftly, balancing on the balls of his feet as he hunched in front of her, catching her chin with his thumb when she would lower it. "Thank you, Cat," he said gravely. "Thank you for that faith. I never intended to be involved in that type of operation." He hesitated a moment, searching out her eyes, then continued. "My boat broke up in some type of underwater cataclysm. I was rescued by Luke and the other two men you met today. They're good people, Cat. But they're from out islands that aren't even listed on Bahamian maps. Luke has a big family, six children. A lot of little mouths to feed. They weren't trafficking in anything hard—and I'm not condoning the practice—but they were just trying to survive." He fell silent for a moment, then lifted his hands slightly in the air. "We were picked up," he said.

He moved back to the bow of the boat, gazing out on the horizon at the ethereal beauty of the setting sun. Cat covered her face with her hands for a moment, fighting the terrible urge to cry, fighting to control her reactions. But her head and heart were both swimming. His boat had wrecked; he hadn't simply deserted her.

She was on her feet before she knew it, moving over to him, tentatively reaching to touch his back.

"Why wasn't I told, Clay? Why wasn't I contacted?"

He turned to her, lightly caressing the straying tendrils of her drying hair. "I didn't know who I was, Cat."

"Amnesia?" she inquired incredulously.

He nodded.

"But they must have taken your fingerprints. You were in the Navy, Clay, they—"

"Cat," he murmured softly. "I wasn't in the United States, or even in the Bahamas."

"Where were you?"

He paused for a moment, and the tension in him suddenly gave her consuming chills. She knew where he had been, and knowing, she determined never to question him again. Her eyes told him that he needn't respond to that particular question in words.

"They tried to find out who I was," he said hoarsely. "But their methods weren't terribly efficient."

"Oh," Cat murmured, stepping away from him in confusion. She had been wrong to judge him without listening to him, and for that she was sorry. But things were still so unclear. He obviously knew very well who he was now, had known for some time, to have founded an evidently prosperous new business.

"I never meant to leave you, Cat," he said. It was a fact, firmly but gently spoken with no plea for forgiveness.

But again Cat was moving without really knowing what she was doing. She turned back to him, slipping her arms around his neck, allowing her fingers to riffle through the the crisp ends of his hair, to touch the satin-sleek bronze shoulders that so enticed her, to feel the powerful tension in his sinewed muscle.

"I'm sorry, Clay," she heard herself murmur, "I had no idea. . . ."

And then she found herself moving closer, pressing against him, parting her lips and inching to her toes to join her lips to his. What she had intended? she didn't know. Something soft, perhaps easy, an apology. But that chemistry was there, that electrical tension that had compelled her years ago, that existed beyond the bounds of time. She felt his arms tighten around her, his hands course down her back, and then his lips begin to move. . . . Sensually. Aggressively. Dominating her advance. She was locked in his embrace, her entire body becoming attuned to his power, heat, and tension. His tongue wedged past her teeth, exploring her mouth fully and savoringly, slow, so slow, and yet determinedly forceful. His hands moved to cradle her buttocks, lifting her, holding her closer, melding her to his body heat, clearly imprinting on each of her contours the perfectness of their fit.

Sensations washed over Cat, engulfing her. It was there, still there after all this time, with only him. That feeling—so intense, so shatteringly hot, a flame that erupted from within, so bright it blinded sun and moon alike, such wonderful, beautiful ecstasy that it was agony.

She didn't want the feeling again. It robbed her of control, of logic, of will. . . . And it could so easily leave devastation. . . .

Clay's lips left hers. They moved in a slow, moist trail along her cheek, creating tremors as they touched upon her earlobe. His teeth grazed over her flesh, nipping gently. A new wash of shivering sensation raged through Cat, evident, undeniable.

"Clay . . ." she protested, attempting to step back. His arms held her in a grip of pure steel. Bracing her hands against his shoulder, Cat sought out his eyes. "Clay . . ." she murmured again.

He smiled, but refused to release her. "Do you know, Cat, as I said before, you never have been sure whether you wanted to seduce me or not."

"Seduce you!" Cat protested. "No—"

"I believe," he murmured, "that you did step into my arms. And I'm also quite sure that you did kiss me, and I'm damned sure, Cat," he added huskily, "that you do want me." Please don't deny that, he added silently to himself. Please, I won't be able to bear it if you do.

For two weeks he had been living in torment. Watching her, his wife and his dream. All those hours of torturous dreaming. Now she was flesh and blood. And every day he had seen her, he had silently and distantly coveted her. Did she know that she tortured him? Appearing each morning in nothing but a scanty bikini that assured him his memory hadn't been faulty. No, Cat was one woman oblivious to her physical attributes. She was a witch of the sea; her slender, elegantly shaped frame was the result of a life lived with nature. Still, it had been agony seeing her golden tanned, silky flesh daily, knowing that her curves were every bit as firm and full as they appeared.

As he looked at her now, he saw the misted depth of her shimmering emerald eyes. Am I dreaming still, he wondered, or is this real? He couldn't let her go now. Somehow he had to make her remember what it could be like, what they had once had together.

"Clay—" she began to murmur again in protest. He silenced her the only way he knew how. His lips seared down hard over hers, seducing as they punished, cajoled and yet branded and demanded. He slipped a hand into the V of her terry-cloth robe, and as he

110

expected, he encountered her flesh, soft and silky and firm, filling his hand. A muffled sound escaped her that might have been a moan, might have been a protest, but if it was a denial, it was a lie. Beneath the graze of his exploring thumb he could feel the swelling of her breasts, the hard rise of her nipples.

Then suddenly he had to see her, had to have her completely. Without releasing his hold, he deftly found the knot of her robe and released it, then, only then, he stepped back. She stared at him, her eyes brilliant and yet slightly glazed with a wondering shock, her lips wet and puffed from his kiss. Her robe hung open, and before she could think to object, Clay slipped his long, broad hands gently around her neck, sliding them along her shoulders to ease the robe from her body to fall to the deck.

Against the amethyst and magenta of the dying sunset, she was a magnificent silhouette. Tall, lithe, as beautifully shaped and curved as a goddess from the sea. As golden as the sun sinking into the horizon. Her hair, that rich, dark hair that had filled his fantasies, swept over her shoulders in a velvet fan, wisps and tendrils waving over her breasts.

She closed her eyes suddenly, thick-fringed lashes forming deep crescents over her cheeks. She is thinking, Clay thought disparagingly, I can't allow her to think. He was about to move for her again, take her into his arms and deny that quarter, but he paused. Her emerald eyes flew open again, and she was moving for him.

How many times had he dreamed it? This creature of divinity, enchantress, witch, striding toward him with that walk that was an effortless sail, hips swaying subtly, provocatively, hair floating with her like tendrils of silk.

He reached out for her, crushing her to him, burying his face into her neck, into her hair. It was still damp, its scent was wondrously clean and fresh and ever so slightly perfumed from her shampoo. His hands moved to tangle into its sable length, his fingers reverently caressed it, and he brought the silkiness to rub against his chest.

All around them was the sea, turquoise waters deepening with night to indigo, the rainbow dusk becoming an endless stretch of the darkest teal velvet. The world seemed to be theirs. It was as if they even owned the heavens.

They should go inside, Clay thought vaguely. But he couldn't bear to break the enchantment of the spell that held them both, and the nearest person was half a mile away. He took her lips again, but his kisses were fevered now. They moved passionately to cover her cheeks, her throat, her shoulders, and then return again to the sweetness of her lips once more. He felt her tremble—he felt his own trembling—and he felt the heat that was rising, igniting, flaring, melding them together in a single torch of desire.

He brought himself down slowly, hands touching and memorizing the nuances of her shape, lips and tongue and teeth following suit, tasting the sweet nectar of her breasts, hips, belly, and thighs. And then when he was down, he drew her to him, demandingly and yet reverently, as though a part of him still believed her a vision, an ethereal spirit who could drift away into the night.

Her discarded robe was their bed. With his wife beside him at long last, Clay released her only long enough to shed his shorts. Then she was in his arms again, his weight beneath hers to shelter her from the hardness of the deck. It was a little like their first time together, Clay noted vaguely. Cat had actually come to him, and then waited, quivering like a bowstring, and then suddenly taken flight, returning his kisses, his touch, with equal fervor, equal passion.

He caught her face between his hands. "Dear God, Cat," he groaned with husky vehemence, "how I want you. There were times when I lived for this . . ."

Cat closed her eyes and shuddered, escaping his hold to lean down and kiss the hollow in his shoulders. Her teeth grazed against his flesh and she tasted the salt of the sea. Tears suddenly flooded beneath her lids simply because she felt so good. She hadn't forgotten the rapture of this pleasure. She had just thought that it could surely never come again. His body beneath hers had the strength of a rock, the vibrance and vitality of the sun. Every taut inch of him was hard with toned muscles, yet his body pulsed a tantalizing comfort, sheltering her, demanding from her. The crisp curls of hair on his chest teased her breasts mercilessly, the strong columns of his legs twined with hers, provocatively edging along the inside of her upper thighs. His hips, crushed to her, left no delusions to his complete and powerful arousal.

And then he was lifting her, bringing her down again, and she was shuddering in earnest as he possessed her in an explosively driving force that left her feeling as if a ray of the sun had indeed burst within her. She gasped, suddenly still, savoring, absorbing the moment, but his hands were on her hips and he was beginning a slow, rhythmic undulation, guiding her along.

And then the rhythm was out of control, building, flying, soaring. There were moments when Cat caught her husband's eyes, and the dark density of passion within them spurred her to even greater heights with the pleasure of knowing she returned all that he gave. And yet still, deep within her, there was a core of fear. She had to be insane, because this ecstasy could only bring agony.

Her fear was ignored because she was insane, half mad with the fire that ruled her body, the sweet deepening ache that pitched higher and higher until she felt she would scream.

And then it felt as if they had joined the velvet night, becoming one with the brilliance of the stars that flecked the heavens. Clay arched, cradling her breasts, gripping her hair, splaying his fingers around her hips to pull her ever tighter in a final shattering thrust.

Cat did scream. The sound was his name, a shivering cry of rapture and fulfillment. And then she was falling to his chest, burying her face into his neck, holding him tightly as the wash of sensations became gentle and mellow.

They lay silent for a long while, the only rustle of movement that of Clay's fingers as they continued to thread with fascination through his wife's hair. And then, just as Cat was realizing she had been a fool because everything was going to be so much harder now, that there would be new pain to rip apart scars that had never properly healed, Clay spoke, tenderly, whispering softly in her ear.

"I love you, Cat," he murmured. "I really can't tell you how much. There were times, so many times, when just the dream of you kept me going."

Cat froze in his arms, terrified to believe his words. Could he mean it? Oh, God, it had been so long. Had he really loved her all those years? Could he really love her now? It was possible. She knew

113

it was possible even if she was afraid to believe, because she knew now that she loved him, had never stopped loving him no matter how she thought she had purged his memory from her life.

"Oh, Clay . . ." she murmured, holding her face tightly against his chest so that she didn't have to face his eyes.

"Do you think you could love me again, Cat?" he demanded softly.

"I'm afraid, Clay," Cat admitted, fingers tense against his flesh. "There's so much I don't know, so much I don't understand. . . ."

"I'm going to talk to you," he promised. "I'm going to try to explain everything. First thing in the morning."

"Why in the morning?" Cat asked, finally pulling her face from him to frown as she studied his.

Clay smiled and shifted, adjusting himself to rise with a swift movement with her still clutched in his arms.

"Because tonight is mine," he told her, brows arching with a devilish twitch. "Because I've dreamed of you until I've almost lost my sanity. Because we're going to drink wine and munch cheese in bed and make love until dawn. Because this is my fantasy, and my fantasy is real, and nothing, nothing is going to intrude upon my dreams tonight. Not even you, sea witch. Tonight you are the fantasy, and you're mine."

As he carried her through the cabin doors, Cat simply had no desire to protest.

CHAPTER SEVEN

She was sleeping so soundly, so comfortably, so very deeply. The blazing light that suddenly caused an instinctive tightening of her eyelids was at first nothing more than an annoyance. Then a sharp tap on her posterior startled her from that hazy cocoon of sleep and her eyes flew wide open.

The light, of course, was the sun, streaming through the now open porthole drape. Cat smiled ever so slightly. Had the sun ever streamed across the sky with such magnificence? Tossing her head and hiding her smile, Cat turned reproachful eyes to Clay, the deliverer of the awakening pat to her anatomy.

He sat beside her on the bed, a grin stretched softly in the firm yet sensuous line of his lips. "It's morning," he told her, shrugging innocence in reply to her reproach. He sobered suddenly, reaching for her hand. "And I want to talk to you. I was thinking—well, actually I was thinking that neither of us had been thinking last night. And I don't think this is the time to add complications."

"What are you talking about?" Cat murmured.

"The facts of life." Clay grimaced.

"Oh." Cat felt herself pinken slightly. "You needn't worry about complications."

"Oh?" She heard the growl in his voice and desperately wanted to avoid an argument in her drowsy state. She knew exactly what he was getting at, and she really wasn't ready to admit the entire truth about her relationship—or lack of one—with Jules. But she didn't want to fight, not after last night.

"I've taken pills since our marriage simply because I discovered they did a marvelous job of regulating my system," she told him a bit huskily.

He didn't reply, but his eyes told her the subject would be discussed again. Apparently he wasn't ready to argue either. He watched her contemplatively for a moment, then smiled and issued a command. "Up!"

Cat groaned and attempted to burrow her face back into her pillow. With the threat of an explosion gone, she had begun to revel again in her feeling of drowsy contentment. "Clay . . ." she murmured, her indignant voice muffled by the pillow, "it was a late night. . . ."

"Noooo, no, my love!" Clay laughed, catching her shoulders and pulling her back forward. "This is a workday, kitten. And you're on breakfast detail because I need to check and oil equipment."

Cat allowed her heavy lids to close again. "Why don't you just throw on a pot of coffee. . . ."

Clay laughed. "Because I'm starving. I had this terribly active night, you see, and the temporary appeasement of one appetite had a tremendous effect upon creating another."

Cat opened her eyes once more to see a mischievous twinkle glimmering deep within her husband's eyes. She flushed slightly and lowered her lashes until her eyes were narrowed slits of emerald, then stretched, pausing with caught breath as Clay leaned over to brush her lips with a gentle kiss. He moved back with a new, strange light in his eyes. Hands reaching tenderly for the luxurious masses of her tangled hair, he began to spread the tendrils in a sunburst fan over the pillow and bedding. He leaned to kiss her again, but this time the gentle movement of his lips turned to a demand, his fingers moved to cup her face, brushed her throat, and clutched her bare shoulders. A soft groan escaped him as he pulled back. "Come on, witch," he commanded huskily, "Get up and get decent, before you destroy all my hard-won resolves for the day!" He stood, smiling as he stared down at her. "And get breakfast going! As a good little wife, you can ease at least one of these aches chewing on my insides."

"Breakfast!" Cat laughed. "You want breakfast! I'm not even sure I can move this morning!" She wasn't lying. She felt deliciously content and satiated, but incredibly tired and drained.

Clay chuckled in return. "Glad to hear I finally learned a way to keep you down. Except that I want you up, acting like a charming little wife, and cooking—"

"Acting like a wife and cooking!" Cat flared, suddenly awake as her eyes narrowed upon him. "After a comment like that—"

"Make it pancakes, will you," Clay interrupted. "I really do feel as if I could consume half the boat." Suddenly he reached down and pulled her to her feet and into his arms. "Oh, Cat! I do love to tease you! It's so easy to stir that wild temper of yours." He laughed again at the outrage and indignity in her eyes, pulling her body close to his, drawing soft patterns over the small of her back. "Let's start this off right—I think you're marvelously talented—far more than a cook and housekeeper . . . and a deliciously erotic lover! But at the moment, would you mind being the cook? We do have a lot to get to before the *Sea Enchantress* pulls up to return Sam and we go to work for the day. I did promise to talk to you, and I thought a nice rational way to talk would be over a cozy and delicious breakfast with a large pot of steaming coffee."

"Pancakes, did you say?" Cat inquired sweetly.

"Ummmm. Lots of them."

"Lots and lots," Cat promised.

Clay kissed her and released her. "That bit about cats and curiosity is certainly true," he teased as he ducked out of the cabin.

"Don't worry about it!" Cat called after him. "Cats also have nine lives, so I suppose I can afford to lose a few over curiosity!"

Twenty minutes later she had the salon table set and a mile-high pile of pancakes positioned beside a pound of crisply fried bacon. Cat had realized while cooking that her appetite was as voracious as Clay's. But when they actually sat down to eat, she found herself picking at her food. This was, she thought pensively, the first meal she had ever prepared for just the two of them. During the first few months of their marriage, their meals had always come from the dining room, just as their suite in the lodge had always been cleaned by the lodge staff. She really hadn't been much of a wife. . . .

"Not bad," Clay commented, helping himself to another piece of bacon and taking a crunching bite. Cat looked into his eyes. There was a teasing glimmer to them, but also a gentle warmth. We've been thinking the same thing, she thought. Clay very particularly wanted this meal this way, not to force me into a role, but just to let me know that it can be enjoyable to be a wife, to do the little things one does for a mate.

Cat smiled and sipped her coffee. "Glad you approve. Am I as good a cook as Sam?"

"Your bacon is far superior," Clay replied gallantly, "but don't ever tell him that I said so. We need his goodwill at the moment. Neither one of us can spend too much time playing cook and bottle washer until we complete this trip."

Cat smiled, lowering her eyes as she sipped her coffee. She wished

117

fervently that he would hurry up and finish eating and start talking. But as if unable to resist a little torture, he did a fair job of consuming most of the food on the table, savoring each bite. How the hell could he eat so much and stay as smoothly taut as a drum? Cat wondered. Easy, he was always moving, always utilizing his body; spending half his life in the sea.

"Clay . . ." Cat finally begged with exasperation.

He chuckled softly, then pushed his plate aside and poured himself more coffee. "Okay," he murmured. He stared at his cup, running his forefinger idly around the rim. "I wasn't stalling you just for fun," he said quietly. "I really don't know where to begin." He sighed, took a sip of coffee, then set his cup back down. "Like I told you," he began, "I lost the *Sea Witch*. I think I must have floated two days on a four-foot-square section of planking before Luke and his crew picked me up. I think I was half dead at that time. I spent another day delirious with fever and dehydration. Luke was the first person I saw and when I saw him, I had nothing for a mind except a sieve. I couldn't remember anything, Cat. Nothing. Nothing about myself, not even what I looked like. And I was sick as hell. Luke took care of me as tenderly as he might a baby."

A soft choking sound escaped Cat; she reached for Clay's hand, but he stopped her, holding up both of his own. "They say, Cat, that amnesia has certain comparisons with being hypnotized. If you know right from wrong, you know it no matter what. And that was one thing that I did know. Luke and his crew were wrong, and they were headed for trouble."

"Oh, lord," Cat breathed. "Why didn't you do—"

"Do what?" Clay interrupted impatiently. "Ask to get off the boat in the middle of the ocean?"

"No, of course not," Cat murmured.

"I hadn't been aboard long before we were picked up," Clay continued. "But long enough to know I was with good men, even if their racket was bad." He fell silent for a moment, tapping his long fingers against his cup. "None of that really matters now, Cat. What does matter, is that I could never forget you. I didn't know who I was, but you filled my dreams. I knew you were a link with my past. But I spent years being haunted and still not knowing. . . ."

"Oh, lord," Cat murmured miserably. "How . . . how long were you held? How did you get away? When did you remember who you were?"

"I was held for four years," Clay said, with only a touch of rueful bitterness. He didn't mention that there had been unsuccessful attempts at escape. "We escaped with the help of a few guards receptive to bribery. The first thing I remembered with any certainty when we escaped was that I had been a diver. I convinced Luke we could do much better salvaging than smuggling, and he turned out to be a magnificent assistant."

Cat felt ill. Her coffee felt as if it were churning in her stomach. So much of his life wasted, his youth, so much pain and bitterness. And she had had nothing to give him when he did return, not even the simply courtesy of pleasure in seeing him alive.

But he had come back into her life, like a sea storm, and there were still so many things she didn't understand. Too much lay between them for them simply to start over.

"You escaped almost three years ago, Clay," Cat said. "And you know very well who you are now."

Clay hesitated. "Yes. I've known who I was since about two months after the escape."

Cat felt her fingers tighten. Her entire body felt cold and tense. Three years. He hadn't come back to her in all that time.

"Cat," Clay said quietly. "I couldn't come waltzing back the way I was. I had too many scars at the time, mentally and physically. I had nothing—absolutely nothing. And I didn't believe you'd be particularly happy to see me. Our marriage hadn't been the best," he said dryly, "and you're a bit of a legend in the islands, my love. From everything I heard, you were living a very happy life."

Cat swallowed. "So why now, Clay? And why all the trouble with the race, and bribing me out here?"

He grinned crookedly. "Because there's only one way ever to get you to listen, Cat. And that's to pound things into your skull or beat you at your own game." He hesitated again. "If I had thought you were really happy, I wouldn't have interfered in your life. But DeVante isn't what he appears—"

"Clay," Cat interrupted, "I really don't see any reason to drag

119

Jules into this. I feel rather shabby about Jules as it is. You did manage to rudely remove him from the picture—"

"Damn it, Cat!" Clay hissed. "You're still missing a big point to this discussion. When you don't want to listen, you simply don't hear!"

"You're right! I don't want to hear you malign Jules!" What was she doing, Cat wondered, creating an argument over a man who no longer mattered? But it did all matter, because she was still so uncertain. Clay was sitting here telling her that he loved her, had loved her, but how could she trust those words when she barely knew her husband anymore, when so many years had passed? When he was freely admitting that only the hearsay of her impending marriage to another man had brought him back? What had he been really doing all that time, and had their lives taken such separate roads that they could never really meet again?

Clay stood suddenly, thoroughly irritated. "The past is over, Cat. The present is our problem, and our future. I've promised to set things straight for you with DeVante—if that's what you want. But what I want to do, Cat, is give our marriage a chance. I've had lots and lots of time to mull over the problems we had and I know full well I was often at fault. But the first thing you need to fix anything, Cat, is commitment. And a willingness to try—knowing that things won't be perfect but that they can be worked through. Are you with me, Cat?"

Cat quailed slightly at the power and intensity of her husband's words. She knew that she loved him; last night had taught her that she had never stopped loving him. That love was the factor that had kept her from ever fully giving her heart again. But loving and living together were different things. She wanted him, she wanted their marriage to be a real one, but she was afraid of him. He was a man who demanded so much, and yet kept so much of himself back. He was, essentially, a stranger. Seven years was a long, long time.

"I don't know," she faltered, staring at her cup rather than at him. "Clay, we really don't know one another anymore. . . ."

He stooped beside her, catching her chin between his thumb and forefinger, tilting her face to his as he gently brushed the skin of her cheek. A small grin twitched at the corners of his lips. "I'd say we were doing just fine," he teased. Then his voice became abruptly harsh. "Were you sleeping with DeVante, Cat?"

"Come on, Clay," Cat protested, attempting to twist her chin from his grasp but failing. "That can hardly be any of your business."

"Answer me, Cat," he snapped.

"Don't start this—"

"Answer me!"

"All right! No!"

His grip eased and his tone lightened, but only slightly. "I'm glad, Cat. Maybe that's not particularly fair, but I'm glad. I can't promise you I'll ever be completely fair, Cat, not if you believe in total liberation. I want to give you everything you deserve, Cat, respect for your intelligence, the right to work beside me. But I also want a wife. I want you to be there for me. I want a normal home. I want dinner and I'm more than willing to help with the dishes. Do you understand what I'm saying, Cat? It might not be the in thing today, but I believe in a little differentiation between the sexes. I'll never lie to you, I'll cherish you, love you, support you, and protect you. But I'll break your neck if you ever lie to me again, or if I ever come across you near another man. Those are my cards, Mrs. Miller, dead flat on the table." He released her chin, standing again. "Think about all that while you make up your mind, Cat. And you can also start thinking about our time out here as a trial period. Because I want your things in my cabin before Sam returns."

"Clay!" Cat blurted in a strangled voice. She really hadn't had a chance to say anything, to think anything. There was so much to assimilate. He had lost so many years in prison, and what she felt was sorrow, shame, and confusion. There were things she wanted to make up to him, but he didn't want anything from her out of obligation. He wanted love and commitment, and he had her love, although he didn't really know, but could she risk the commitment of his demands? He admitted it wasn't fair, but he had been glad she hadn't been sleeping with Jules.

But where had he been sleeping? And was he willing to give the total fidelity he demanded?

"Clay," she murmured again, "I need time—"

"You take your time in my cabin," he said abruptly. "I'm not sending Sam off the boat again to seduce my own wife. And I'm not playing games. We're not going to play this as a whimsical affair with you deciding you do and then don't. You're great at that, Cat. A little torture, and then a giant step backward. Because you're not sure of what you want. Well, I'm going to be sure for you. You're a very healthy, marvelously sensual creature, Cat. You'll never convince me that you don't want to sleep with me, you never could. So save us both some trouble. Transfer your things to my cabin."

He was shaking, Clay realized, at the same time he was realizing he was a fool. What in God's name was he doing? The sure way to raise defiance in Cat was to command. What if she denied him now?

He turned abruptly on his heels to leave her before she could realize he was anything but adamant and forcefully determined. If she fights me, he thought sickly, I will have to fight her back. She has to believe me. . . .

"Clay!"

Her voice, stilted and tight, stopped him. He turned back to her, noticing that her emerald eyes were wide and her face was pale beneath its golden tan. But she sat very straight, her chin lifted.

"Who is Ariel, Clay?" she asked.

He hesitated for only a fraction of a second. "I told you, Cat, Ariel is Peter's wife."

Cat watched as he exited to the deck, pulling the smart French doors closed behind him. She was shivering, and the day was hot. She had wanted him to talk, and he had talked. But she was still so lost, so unsure.

He had definitely laid his cards on the table. His list of demands was very straightforward! But could even last night change the distance that lay between them? They were both older now, more mature, aware that the greatest passion was not the only ingredient necessary for a marriage.

He seemed so sure! Cat thought. So positive of all that he wanted, so positive it could work out.

Too damned sure. He was already back to ordering her about.

But was what he asked too much? He was a bit of a chauvinist—and frankly willing to admit it with little apology. Yet was that so

122

terrible? He was ready to give so much; he just wanted her to be a wife. And if he were a man she wanted to change, could she possibly love him?

Cat idly began to clear away the breakfast dishes, mechanically cleaning the galley. What kind of choices was he giving her? Demanding that she share his cabin, while still promising to straighten things out with Jules if that should be her ultimate desire?

He doesn't know that I could never go back to Jules now, she thought, which was good. Clay had come back into her life and had overwhelmed her. She didn't want him knowing the extent of the power he wielded. Her independence was still very precious. And even though her heart was willing her to be the wife he desired, he had to know that she would never be a sweet, docile creature waiting to jump at his command.

Oh, lord, she thought, I do love him, but if he wants me in his cabin, he's just going to have to learn to ask nicely.

If I could only really understand him! she mused miserably. He tells me about the time he has lost, but I can't really envision what it must have been. All those days, night, weeks, months, years—lost! And when it was over, he didn't trust my capacity to give, he couldn't come to me for help.

That hurt, it hurt badly. Had their marriage been that bad? Cat wished that she could somehow tell him now how deeply she had loved him, how she too had realized all the mistakes she had made when it had been too late to rectify them. But she couldn't tell him, not when he still held himself back. He told her things, but he had yet to share his feelings, to explain the three-year gap in which he had known his identity and rebuilt his fortunes without bothering to inform his wife he was still alive.

He was a different man from the husband she had known. She would have to tread warily, learn to know him again before offering the love he demanded. A certain holding back on her part would be simple survival. She couldn't bear losing him again. He had suffered hell, and she had also suffered a hell of a different kind.

"And who the hell does he think he is?" she muttered aloud suddenly, remembering that he had cunningly taken her in the boat race, forced her hand with a ridiculous debt, picked her bedroom

123

door lock, made her appear a wanton fool before Jules, and to top all else, had hurled her to the floor.

"The hell if I *will* jump at any of your commands, Clay Miller!" she muttered again in a hiss, drying and stowing away the last dish. He might be a different man, she thought irritably, but certain things about him hadn't changed a bit!

The sound of activity from the deck alerted her to company from the starboard side. Cat dropped her dish towel and hurried out the cabin doors.

Freshly filled air tanks for the day lined both port and starboard sides of the *Sea Witch II*. Their flippers, masks, weights, and regulators were also ready and waiting. Clay had been busy. Cat noted all this quickly, then turned her eyes toward the *Sea Enchantress* pulled alongside them. Sam was in the process of leaping back to the *Sea Witch II* and Clay was taking his place aboard the *Sea Enchantress*.

"Mornin', Mrs. Miller!" Luke called out from the helm of his craft.

"Good morning," Cat called back, attempting a smile but frowning instead, her eyes narrowed on her husband's departing form.

Clay must have sensed her scrutiny. "I'll be right back, Cat. We've sonar equipment on the *Enchantress*. Peter picked up something large last night and I want to check it out."

The *Sea Enchantress* roared into full motor before Cat could reply, her eyes on the bow until she lost sight of the occupants. The mysterious Ariel had appeared on deck. And Cat had had a view of the boat's bow long enough to see her softly smiled greeting to Clay and the tender light in Clay's eyes as he gently replied.

"You listening to me, Cat?"

"What?" Cat started as she realized Sam had been talking to her.

Sam eyed her suspiciously, but decided against questioning her distraction. "They weren't expecting the sonar to be much help, not with all the wrecks that are down there. But you should have seen it, Cat, a blip as big as the sun."

Despite herself, Cat felt a surge of adrenaline through her system. "So they think we've found it?" she demanded. "Really, Sam?"

A wide white grin broke out across Sam's leathered face. "The way Peter sees it, missy, we just might have. That galleon was a

124

mighty big ship when she sailed the seas. And that husband of yours has a lot of faith in your theory about the *Santa Anita* being out here."

Cat lightly lifted a brow at Sam's tone. It was reproachful. Cat knew that Sam had fully accepted Clay's return. Sam had always thought that the sun rose and set on Clay. He didn't say anything to her, but Cat was aware that Sam thought she should have welcomed Clay back from the beginning with open arms and no holds barred. She couldn't help feeling a marked resentment. Sam had been her teacher, friend, and mentor since childhood, yet it seemed as if he were cheerfully willing to hand her over to the devil and expected her to appreciate it!

Cat was tempted to tell Sam exactly what she thought of his loyalty—or lack thereof—but thought better of the idea. "If anyone should have faith in me," she said with a smile, "it's you, Sam. We've been together long enough."

Sam cast her a wary eye. "Sure, Cat, I know you know what you're doing. But I couldn't have helped you any. You needed that man to come back."

You're right, Cat thought bitterly, but I needed him to come back years before he did.

Cat idly pretended to check the gear on deck. "Did you have a nice night, Sam?"

"Sure did," Sam replied evenly. "Did you?"

Cat flushed slightly and grimaced. Sam had known her a hell of a long time.

"What do you think of Clay's crew?" she asked.

"They're good people, and he's trained them well. They know exactly what they're doing."

"How about Ariel?" Cat asked, attempting to sound entirely casual. "Peter's wife. I haven't had a chance to meet her."

Sam crossed his arms over his chest and leaned against the cabin wall. "You know, missy, you could just about melt any heart and connive information from a stone except that I know you, and it seems to me you're after something. Ariel seems just about as sweet as she can be. She's no concern of yours. You're going to like her very much."

125

Cat was about to respond when she heard the roar of the *Sea Enchantress* returning. She and Sam both watched expectantly as the sister boat pulled alongside and Clay hopped lithely to the rim of the hull to jump back to the *Sea Witch II*.

"This may be it, Cat!" Clay called enthusiastically, gathering her gear and stuffing mask and flippers into her hands. "Sam, turn her about. We need to backtrack almost a mile. We were there—right where we should have been—just a few days ago. What a stupid oversight!" He sat, leaning overside to wet his flippers before sliding his feet into them, then waving at Luke as the *Sea Enchantress* pulled away.

Cat also waved to Luke, noticing that he alone sat at the hull, then turned back to Clay. "What stupid oversight? What are you talking about?"

"Drop-offs, Cat. We were looking right on the reef. I think we missed some type of a drop-off—maybe a blue hole or cave in miniature, and probably just ten feet deeper. . . ."

His positive excitement infused Cat. While Sam sped along in the wake of the other boat, Cat busied herself wetting flippers and mask and donning her weights and tank with Clay's help. For the moment, problems were forgotten. She could think only of the *Santa Anita*. Was she down there? Would today be the discovery, the ultimate triumph?

As Sam brought the *Sea Witch II* to a stop, the *Sea Enchantress* continued onward to put the distance of a half mile between the two cruisers. Cat was able to see that Peter Gruuten and Ariel were also preparing to dive. For a moment the pretty, fragile blonde looked up and caught Cat's eyes. Ariel smiled. Her smile was as gentle and soft as her delicate heart-shaped face.

Cat smiled in return, puzzled with her reaction to the other woman. She kept feeling that Clay was hiding something from her, and yet she couldn't look into Ariel Gruuten's eyes and believe that she was anything other than what she appeared—genuinely sweet . . . offering a shy friendship.

"Dive flag up, Sam!" Clay called cheerfully. Cat jerked around as she felt Clay's arms around her, securing the sixty feet of nylon line that was their communication and safety bind.

126

"Let's go," he said, his eyes incredibly tense in the depths of his mask. "We're going to work toward the *Sea Enchantress,*" Clay said crisply, "We'll go to seventy-five feet, and watch for ridges and caverns. When we meet Peter and Ariel, we surface. Got it?"

"Oh, yes, sir," Cat murmured with a trace of sarcasm. He did have the capacity to sound like a whip-cracking headmaster of a military academy. He caught the acid in her tone and was about to reply, but Cat floundered by him—graceless on deck with her unwieldy flippers and tank—to take position to enter the water. What a stupid time to be petty, she thought remorsefully. We just might be reaching out to touch a dream.

It's Ariel, she thought sadly. I can't pinpoint what's wrong, but something is. . . .

Her thoughts left her abruptly and she almost careened unprepared into the water as she glanced northeastward to notice a third cruiser moving into the area. She caught herself, and turned curiously to Clay, who was preparing to jump beside her.

"Clay, are you expecting a third boat?"

"No, why?"

Cat pointed toward the newcomer, still too far away for the name to be read.

Clay twisted his lower lip and bit it thoughtfully. Then shrugged. "I'm not expecting anyone, but then these are open waters. Probably another group of pleasure-seeking tourists." Still, he glanced back to Sam, who was raising their dive flag. "Keep an eye on that craft, eh, Sam?"

Sam nodded, giving Clay a solemn thumbs-up sign.

Clay switched back to face the sea, securing his mask to his eyes with the practiced touch of a finger. "Ready?"

Cat nodded and they entered the world of the sea with dual splashes. As she followed Clay into the crystalline world, she quickly noted that he had been right. They had totally ignored the possibility of the *Santa Anita* being off the reef. Excitement grew within her until she felt giddy. They had been here before. They were passing a sandy ledge where several of small nurse sharks—docile fish, generally harmless to man unless unduly aroused—seemed to find a comfortable refuge. Cat could easily recognize a sector of stunning elkhorn coral, the remains of a small sailboat snagged beside it. But what she didn't recognize, and hadn't noticed before, was the drop-off. Just as Clay had suggested, the reef suddenly seemed to disappear. They began to descend deeper than they had ever been before.

It wasn't a blue hole—not in essence. But for a fair patch of space the ocean offered something very close. The coral they had previously traversed was a mock covering of the ocean floor, actually far below and darkened by the shadowy ledge of the coral.

Clay was tapping her shoulder. Cat turned to see him place both his hands upon his own upper arms. Be careful. She saw the message as clearly in his eyes as in their prearranged pantomime. She nodded, pointing to the left. Clay nodded in return and proceeded to the right to explore.

Alone, Cat could hear only the sound of her own air bubbles. She had a strange feeling. The water was much dimmer than it had been before, and they were too deep to encounter the brilliant little fish that abounded in the shallower, close-knit coral. Sea fans and algae did cling to the walls of the little pocket in the reef, and occasionally a larger fish swam by. Something startlingly larger than she bumped against her as she surveyed her immediate surroundings. Hoping she wasn't being tested for edibileness by a member of one of the nastier shark species, Cat tensed, holding her underwater flashlight close to her and feeling the race of adrenaline but ready to butt the creature into disinterest. She had encountered many sharks while diving, and she knew she was much safer as one among them than a swimmer thrashing on the surface, and that nine out of ten of the creatures could be easily discouraged from attacking. Sharks preferred their meals to be natural prey from the sea, smaller than man, who appeared tremendously large in the water. Still, any shark could attack.

Cat expelled another burst of air with mammoth relief as she realized the creature butting curiously against her was nothing more than a grouper—an old fellow, she decided with an inward chuckle, to have reached such a size. Cat reached out a gloved hand to touch the side of the inquisitive fish, then reminded herself she was down here for a purpose, and that her time would be limited because today they would have to pause during their ascent to the surface for decompression time.

Swimming in an opposite direction from Clay, Cat scanned ledges and crevices and searched the sandy bottom. Occasionally some piece of encrusted timber or rock would attract her attention, but upon closer inspection Cat would realize that she had discovered only a bit of more modern wreckage.

Her mind began to wander. Even here, in the haunted world beneath the sea, her body responded with tremors when she thought of the night she had just shared with her husband. So many passions had lain dormant so long and had been so thoroughly reawakened. In his arms, Cat knew, she was willing—no, eager—to forget everything and promise anything. But could things change? Had their marriage stood a chance when it had been so disastrously interrupted?

If only I could believe that he loves me, she thought miserably. If only I could understand the years he waited . . . if only I weren't so pathetically jealous! she added ruefully. But had she ever had cause? They really hadn't discussed their past problems, they had just admitted that they had existed. And Clay, too, had acknowledged his own steaming jealousy.

And it all came back to a question that had supposedly been answered: Who was Ariel?

Until she had a legitimate answer, Cat decided sadly, she preferred that Clay think her a little heartless. She wanted him to believe that she still harbored feelings for Jules. Of course, she did still have feelings for the man she had been about to marry, but those were of gentle remorse and apology. Clay had to be very wrong about Jules; he had never been anything but courteous and protective. He had offered everything while demanding nothing.

They're definitely opposites! Cat thought of the two men she had cared for in her life.

And then, once again, she wasn't thinking. She was staring. Rising with chameleon coloring from the sandy flooring was a ledge that didn't belong. Cat suddenly realized that she had been swimming alongside it for several feet and that it extended ahead of her for several feet more. She stretched out a hand to touch it and a thrill of excitement ran through her. Timbers. Eroded by sea and time . . . but she touched timbers.

Cat swam back a few feet swiftly to gain perspective on her find. She tried to control her rampaging heartbeat with stern warnings: They had come across many wrecks; she could not count on this being the *Santa Anita*.

But damn! It looked like the structure of a bow, and if her estimates were at all correct, it was a bow that must have once been a proud thirty feet in width, a bow with a fo'c'sle built low and square, set back from the stem where it would catch less wind, take less chance of tilting the bow. A bow that could well belong to a long-lost galleon of the heyday of the Spanish Main.

Fascinated, Cat moved back in once more to touch the encrusted timbers. It was easy to see how they had missed the structure—even with its size so obvious! Coral extended over the wreck, creating a false bottom, and ocean life had thrived upon the ghost ship. Her planking had been covered by algae in the dim recesses of the cavelike formation; she had literally become one with the sea and silt, coral and sand, and thriving molecular life.

Cat was tempted—oh, so tempted—to prowl her discovery on her own, explore the eerie shell that remained. But Clay would, she knew, literally break her neck. Wrecks with their rotting timbers were very dangerous but oh, so compelling. A little like Clay, she thought wryly. She couldn't stay away from him, he was magnetic, but probably more dangerous than any menace in the sea.

Cat pulled sharply three times on her end of the nylon cord. The lure to explore further was strong. After all, she had called him. Cat propelled herself upward, shimmying carefully between planking and the living growth of coral that housed over it protectively. She found the rim of the ghost structure and paused, bubbles from her regulator silent as she held her breath.

The wreck was in a sad state of corrosion, and she would never be brought to the surface intact. But she was the *Santa Anita*, she had to be. Her full structure could only be that of a galleon, and just as they had lain for that lost battle centuries ago, her cannons lined the deck, proud armaments that never had a chance to fire.

A rude shake of her shoulder informed her that Clay had reached her. She knew he was angry that she had taken the first step alone. But as she turned to him, her eyes brilliant behind the glass of her mask, his anger faded. She saw a smile form on his lips and his deep jet eyes gentle as they recognized the extent of her thrill. His arms came around her and he hugged her, swirling her in delirious circles beneath the sea.

Cat was absurdly tempted to rip out her mouthpiece and meet his lips. His touch, even in the sea, was a wild stimulant, coupled with the exuberance of triumph, and the effect upon Cat was devastating. The *Santa Anita* was more than the find of the century. It was something very personal. They had found her together, and in those moments Cat admitted to herself that Clay would always be able to call the shots, beat her at her own game, as he said. He was more than her match, he was a power she would always bend to because the power he wielded was that which controlled not only her senses but her heart, and her every reason for being.

His hand slid tenderly and yet erotically down her bare shoulder to her gloved hand. Fingers entwined, they moved over the decking of the galleon.

Her flooring was littered with holes, and it was easy access to reach the innards of the ship. As never before, Cat felt a wonder and sadness grip her. The oak chairs and dining tables had withstood the ravages of time, as had swatches of fabric, bits and pieces of cutlery. It was eerie in the darkness of the graveyard ship with only the power of their flashlights to illuminate the fragments of a culture long past.

Cat held tightly to Clay's hand as he led her along. She had never known fear before, but here she was afraid. Her ray of light caught upon the evil grin of a moray eel that had found a home in the cave of a barnacle-covered desk. Probably the captain's desk, a place where the riches of the Aztecs would be counted and prized. Those riches, Cat knew, would be deep, deep within the bowels of the *Santa Anita*.

Clay came upon a hatch to the deck below. He set upon it with the strength of his hands only, and Cat was suddenly overwhelmed with panic. She touched his shoulder to stop him, but with a strange

131

creak the rusty mechanism gave. He was slipping through the hatch, and she had no choice but to follow.

A scream rose in her throat as their light illuminated a scene preserved in this watery prison. They had come to a bedchamber, sealed with the sinking of the ship until their appearance now. A chamber where passengers had come for safety from the impending battle. The skeletons dressed in decayed remnants greeted them in various stages of decomposition and posture. It almost appeared that one of the skeletons beckoned them with an eerie smile to join him as he wavered in a drunken dance by the porthole.

Cat was ready to bolt in panic, heedless of decompression, heedless of breathing period. Clay caught her hand, forcing her to precede him slowly out of the hatchway.

With dim light filtering through their coral blanket, and the vision of macabre skeletons no longer facing her, Cat ridiculed herself for her panic and determined that Clay not think her too squeamishly female for the task ahead. The *Santa Anita* was her dream come true, she couldn't turn it over to him.

She forced a calm smile into her features, pretending that nothing was wrong. Turning from Clay, she decided to take a closer look toward the aft, a section that had apparently taken the fire of an English cannon.

Clay sternly caught her hand, his eyes intense jet. She shook her head, attempting a protest. Clay jerked her hand once more, then tapped furiously upon his diving watch. Cat stared down at the minutes past, wondering if she could wish more time into existence. But Clay was never lost to euphoria or panic. He didn't intend to give her a chance for any more stalling. He began a slow ascent, dragging her with him.

They paused for their first decompression stop just above the coral ledge. Minutes that seemed like ages passed with Clay eyeing her sternly and clutching her hand all the while. It wasn't until they reached the sandy ledge just thirty feet below the surface that either realized there had been other divers near. And what Cat saw sickened her far more than the pathetic bones in the wreck. She immediately felt a boiling rage creep into her bloodstream. The nurse sharks had been savagely attacked. Even as she watched, a number of the

132

creatures ripped through the water in spasms and throes. Every one of them had been hit with a high-powered spear gun.

Horrified, Cat stared on, wishing desperately she could do something to still the agony of the fish. She wasn't in love with sharks—any sharks—but neither could she agree with senseless slaughter of the sea creatures. Why? she wondered. Why on earth would anyone inflict such a cruel massacre upon nurse sharks?

She suddenly felt her hand being wrenched none too gently. Clay was pulling her toward the surface, and before she knew it, she was breaking surface. She spat out her mouthpiece as Clay emerged beside her. "Why were you dragging me like that? Didn't you see what had happened?"

"Of course I saw," he grated harshly in return. He waved his arms over his head toward the *Sea Witch II*, a signal for help. "I dragged you up, you little fool, because while you were floating there gaping, every shark in the vicinity was congregating! That blood will be pulling in the real predators by the hundreds."

Cat shut up, stunned. He was right, of course.

In just seconds Sam pulled the *Sea Witch II* up beside them and hurriedly helped first her, and then Clay, from the water.

As soon as they were on deck, Clay furiously spun on her. "That upset you, huh, Mrs. Miller? Good. Because you have your precious Jules you insist upon defending to thank for the incident. That nice decent man is so determined to keep you from claiming the *Santa Anita* that he isn't at all adverse to the idea of turning your diving waters into a feeding frenzy!"

133

CHAPTER EIGHT

"You're insane!" Cat cross-charged furiously, fumbling to remove her tank and doing a poor job of it owing to her state of agitation. "I know you don't think much of Jules, Clay—and I'm sure it's a form of jealousy, since you seem to think that I'm a piece of property he was rude enough to intrude upon—even though you were nowhere near! But to accuse him of being lethally malicious! You're pushing things way too far!"

"Am I, Cat?" Despite her determination to resist him, Clay spoke while forcefully turning her around to assist her with her weight belt and tank. "You're blind!" he told her, angrily jerking a strap. "And you're in for one rude awakening." Clay turned to Sam, caught as he so often was, silent in the midst of their arguing. "Did you get a look at that boat, Sam? Did you recognize anything about it?"

"Yeah, I got a look at her," Sam said, his eyes darting from Clay to Cat. "And I've never seen her before."

"You see!" Cat hissed. "Sam would recognize a boat that belonged to Jules—"

"Hold on, Cat," Sam said. "I didn't recognize the cruiser, but I think I have seen one of the divers. You can tell for yourself anyway —she's still anchored dead ahead of us. What happened, anyway?"

"We found her," Clay said tensely. "We found the *Santa Anita*."

"You found her!" Sam shouted incredulously. "And you two are bickering over a boat."

"There's more to it than that," Clay explained. "Those divers were down there slaughtering nurse sharks, literally chumming the water enough to call out a great white all the way from the coast

134

of Australia. At best, someone is trying to destroy our salvage operation; at worst, they want us entirely out of the picture—dead."

"Jesus," Sam breathed.

"Get out the signal flags, will you, Sam?" Clay asked. "I want to make sure Peter and Ariel are back aboard the *Sea Enchantress*."

Little chills of fear rippled along Cat's spine; she had forgotten all about their co-divers. Thank God their signals were immediately answered. The Gruutens were safely aboard the *Sea Enchantress*.

"Shall I tell them you found the *Santa Anita*?" Sam asked Clay, hands by his sides, holding the flags.

"No!" Clay said tensely. "Not with that other boat in viewing distance. Just tell them we'll rendezvous at six for dinner on the *Witch*."

Sam did as directed and turned questioning eyes back to Clay. "What now?"

"A beer," Clay said. "And a little planning. We need to register our claim, but we should bring something up first—a plank, anything we can have carbon-dated."

"That's it?" Cat demanded.

Clay turned to her, as if suddenly aware of her presence. "What do you mean, that's it? Now that we've seen her, I can start thinking about the best ways to bring the most up. We'll never float her, Cat, you do realize that—"

"I'm not referring to the *Santa Anita!*" Cat flared furiously. "A pack of idiots was down there killing nurse sharks with illegal spear guns and you're not going to do anything? You can still see their damned boat! Don't you think you should do something? Find out who they are—"

"Cat!" Clay lashed back, his voice a whip crack. "I know who the boat belongs to, and the owner isn't going to give a damn if I go lecture him on the cruelty and danger of indiscriminate killing! If there is anything that I am going to do, it's keep a good eye on the movements of that cruiser. And its inhabitants, before I take a dive."

Cat grit her teeth for patience before speaking. "I'm telling you, Clay, it isn't Jules. Those divers are probably a pack of idiot tourists who shouldn't have been certified in the first place."

135

"Sure, Cat," Clay said with ill-concealed disgust, "whatever you say. You refuse to see anything until it slaps you right in the face. Well, you can just stand there all day deciding on how you're going to reprimand those terrible 'amateurs' for slaughtering those sharks. Sam and I have work to do. You're invited to attend the session if you can break away from your outrage. We can make some solid plans now that we know how the *Santa Anita* lies. . . ."

His words trailed away as he turned and walked through the cabin doors, leaving Cat with the choice to follow or not. Sam shuffled his feet a little uneasily, glanced at Cat, smiled a trifle apologetically, and followed Clay.

Cat stared after the two of them, still steaming. How could Clay believe Jules to be not only spiteful but dangerously so! "Men!" she muttered with disgust.

Clay was wrong. Very wrong. And as usual he was taking nothing she had to say into account. "Damn him!" she hissed. Just last night he had told her he loved her, that memories of her had kept him alive. He had asked that she love him again. He had made love to her through the night, demanding that she be his while still promising that in the end, were it her choice, he would rectify things with another man. This morning he had begun to explain his past, and then had become more autocratic than a sergeant major!

Cat stared after the closed cabin doors. Her steaming anger simmered to a very low boil. "Do you know, Mr. Miller," she murmured, "there is nothing more I want out of life than for the two of us to actually have a chance to make it. But you gave your list of demands—and you forgot to ask for mine! And the first thing on my list is that you learn to listen to me and trust in my opinion at least once in a while—on matters other than history and the sea!"

Cat could hear her husband's voice, velvet and authoritative, from where she stood on deck. He was discussing flotation of the *Santa Anita*'s wide range of cannons by air bags.

Cat knew precious little about the actual and mechanical labor of salvage. She doubted her presence would be influential. And she had suddenly decided that Clay had no intention of listening to her regarding the sharks and Jules. And if he wouldn't listen, she had to prove him wrong.

Besides, the divers from the other craft did need a warning. The explosive spear guns they were using were illegal in Bahamian waters as well as discourteous and dangerous. They needed to be told that their bloody entertainment was foolhardy and possibly deadly.

Moving quietly on deck, Cat retrieved her flippers and mask. The third boat was less than half a mile away; she could swim it easily with snorkel gear, have a stern discussion with the kids—they had to be kids, surely adults wouldn't have done such a thing!—and then return, before she had even been missed. Then she could coolly inform Clay as a fact that he had been very, very wrong.

She glanced at her watch. Almost thirty minutes had passed since they had left the water. She would wait another thirty minutes to assure herself that the waters had settled. No, she would wait even longer for safety's sake. She wanted to prove a point, not that she was an idiot.

Cat left her mask and flippers ready near the tiller and entered the cabin, pouring herself a cup of coffee as she listened idly to the operations discussion going on. Like her, Sam had never taken part in an actual expedition before, but he seemed to understand all that Clay was talking about.

Neither man paid much attention to her as she leaned against the sink listening. Clay thinks that he has spoken and that's that, Cat thought wryly. Cat suppressed a small smile. She could remember her mother, whom she had always thought to be such a serene woman, often agreeing with her father and then turning around and doing what she thought right anyway. It wasn't a bad lesson, Cat thought. Her mother always proved her point quietly, never setting Jason up for any humiliation.

Except I do want a little humility out of Clay right now! Cat thought. Just this once. . . .

Clay and Sam were still talking about tonnage and air bags and the amount of time it would take to strip the *Santa Anita* of her monetary and historical treasures. Funny, Cat thought vaguely, she had always thought merely of finding the galleon, not of the work her salvage would entail. Of course, she had always dreamed of raising the ship intact, and even without Clay telling her, she had realized that to be an impossibility. Her mind began to wander again with dreams of finding the actual treasure trove—the Aztec crown jewels.

"Shouldn't you be doing something?" Clay demanded.

Startled from her pleasant reverie, Cat jumped, then flushed with annoyance. She met the incredibly dark depths of her husband's eyes with her own raised in irritated query. How could anyone make such drastic changes? she wondered. Last night the most tender of lovers . . . today, the most arrogant of taskmasters. And either way, Cat thought, he had the ability to compel. He had acquired a tremendous ability to manipulate. Like a fly lured to a spider's web, she was enticed by gentle seduction until the trap was set to spring. Even now he held her in a spell she seemed powerless to break. She could literally feel the heat of his eyes, searing her, mind and soul, yet all the while offering the intensity of a caress.

"Doing what?" she snapped, breaking the strange spell.

Clay leaned back against the booth, his eyes still holding hers as he reached for his pipe, filling it from a leather pouch and striking a match to the bowl. With just those simple movements, she could see the ripple of bow-tight muscles in the breadth of his sleek chest, the steel in his long fingers.

"Your things," he said quietly. "Luke and Billy will be diving in the morning for a piece of the wreckage and will head back in to stake our claim. Peter and Ariel will be coming aboard the *Sea Witch* tonight so that we don't lose any diving time. They're going to need your cabin."

Damn him a hundred times over, Cat thought. Had he suspected she would fight his edict over principle? Now she was trapped. She could only refuse by creating an awkward and childish scene.

But surely, she thought, these people all know that Clay and I aren't your usual couple. They know he hasn't been with me for years because he's been with them.

Cat slowly took a sip of her coffee, thinking with her mind in high gear as she returned her husband's stare. I can't go back to what we had before, she thought with panic. We have to change. I'd rather have nothing at all than a life where he dominates and then leaves.

138

She set her cup down in the stainless steel sink and smiled sweetly. "Sure," she murmured. "But no one rinsed the gear. I'll just take care of that first. You two keep talking, since it certainly does sound like you know what you're talking about."

Cat knew her easy agreement had surprised both Clay and Sam, but as they seemed to accept her words at face value, she smiled again and left through the cabin doors. Plenty of time had passed now.

Just to ease their suspicious little minds, Cat did run the deck hose. She rinsed all the diving paraphernalia left so haphazardly on deck. But then she slipped into her mask and fins, and quietly eased her body over the edge of the port side and into the water. A quick glance told her the direction to take to reach the third boat—Jules' boat, according to Clay. In just a few minutes she would disprove his haughty assertion.

With slow and easy strokes and the swift power accredited her by virtue of the massive fins, Cat was shortly within reach of her mark. Pausing in the water ten feet from her destination, Cat was able to read the boat's name: *Chrissy*.

She was a handsome yacht, about forty-five feet in length. And more than that, she was a boat Cat was sure she had never seen before. Clay was wrong. Cat knew every pleasure craft that Jules owned.

Pulling her mask from her face, Cat swam toward the ladder cast over the aft. Catching hold of a rung, she began to climb aboard, calling out, "Ahoy, there!" She slipped off the awkward flippers and tossed them aboard before attempting to step into the craft. No one had appeared on deck and she called out again. "Hello! Is anyone here?"

The main cabin door squeaked slowly open and a man appeared. He was almost Clay's size, Cat thought, inadvertently taking a step backward and almost returning to the water she had just left. And he wasn't a kid. His leathered face and limpid, narrowed blue eyes gave him the appearance of a man of at least forty, and he was evidently quite surprised to see her.

He said nothing, and Cat began to feel her first qualms of uneasiness. She began to speak, willing nervousness from the authority in her voice.

"Listen," she said coolly, "I thought I should come over and warn you about a few things. Those spear guns you're using are illegal in Bahamian waters, and the Bahamians are very sticky about their laws being obeyed. If the water patrol comes by, you could find yourself under arrest. But more than that, what you're doing is much more than rude. I'm sure you've seen our diving flags up. Killing those sharks for fun is cruel and also dangerous. If you do something like that to some of the divers out here, they'll come after you. A lot of Bahamians make their living from the sea, and they would think it only justice. . . ."

Cat's voice trailed away as two other men of similar shapes and ages suddenly joined the first on deck. They all proceeded to stare at her silently, and a grip of panic knotted into her stomach. She stood straight, determined not to display her nervousness, and began to speak again. "Please be more careful and considerate from here on out. I would hate to be forced to call the water patrol."

Cat bent to retrieve her mask and fins, the knot in her stomach tightening as she gasped. It had suddenly hit that she recognized the man on the left. She didn't know him, but, as with Sam, she had seen him before. He captained one of Jules' salvage barges.

Oh, God! Cat thought, her shock so great that she felt physically ill. Clay had been right and she had been a fool . . . none so great as a fool determined . . . but Jules? No, she still couldn't accept the fact that she had entertained the idea of marriage to a man who would do such a thing.

Maybe they weren't working for Jules. They were out on their own. Cat thought about Jules, his Gallic charm, his determination to consistently be nothing less than gallant, except for their one argument over the salvage of the *Santa Anita*. . . .

She abruptly realized that she had gasped and then frozen, and that now the men were looking from one another to her. Cat desperately attempted to repair the damage done by her startled sound of recognition. Her free hand moved to grasp the ship's rail as she prepared to spring for a quick escape.

"Stop her," the burly man she had recognized snapped. "She

knows me, we can't let her go now. DeVante will have to deal with her."

"No!" Cat cried, her protest sick and stunned. They were working for Jules. A man she had laughed with, a man she had cared for deeply, even thought she had loved. . . .

They moved after her from three directions, their steps assured. Cat finally galvanized into action, springing from the deck.

But too late. Her foot was caught, and though the intent had been only to restrain her, not hurt her, the fury of her own spring sent her head crashing against the hard planking of the deck's edge. The sharp pain seemed to split her skull, and then she wasn't feeling anything at all. The world dimmed, then disappeared in a cloud of fog.

"I don't intend to stay out here for the majority of the work," Clay told Sam, after telling him his time-estimate for bringing up all that was salvageable was several months. "I'd like to find the jewels," Clay continued, "or rather, I'd like Cat to be able to find them. They were her dream, and finding the ship was her theory. But other than that, Sam, I want to get back to Tiger Cay. I want to start building a home life." Clay laughed. "I think I'm getting old, Sam."

"Maybe," Sam laughed in return, taking a long sip of beer. He frowned then, more aware of Clay's past than Cat, and much aware of the hardships endured. Sam had never met a man he respected more than Clayton Miller, and he had determined from the beginning that Cat needed to be back with her husband. But getting Cat to accept the husband who was more than a match for her own fiery temper was proving a slow process.

"Clay," Sam demanded, his frown deepening, "do you really think DeVante is trying to sabotage this operation?"

"I don't think it, I know it, Sam," Clay said firmly, his frown matching his friend's. "DeVante is in hock all over the place. He took a few chances too many that didn't pan out."

Sam narrowed his dark eyes. "How do you know that?"

Clay shrugged, his voice somewhat bitter. "I've been keeping tabs on Cat. I heard some things about DeVante within the business—

141

not fact, just rumor. But when I heard about him and Cat, I couldn't take a chance on rumor being true. So I checked up on DeVante. I called various banks and business concerns, and in a few instances I was able to have him spied on. He always suspected that Cat could find the *Santa Anita*. He simply hadn't expected she'd be so stubbornly determined to find the ship herself. And he couldn't take that chance, not unless she married him. And Cat was dragging her feet not even knowing that she couldn't marry him because I was still alive. DeVante is in trouble, Sam. He doesn't know that we've found the ship, but he knows we're close. He has to get us out of these waters so that he can search himself. As of tomorrow, though, it will be all over. Our claim will have been secured."

Sam began to reel off a few of his opinions regarding Jules in very explicit language. Clay firmly contained the twitches that were about to spread a grin across his entire face. Sam adored Cat. He was the finest protector alive. "You mean," Sam demanded, "that DeVante never cared a thing for Cat, he was always after her property and her knowledge?"

"No," Clay interrupted, his voice harsh and guttural. "At least," he added dryly, "I don't think so. He used to boast of her in every port and about how he was the only man she would ever give more than a hello and good-bye. He wanted her, as if she were a special jewel to covet. So in his rather warped way, it seems he does care about her. From what I've been told, he wants her almost as much as he wants the treasure."

Clay could feel himself tightening as he said the words; his features seemed to tense painfully and he could swear his blood steamed. He had always tried to be logical when he thought of his wife all those years, but logic hadn't always tempered his feelings. The vision of Cat, naked, her lustrous hair streaming over her shoulders as she approached him, her body so lithe and yet fully shaped, her lips curled in a tantalizing smile, plagued him each time he closed his eyes. He loved her, she was his. Thinking of her in the arms of another man almost made him sick with a possessive rage. But those were gut feelings. Rationally, he had to assume that another man had taken his place and he forced himself to understand. If Cat had been happy, he wouldn't have interfered. He hadn't lied to her. If she knew the truth about DeVante and still chose him over Clay, he would exit from her life.

Or so he had thought. But now he had held her again, felt the passion of her body respond to his. She was no longer a vision, or a fantasy. If she wasn't already aware that she was his, he would simply have to make her so, by fair means or foul—and he admitted freely that a number of his means already had definitely been in the "foul" category.

"Where the hell did she get to, anyway," Clay murmured, suddenly realizing that it had been some time since she had sweetly smiled and volunteered to rinse all the gear. Suspicion sent a shiver down his spine. It wasn't like Cat to take to a command so readily, and although he had carefully phrased his words to make his desires sound like a logical explanation, Cat had known she had been issued a challenge.

"Something is wrong," Clay said tensely, standing to rush out on deck with Sam behind him.

"Her mask and fins are gone," Sam reported tersely.

"Oh, God," Clay groaned. "What has that fool woman done?"

But it was himself he wanted to kick. He had been the fool. A sane man didn't tell a woman that a man she had loved was crooked as a mountain road and simply expect her to believe it. He should have done something, gone with her to challenge the divers.

I wanted her to believe me because she loved me, he thought with rueful remorse. I wanted that faith from her, and I was asking too much. And lord, he thought in a sweat, he didn't know how far DeVante would go, or just what orders his "workers" had been given.

"Let's get the dinghy down," Clay said to Sam. "We'll move in quietly. . . ."

As they began rowing silently to the other boat, Clay could think of nothing but the admission he had forced from Cat. DeVante had never shared her bed.

The steam within Clay, the gut feeling he knew to be chauvinistic but still undeniable, began to grow. If Cat was touched, harmed in any way . . . Clay felt he could easily draw and quarter another human being.

But what if DeVante was on the boat himself? What if Cat did love him, was willing to forgive him once they had talked? So far, the man had been guilty of no more than a little illegal spear fishing.

Sorry, Cat, he whispered inwardly. I'm a liar. I'll never let you go. You are my wife and I'll fight you from here to hell and back to keep it that way.

And yet it wasn't really his wife's feelings he was worried about as they approached the intruder's boat. He was simply praying she hadn't gotten into any trouble.

Cat groaned softly, and it was her own groan that brought her back from the depths of the clouds. She wasn't at all disoriented. The sound of her moan registered as a warning. She remembered immediately all that had happened, and she kept her eyes tightly shut as she tried to feel her environment and those around her.

She was lying on something soft . . . a bed within the cabin? . . . and as the ringing ceased in her ears, she could hear conversation.

"What do we do now? We should just have let her go. We hadn't really done anything—"

"Don't be a complete ass!" someone interrupted harshly. "She knew me. The only thing we can do now is get her out of here and to DeVante. He can deal with her, use some of that charm and maybe even get her to hand over her claim."

"What good is that going to do? Miller is still sitting over the *Santa Anita*, and Miller is her husband."

"A husband who hasn't been around in a long time," the harsh voice snickered in return. "I think DeVante will be happy to get his hands on her." A laugh sounded. "In fact, I think DeVante will be pleased with the idea of a little revenge. He treated her like the virgin queen, then walks in to find her bedded down with a man she was claiming to be a ghost. Yeah, I think DeVante will be happy to have his 'fiancée' back. I don't think he'll let her act much like a little ice queen anymore."

Her stomach was churning so violently that Cat had to swallow to keep herself from becoming physically sick. Oh, dear God, she prayed, forcing her eyes to remain closed with every ounce of her willpower, I have to get out of here.

The task of trying to retain a survival calm almost became impossible as she felt a finger trail over her arm. Another laugh sounded, one that held a hoarse, lascivious tone, sending chills of alarm warnings through Cat's system. "Can you imagine leaving a woman built like this alone for all that time? Damn it, feel that skin. . . ."

Do something! Cat's mind raged, but desperation kept her from falling apart in panic.

She could defend herself, but against three? She forced her mind to retreat to her teachings by Lee Chin. "We are a small race!" the young man had told her with a laugh. "And so we learn to make our adversaries use their power and strength against themselves. Channel your energies, your power is in your center, and the center is a circle of balance and grace. . . ."

And so she had spent days studying the art of T'ai Chi, learning to control her mind, to perfect the movements of the body. "It is not all hostile," Lee had told her. "It is also training in peace of mind, in the beautiful possibilities offered the body. . . ."

And at the time it had been peace of mind, it had been enjoyable, and she had gone on to learn a few of the more aggressive techniques of judo. Cat had been so fond of Lee, so touched by his honorable declaration that he couldn't pay her but he was at her service, as he was not a man ever to forget a debt . . . so young, yet so responsible.

But Lee, Cat thought desperately, I failed once. I failed against Clay, but then Clay had obviously had some training. Among the cutthroats and thieves in prison he had learned a lot about survival. It was unlikely that these thugs knew anything but using brute strength.

Cat opened her eyes into slits. She was right inside the cabin door, not more than a few feet from it. Only the man who had touched her was actually near her. If she could escape him, the element of surprise should take her out to the open. And then, pray God, the sea would offer release. And if she was lucky, Clay and Sam would

145

be worrying about her by now. They should be out on deck, searching the water.

Cat let her eyes open wide as she feigned a look of total disorientation and panic. As if in alarm, she reached out a hand and mumbled a very pathetic, very feminine "Pleeease . . ."

As she had hoped, the man before her, the evil laugher, reached out his own hand to take hers; the look in his eyes showed him rather pleased with her apparent submission.

His macho arrogance was about to do him in, Cat thought with a grim smile.

"Watch her, Al!" someone shouted.

But it was too late for Al. Cat shifted, springing from the salon couch just as Al's own weight brought him down upon it with a heavy thud. Cat didn't wait to appreciate his stunned expression. She was headed out the door.

She had just made the deck when she felt herself wrenched back cruelly by the hair. Shifting low, pivoting from her "center" as she had been taught, Cat wedged a foot behind that of her attacker, and leaned forward. Once again it was the man's own weight that brought him sprawling to the deck.

But there were three of them. Dismay began to chill through Cat. How long could she keep this up? They were falling. They were cursing. She was doing a fair amount of damage. They kept coming back up. Her strength was failing her, her breath was coming in terrible short gasps.

She got a good look at Al's livid face as he came for her a third time. He was the angriest of the men—the first to be tricked. Uneven and yellowed teeth were bared in the frame of lips drawn into a snarl.

"Oh, honey," he hissed, "you just wait till I do get my hands on you. You're gonna pay. . . ." His tone became a slimy and threatening caress. "I'm gonna make sure you ain't no ice queen when DeVante gets ahold of you."

"Hey, Al," one of the other men warned uneasily, taking up a position so that the three of them surrounded her in a narrowing circle. "Don't get any ideas about touching her. I ain't in this for kidnapping or rape. And DeVante will have your hide."

146

Al took a lunge toward Cat that she managed to sidestep, apparently infuriating him further while she still fought wave after wave of debilitating panic. She had held them off so far, but her resources were fraying. If two of them got hold of her at the same time . . . And the world kept dimming on her. If she didn't keep blinking, she saw black. She was nauseated, terrified that at any minute she would pass out cold.

"DeVante didn't tell me we were going to tangle with a wildcat," he hissed in reply to his cohort. "This bitch has clawed me good. DeVante won't mind me having a turn after all this tigress has lashed out to me."

"DeVante might not mind," a voice with the ice-edge of a steel sword suddenly drawled out in sliced anger all the more deadly because it sounded so terribly controlled.

Cat spun around, sure that she would faint now with relief. Clay was coming over the aft edge of the boat with Sam in tow behind him. "Cat," he hissed, his eyes not on her but on Al, "I can see you're doing rather well with those little dance steps of yours, but do you think we could stop messing around now? Get in the dinghy."

Cat moved instantly to obey him, with Al growling behind her. She could barely breathe as she imagined him reaching for her again.

"You're crazy, Miller, if you think I'm letting her walk right off this boat—"

"Don't touch her!" Clay lashed out instantly, and Cat realized he held a small pistol. "I brought this just to make sure we could make a quick retreat. I'd like to stay and fight this out—you're a bit bigger than my wife and I'd like to see how you'd fare against a man your own size—but I'm really afraid I'd be sorely tempted to kill you. In fact, you stretch one of those grimy fingers toward her again, and I'll be real, real tempted to shoot it right off. Sam—" Clay still kept his eyes upon the three men of the *Chrissy.* "Get Cat into the dinghy now!"

Cat started to move, but not quickly enough. She was stunned with the relief of Clay's appearance, and totally off guard when Al's fingers closed over her shoulders. A small gasp escaped her; she

147

attempted to struggle, but she was worn and weak, unable to break the grip around her throat.

"You're not going to shoot me, Miller," Al challenged thickly.

Cat was dazed but still vaguely aware that Clay's apparent control was very deceiving. She knew his temper, that his rage was murderous despite the calm drawl of his voice. "You're right," he said softly, too softly. "I'm not going to shoot you." The small pistol was tossed almost negligently overboard to the dinghy. Clay turned to Sam, lifting a brow. "Care to join me on deck, Sam?"

"A pleasure," Sam agreed.

"There's three of us!" Al snarled.

"You are at a disadvantage," Clay said coolly. And then he was approaching Al, his footsteps the calm, assured ones of a great cat stalking prey. For just a split second his eyes touched upon Cat, then narrowed. Cat felt a searing on her forehead where his vision had brushed it. She became aware of a sticky sensation and that Clay had seen the trickle of blood against the bruise at her temple—a result of her collision with the planking in her first escape attempt. Until now, she hadn't had the time to realize she was hurt.

Cat gasped and a cry escaped her as the hold on her throat tightened momentarily. But then she was instantly released. Clay's hand had come upon the arm of her attacker.

"Get in the damned dinghy, Cat!" Clay roared.

Cat found the energy to run. She saw Sam fell one of the other men with a single well-aimed blow delivered by his giant hand. She heard a thud behind her that made her pause. The cocky Al was also down; Clay had brought a bloodied knuckle to his mouth, then he shook his hand, looking down at the man who lay in a heap at his feet, as if he wished to do him further injury. Dear God, Cat thought swiftly, Clay looked as if he were still ready to kill. . . . "Clay!" she cried out.

"Sam—get her into the dinghy!"

Cat was only able to see that the third man of the *Chrissy* was moving backward. "I didn't want any part of this," he was pleading. "I was the one telling Al to leave her alone. . . ."

Cat was grateful to hear the sound of Clay's voice rather than the repercussion of action as Sam grabbed her arm to follow her husband's directive. "You just get this garbage back to DeVante," Clay hissed. "And don't ever let me see your face again unless you want it rearranged."

Thank God that Sam was there to help her, Cat thought, because she was shaking so badly she barely made the step over the side of the boat. She heard Clay continue to talk as she took up a shivering position in the dinghy. "You make damned sure to tell DeVante it's all over. The water patrol will be around soon and they'll be staying here until the salvage operation is complete. You're getting off easy. Any more trouble and you'll be paying with lots and lots of years out of your worthless life." Clay hesitated a moment, his voice lowering. "And if my wife is touched again, you'll be paying with your worthless life itself. Do we have an understanding?"

Cat couldn't see the one man of the *Chrissy* still standing, but he must have been convincingly and eagerly agreeable. Clay was in the dinghy only a second later, picking up the oars.

"Clay—" Cat began miserably.

He spun on her with such fury that she was stunned into silence. "You little idiot!" he shouted. "All of this over your damned Frenchman! Because you just can't bear to listen! Let me warn you, Mrs. Miller, another stunt like this one and you'll find yourself chained in a cabin!"

Cat opened her mouth to protest, but no words would come. She sat in shivering misery, aware that Sam's eyes condemned her silently just as Clay's words had. She had been an idiot . . . so trusting . . . so stupidly sure of herself.

The oars suddenly ceased movement in the water. Clay reached out across the feet of the dinghy, gripping her chin as he examined her temple. There was no tenderness to the touch of his fingers; he was swearing soundly.

His eyes continued to flame as he abruptly released her. "You'll heal," he said curtly.

Cat grit her teeth to fight back tears. She knew the wound was superficial; she could barely feel it. And she knew she had been wrong, her determined persistence had put her into an extremely perilous position. But she hadn't expected to be the recipient of Clay's raw anger. She was sore and tired, stunned and shell-shocked, bewildered, confused—and scared silly, and she needed his comfort.

The taut, grim mask of his face assured her that he offered none.

Their return to the *Sea Witch II* was a tense and silent affair, with Cat struggling with an inward battle as strenuous as that which had just drained her physically. She fought to retain her dignity against a man treating her like an errant child. But her dignity broke as she tried to crawl aboard the *Sea Witch II*. She was too tired . . . she was shivering uncontrollably. Her steps faltered and she almost tripped.

Clay's arms came around her and she was lifted into his iron hold. But there was no tenderness to his touch. He stormed through the main salon to his cabin and tossed her unceremoniously upon the bed. He bent to touch the bruise on her temple, his touch gentle despite his ill temper. A muffled curse escaped him, then he was striding out of the room. Cat struggled to sit, but before she could fully rise, he was back, an ice pack in one hand, pills and a water glass in the other. He handed her the glass and the pills, stared at her until she had swallowed them, then pressed her back against the pillow. "Aspirin," he informed her abruptly. "The cut isn't a half inch, and the bruise should be gone tomorrow." His control suddenly exploded. "Damnation! Do you know how lucky you are? Do you have any idea of what could have happened?" His query ended in a sharp tone and he spun away from her, twisting back to issue one more impatiently snapped decree. "Don't move!" he warned her curtly. "Not a damn muscle! We'll discuss this as soon as I think I can do so with half a pretense at sanity!"

The tears Cat had been fighting for what seemed like an eternity cascaded from her eyes as he left the cabin, the door slamming behind him with a furious, thundering thud.

CHAPTER NINE

Cat remained upon the large bed of the master cabin for a long time, not so much because she had been commanded to do so, but because she really couldn't rouse herself to do otherwise. She had never felt so physically exhausted and bone-sore, nor had she ever succumbed before to such overwhelming confusion and self-pity.

After all she had been through, how could Clay be so cold? So lividly angry that he couldn't even bring himself to speak to her?

Trying to gather her shattered spirit together, Cat gave vent to a long list of hissed names that—in its entirety—did not adequately describe what she was feeling for her husband. But at least the effort did help ease her battered soul.

He had come just in the nick of time to save her, the perfect hero, but there the line had been drawn. Heroes were not supposed to raise hell with those they rescued, nor abusively toss them upon beds with orders that they not move a muscle.

But it wasn't only her husband's erratic fury that had left her feeling so shattered; it was the terrible knowledge that he had been right. Jules had been more than willing to use her. He had ordered men to follow her and Clay, to destroy their efforts, and apparently they had been given free rein to deal with her in the event of trouble.

But how had Clay known what Jules had planned?

Cat started shivering again. She set aside the ice pack and winced as her fingers brushed her temple. She finally managed to raise herself from the bed then, feeling absolutely filthy and as if she could never wash clean. But surely a shower would help. It might partially eradicate the memory of being touched by the scavengers aboard the

151

Chrissy. It could help clear her mind of the catastrophe that might have occurred had Clay not made his timely appearance.

There was a private bath in Clay's quarters; she had learned that just last night when the world had looked so miraculously beautiful and bright. Things had certainly changed.

Cat began to wish she had listened to Clay and moved her things into his cabin. It was inevitable that she would eventually follow his decree, and if she had simply become resigned to his ways earlier, she would have her own clothing to change into now. But she hadn't moved her things into the cabin, and in her present state she wasn't up to another battle with Clay—which would surely ensue if she did attempt to leave his cabin at the moment, even if it were only to procure some of her own clothing. It was all she could do to drag herself around to find an oversize navy velvet robe.

Cat slipped into the tiny head adjoining the cabin and clenched her teeth against the spurt of water from the shower stall, which simply refused to become warm. Still, the cold was invigorating. It washed away the salt that had dried on her skin. The movement was also good; if she had stayed stationary any longer, she might have been really sore in the morning.

Cat blanched and swayed slightly as she forced herself to face what had almost happened. She clutched the tile wall, teeth chattering. She had always believed herself so capable, but then she had walked around with her head in the clouds. She was the mistress of Tiger Cay, respected among the islanders, protected by Sam. Never in her wildest dreams had she feared a possible assault, the horror of rape.

Cat turned off the water and shakily attempted to wring out her hair, doing a very bad job of it as she gingerly tried to avoid touching the sore spot created by the bruise. Her head wasn't pounding, as she had expected it might; it merely plagued her with a slow throb, and even that was dimming thanks to the aspirin and ice.

She stepped from the shower and grabbed one of Clay's massive chocolate towels, wrapping it securely around herself and just standing there as she once again fought a spasm of shakes.

No wonder he's so furious, she told herself. I wouldn't listen, I just had to take matters into my own hands. But I'm not a fool, I've handled my own life very well for the past several years. We all make mistakes. But the mistake she had made today had been a very serious one.

"Well, I can't change it," she said aloud. But to herself she countered, I can accept what I've done, I can understand his anger, and instead of shutting off and retaliating with further anger, I can try to make him understand why I felt that I had to do what I did.

A light tapping at the cabin door interrupted Cat from her thoughts. She shrugged quickly into Clay's robe, belted its huge folds around her, and rushed for the door. Maybe it was Clay, and they would have a chance to really talk.

But it was Sam. Of course it was Sam, Cat thought, disappointment giving rise to bitterness. Clay wouldn't have knocked. In his opinion, it was his room, she was his wife. Why knock?

"I brought you some tea and toast, missy," Sam said, handing her a tray with a small ceramic pot and a covered dish.

Cat smiled. She felt a little like a chastised child receiving comfort from an older sibling. "Thanks, Sam," she said, accepting the tray.

"You okay?" Sam asked, his eyes probing hers with concern.

Cat nodded, a catch forming in her throat. Even if the man who claimed to love her wasn't overly concerned with her well-being, at least Sam was. "Yeah, Sam," she said huskily. "I'm fine."

He stretched out a hand to lift a tendril of wet hair and check her temple, obviously deciding for himself that the damage was light.

"You eat that toast," he told her. "I know you, when you get the least bit agitated, missy, you don't eat."

"I'll eat, Sam, I'll eat!" Cat promised.

Sam lowered his eyes and shuffled his feet. "I'll bring your things in for you in just a few minutes. You want to rest up a bit. Tomorrow night is a celebration."

"A celebration?" Cat mumbled blankly. What could they be celebrating? The day had turned out horribly.

"The *Santa Anita*," Sam said softly. "We found her, remember?"

"Yes, yes, of course," Cat murmured. Had that been only this morning? The realization of the dream? The dream did not seem as golden as it once had, now that she knew what men would stoop to for treasure.

"You want anything else?" Sam asked, almost apologetically. Cat lowered her lashes to keep him from reading the reproach she was feeling. He was concerned for her, yes, but he was also subtly telling her that he was not about to aid a rebellion against Clay. She had been confined to quarters and she had best stay there.

"No, Sam," Cat said. "I don't need a thing."

Sam cleared his throat and hesitated. "Cat, I know that Miller can be a hard man. A real hard man. But he was awful scared, missy, awful damned scared when he saw that you were gone. And you can understand why, Cat, you were messing with ruthless people. Now, I know that you can handle yourself, lady, Miller knows that too. But there's times we can get in over our heads. You were hell bent on getting in over your head. He's angry now—I don't deny that. But that man is angry 'cause he cares so damn much. You think about that before you read him the riot act."

Sam stopped talking abruptly and flushed, then mumbled something and turned from the door. But as his footsteps carried him away, Cat could make out his mutterings. "Damned woman like that needs a damned man like that and *that* is just the way it is. . . ."

Cat bit her lip thoughtfully and slowly smiled.

As she closed the door in Sam's wake, she realized that she was starving and immediately decided to consume the contents on the tray if not the tray itself. The tea tasted delicious, and the toast even better. A feeling of calmness finally slipped over her and for the first time since she had returned from the skirmish aboard the *Chrissy,* Cat felt as if she would be able to come to terms with the events of the day.

When Sam returned with what little wardrobe she had packed for the salvage trip when her daily work outfit consisted of a bathing suit, she was cheerfully ready to thank him again.

And when Clay himself finally arrived in the room, his temper apparently calmed, but his eyes still very dark and warning, Cat was also ready to greet him.

She had chosen her casual outfit carefully, although it was simple. She wore a white cotton halter dress and a pair of matching thin-strapped sandals. White, Cat knew, was a color she wore well. It

154

contrasted with the dark sable of her hair, it complemented the deep gold of her skin. And her dress was similar to one she had worn for Clay many years before.

She had brushed her hair studiously to a high shine. It fell down her back and waved over her shoulders in a lustrous mass, and the soft tendrils that framed her face hid any sign of injury. Clay had never minded braids or coils or upsweeps, but Cat was also aware that he preferred her hair down . . . simple, natural.

When he entered the room, she sat serenely at the foot of the bed. She met the wary look in his eyes with her own eyes wide and regal, but soft, her fingers folded placidly in her lap.

He crossed his arms over his chest and leaned against the door as he watched her. "How are you feeling?" he finally asked.

"Fine," Cat said quietly. She offered him a small smile. "Sam brought me some tea. It did the trick."

Clay nodded curtly, then suddenly he was striding toward her, clutching her arms in a fierce hold as he bent one knee upon the bed and glared tensely down at her. "Damn, Cat," he muttered vehemently, opening his mouth as if he were about to say more, then clenching his teeth back together.

Suddenly and somewhat roughly, Cat felt herself pulled into his arms and they fell to the bed together. She lifted wide eyes to Clay, unnerved by the smoldering that remained in his. But there was something else in the jet depths that magnetized her; a pain so deep it froze in her throat any words she might say.

His eyes followed a callused finger as he touched her forehead, drawing a soft line downward over her cheekbones along the line of her chin. He touched her lips next, encircling them; then his view shifted and he touched the satin of her bare arm. "I think I really might have killed him if he'd harmed you any further," he muttered hoarsely, more to himself than to her. "Christ, Cat, I was sick thinking about what might have happened to you. . . ." He stared into her eyes for an instant, then his lips crushed down upon hers, demanding, passionately bruising. With that same intense heat his kisses roamed to cover her face, then his lips returned to touch hers, commanding admission, his tongue delving deeply in a sweep that fully raided and claimed the recesses of her mouth.

155

Cat trembled with the intensity of his administrations, feeling the shiver of desire race up her spine despite the situation. A fire was ignited within a deep core, and when he shifted his face from hers, burying it in the wealth of hair that fanned beside her neck, and brought his hand coursing over her breasts to her hips, she moaned and curved her body instinctively closer to his. There's so much I need to say to him, she thought vaguely.

Clay, too, it seemed, needed to talk. He lifted his head and stared into her eyes. "I can't do it, Cat," he murmured. "I'm a very jealous and possessive man . . . just the thought of them hurting you . . . touching you. . . ."

Cat returned his stare, her emerald eyes dilated as she nodded, at a loss at how to reply. She wanted his touch to continue, as she always did, and yet she was frightened, forced into an abrupt awareness of the man she loved. He was a shockingly vital man, everything about him intensified. His tempers were thunderous, his will as strong as steel, his passions insatiable. He would always demand because that was his nature. He was stronger than the sea they both so loved, but was she strong enough to handle such a man?

As he thoughtfully massaged her hair, Cat finally found her voice, a little nervously. "You should shower," she murmured. "Aren't Peter and Ariel coming aboard soon?"

For a moment it seemed as if he hadn't heard her. His hand slid along the curves of her body once again, almost idly finding the hem of her dress and slipping beneath the hem. The slow, absent feathering of his fingers against her skin was almost unbearably arousing. His fingers grazed teasingly over the tender flesh of her inner thigh until she was sure she would cry out. Cat swallowed back a gasp, murmuring, "Clay! Your friends . . . Peter and Ariel. . . ."

He nodded vaguely and stood, unselfconsciously zipping down his cutoffs as he walked toward the shower. Cat followed his movements with her eyes, flushing slightly as he casually shed his pants and kicked them aside, leaving her with a full view not only of the glistening bronze shoulders, to which she had grown accustomed, but also of his full state of arousal within the angle of his trim hips.

Cat suddenly felt her teeth begin to chatter. What is the matter with me? she wondered. His physique was nothing new to her. In their married life they had always been perfectly comfortable with one another. But she was nervous. He was the man she had married, but yet he wasn't. So much still lay between them.

He turned as if he were about to say something, then suddenly paused, his eyes studying hers.

Cat grew even more nervous as she saw his eyes darken even more deeply, his features tense. She was unaware that he, too, was seeing the state of her arousal, skirt hiked high, baring long slender legs that curved invitingly, her hair disheveled and fluttering across the white of the spread like raven's wings, her lips moist, still slightly parted, her emerald eyes magnificently dazed.

He had been so worried about her, torn between the anger he couldn't control and deadly fear. He had meant to leave her alone until they could both talk, really talk. But it was obvious she was feeling just fine. And almost having lost what was his, he was suddenly unable to resist the temptation to claim it.

As he watched her, her lashes framed thick crescents over her cheeks. Her eyes flew back open, and she rolled from the bed, her cheeks flushed a beautiful pink as she started for the cabin door, faltering as she murmured, "I . . . um . . . I'm going to go out and get a drink—"

Her words cut off as she was spun around, into his arms. Cat could find nothing to say as she stared into her husband's eyes, mesmerized. She didn't think it would really matter if she had anything to say or not. His fingers moved deftly against her nape and the halter dress fell to the floor. Cat was crushed instantly into his arms and returned to the bed with a strangely tender savagery.

"Clay—" Cat murmured, fingers splayed against his chest as the intensity of his dark eyes flamed like fires of hell. But she had no chance to say more; her hands were nothing against his power as he lay over her, catching her hands and entwining them with his as he pressed a kiss against the pulse that beat at the base of her throat. "You make me crazy, Cat," he groaned, "and you will not walk out of this room . . . not yet."

His hands deserted hers to rake through the sides of her hair as he held her still and kissed her lips devouringly, his tongue plundering soft crevices ruthlessly. Cat was stunned by his ferocity, yet still

157

she couldn't deny that his fevered need sent her senses reeling. Deep within her abdomen something almost agonizingly sweet and potent had begun to burn. She felt the quivering of his body beneath the demanding power and knew that he was driven to his state of rough demand by haunted emotion. The fires were set; she could not protest him, only answer his need with the wild passion it decreed.

She controlled a cry as his hold upon her hair tightened, but then she gasped aloud as his right hand deserted her hair, moving instantly to her thighs, teasing through the the film of lace. He lifted himself from her, then stared at her slender body, running his hand up and over her abdomen to her breasts and back. "You just don't know, Cat," he whispered hoarsely. "I wanted you for so long, so long. And then you were mine again. The thought of another man touching you, feeling the silk of your skin . . . that riff-raff thinking he could have you . . ."

His lips fell to the flesh of her collarbone with a sizzling moist heat, fiercely tender. Then they moved lower, touching, caressing, massaging her breasts, and he took the peaked nipple lightly between his teeth. Cat cried out, kneading her fingers into his back, vaguely acknowledging a groan of pleasure from him as her nails wove a soft, punishing pattern.

He drew away once more, catching her wide eyes. "You're mine, Cat," he murmured. "Mine only."

Cat nodded, understanding fully the devil that haunted him. Today had been traumatic for them both. She smiled tremulously, the words she finally found herself able to say coming out in a ragged pant. "I love you, Clay."

"I love you, Catherine. . . ."

Cat lifted her arms, stretching them out to her husband. Momentarily he allowed her to entwine him, her fingers luxuriating in the muscles of his back. But then he was slipping from her to remove the last of her garments, sliding her panties slowly and sensually from her legs, following the erotic roll of his fingers with wickedly exotic flickers of his tongue. "Clay!" Cat gasped and pleaded, curling and writhing and arching in a frenzy to reach him, to make him end his magical torment. In a remote corner of her mind she knew she no longer needed to make an apology—nor did he. She understood the intensity of his feelings . . . sometime, they would talk. But he knew as she did that they somehow managed to communicate in the whispers of their physical love as they never had before.

I love you. . . . The three little words were all he had craved. All she had been so afraid to give until he had come to her with that fierce savagery she had finally understood.

"Clay . . . oh . . . Clay!"

He raised himself above her, smiling as her soft slender leg moved against his, offering the sweetest of surrenders and invitation.

A gasp, a sigh, a whisper of luxurious pleasure broke from her as her body shuddered with the pulse of his passion finally surging into her, filling her, joining fire to fire and climbing to rhythmic heights. Cat was dizzy as the world became just the two of them, and yet within that world she was achingly aware of every sensation: the rough hair of his thighs grazing hers, the hardness of his chest, the taut grip he held upon her arms unless he released them to touch her breasts, to bring his hands beneath her to cradle her buttocks and press her ever closer to the driving rotation of his hips.

"Cat . . ." he murmured, meeting her eyes as his voice caressed her. And then, as his body shuddered with the final strong courses preceding ultimate ecstasy, he whispered, "I love you. . . ."

She felt his words. They filled her as sweetly as the warmth that swamped her with the seeds of their mutual release. They held her as they clung to one another, slowly descending back to earth, temporarily satiated and savoring the delicious glow of love's aftermath.

For many minutes they were still. Then Cat shifted to curl against him, running her fingers wonderingly over the damp hair that curled crisply over his chest. She was startled when he gripped her fingers.

"Did you mean that, Cat?"

She lifted herself up on an elbow and smiled into his eyes. "Yes," she said softly.

He lifted an eyebrow. "That wasn't just because you discovered you're no longer enamored of Jules?"

Cat hesitated. "Clay—I . . . I knew I would never go back to Jules long ago. I just couldn't see your condemning him out of jealousy.

159

I really thought you were wrong, and that the only way to make you see it was to prove it. But I was the one who was wrong, I had to find out the hard way. Oh, Clay! I am so sorry—"

"Hush!" Clay murmured. "We've both been very wrong. But maybe we're on the track to both being very right. We still have a lot to learn about each other, Cat. And we both need to learn to trust!"

"But, Clay," Cat whispered. "How did you know about Jules?"

Clay shrugged. "I checked up on him, my love. And I know several islanders well enough to have a man watched."

Cat bit her lip uneasily, but Clay chuckled. "The grapevine is also great—if you learn how to listen to it!" He smiled, brushed a kiss on her lips, and rolled across the bed to pounce lithely to his feet.

Cat frowned. "Where are you going? We were finally making a little headway."

Clay chuckled softly. "You were the one telling me we had people coming on board! And you're right—one of us needs to at least say hello when we have guests right outside the boundaries of our bedroom. Personally, I'd just as soon stay here."

"Oh, lord!" Cat gasped, her body, from face to toes, flushing scarlet.

"What?" Clay demanded quickly, his brows raised.

"Outside our door? Oh, Clay! I—oh—"

Clay burst into deep laughter. "Don't worry, sweetheart," he said, lips twitching as he assured her. "You are a vocal little sea witch, but I promise, your sweet words and murmurs were for my ears only!"

He turned for the shower and Cat threw a pillow after him. "How dare you laugh at me!" she charged, but she was laughing herself because her aim had been very good and the pillow caught him right on his well-formed rear.

Clay spun back, a brow lifted in vengeful indignity, but his lips still twisted in a grin. "Watch it, witch, or we'll see just how much I will dare!"

Undaunted, Cat sprang from the bed and raced past him.

"Hey—I have to shave!"

"Which will take you a while! I just want to hop beneath the shower and rinse off! Two minutes."

Five minutes later Clay was eyeing her dryly as she briskly toweled her skin to a pink glow. "Okay," he muttered, snatching the towel from her and twirling it to flick it against her buttocks. "Out of my way—I'm a busy man and you have nothing to do with the evening but loaf!"

"Ouch!" Cat protested, lifting her chin as she sailed past him indignantly. "And what do you mean, I have nothing to do but loaf? I can think of several things I could usefully do."

"Don't bother to think of any of them, my love. Because you're going to stay right in here tonight—and tomorrow—and take it easy."

Cat lifted her brows in rebellious inquiry. "Why?"

"Have you forgotten today already? Have you forgotten what almost happened?"

Cat swallowed uncomfortably. He hadn't forgotten, and even though they had talked and admitted many things between them, he was still a little angry but also concerned.

"I'm really all right, Clay."

"You'll make me a happier man if you'll stay put and take it easy for the remainder of the evening. I'll have Sam bring you a tray later, okay? I've got to discuss a few things with Peter and I'll—I'll be late. Have yourself something to eat and then just rest—please?"

Cat nodded slowly, and then suddenly laughed.

"What's so amusing?" he demanded with a little growl.

"You—you're telling me I need rest, but I don't think the time we just spent together could actually be classified as rest!"

Clay grinned in return with a little shrug. "I guess not, but that's all the more reason I want you rested now. When we are together, you won't have to worry about being too tired!"

"Typical, typical male!" Cat laughed. But as he grimaced and scooted into the shower, she shrugged with a little smile and slipped back into bed. She really didn't mind listening to him at all when his words were laced with concern and love.

She yawned suddenly and realized that he was also right. She needed some sleep, she was very, very tired. And now, contentedly tired.

She was sound asleep before Clay finished his shower.

She was glad she had taken Clay's advice. She slept until noon the next day and awoke feeling marvelous. He appeared in the cabin just minutes after she opened her eyes, smiling devilishly as he sat at her side with a breakfast tray crammed with cutlery, cups, and food.

"Thought you might be starving," he offered.

"I am," Cat admitted, stretching luxuriously with a happy smile.

"Breakfast for you, lunch for me," Clay said, pouring them each coffee. He lifted his eyes innocently to hers. "And then . . . well, do you feel rested?"

"Oh . . . very . . ." Cat murmured gently, her voice sweetly throaty, yet entirely guileless. And then they both started laughing, and they ate their meals like young lovers, buttering one another's toast and pausing between bites just to touch or to kiss.

They spent a wonderful afternoon together, making love, talking randomly, drifting into dozes together, waking up to make love again. The sun was streaking fast westward when they realized that the sounds of cooking and conversation were rising from the galley and kitchen.

"I think we'd better get out there!" Clay laughed.

"Ummm . . ." Cat agreed.

Again they squabbled over the shower; again Cat won first dibs. She grew silent as she went quickly through her drawers for clothing, and Clay watched her from the shower door with an ear-to-ear grin.

"Cat—I can read you like a book! You're already worried about going out there because you're sure everyone will know what we've been up to! And you're turning the most delightful shade of pink again! Relax! We are married, remember?"

Cat allowed her hair to fall over her face, shielding her eyes, as she quickly stepped into another cool cotton halter dress. "Yes," she said softly, "I remember."

Cat heard the soft click of the shower door closing and turned to

162

the mirrored wall cabinets to hastily draw a brush through her hair. Then, before she could allow her nerves to keep her locked in the cabin for the night, Cat breezed out of the door and down the short hallway to the main salon.

Luke and Billy were conspicuously absent, but Cat remembered that they had gone to stake the claim for the *Santa Anita*. Sam was in the middle of the preparation of a delicious-smelling dish he worked on over the galley's gas stove. Peter Gruuten, the tall, handsome German, sat beside his wife at the vinyl-covered booth surrounding the lacquered table. The three were chatting amiably away.

It was the first good look Cat had had of Ariel, yet all her previous assumptions had been correct.

Ariel was very, very pretty. She was a petite woman, her delicate face and fragile hands very feminine. Her hair was a stunning natural blond, a shade that complemented an almost ethereal blue in lovely almond-shaped eyes. And as she noticed Cat and glanced up, a smile formed on her lips that was as lovely and beguiling as her features. But her brows were knit in a frown of concern.

"Catherine!" she murmured, rising from her husband's side as all conversation stilled. "Sam has been telling us what happened. My lord! How awful for you! Are you okay?"

After the wonderful day she had spent, Cat had to think a minute to realize what Ariel was talking about. "Fine, thanks," she murmured quickly, accepting the blonde's tiny hand and wondering at the woman's sincerity, as they hadn't really met before.

Sam glanced up from his steaming pot, smiling. "She must be just fine, Ariel! She's been locked up in there plenty long with Clay."

Cat felt a flush creeping along her flesh, but she couldn't really take offense. Sam always had a carefree air about his broad white smile that was impossible to resist.

"You leave her alone!" Ariel chastised with a touch of steel in her soft voice. For all her tiny size, Cat thought with admiration, it was obvious that Ariel held her fair share of authority. She smiled again at Cat. "If you're absolutely sure you're okay," she said brightly, "it's time we break out the champagne! In honor of Mrs. Cat Miller!

Oh, Cat! I never thought I might be in on something as spectacular as the discovery of the *Santa Anita*!"

The enthusiasm and victory that had been Cat's the morning before were returned to her as she was kissed by both Sam and Peter, and hugged by Ariel. She was treated to the visions of the sparkling dreams in their eyes, and rained upon by the exuberance of their congratulations. Was it possible, after all the trauma the previous day had wrought after the triumph of discovery, that she could once more feel so on top of the world about the quest into the sea? That she could enjoy the fellowship of other salvage divers . . . Peter . . Ariel?

Though she barely knew the two, they were a breed who lived with and for the sea, respected her, loved her, and the camaraderie she shared with them was spontaneous.

And yet still, as the initial toasts quieted, Cat found herself watching Ariel. Why? she wondered. It was very apparent that she and Peter were happily married. They touched one another often, a special gentleness touched their eyes when they looked at each other. Both Ariel and Peter appeared very, very comfortable. They, like the others, seemed totally oblivious to the regularities surrounding Cat and Clay's relationship. Everyone knew she and Clay hadn't seen each other in years, yet they behaved as if everything were perfectly natural and normal.

Are things natural and normal? Cat wondered. How could they be? She believed now that Clay did love her, and she had no intention of pretending to either him or herself anymore that she didn't love him.

They had touched upon a few of their problems, they were learning to accept certain things as one another's nature. Age seemed to have granted them both the wisdom that although you didn't change a man or woman you loved—and if you loved one, you didn't really want to change him or her—but that an understanding of what really hurt the other could make one think carefully about his or her actions, talking and explaining, thinking before acting.

Yet had they come far enough? They were treasure seekers now, questing for magic, groping and fumbling toward one another. Was that enough to form a real life together without being haunted by the past?

Cat found herself taking a turn at the bouillabaisse pot, her thoughts turning inward as she stirred the concoction of seafood, and she was unaware that she had withdrawn into her own world until she was tied back to reality by the soft sound of Ariel's voice.

"Are you really okay, Cat? That must have been a really terrible experience."

Cat smiled. "I really am fine, thank you."

Ariel took a sip of her champagne, lashes lowered as she stared at the rim of her glass. "You're a very remarkable woman, Cat," she said quietly. "Clay always said you were." She hesitated a moment, then her beautifully opaque eyes turned up to Cat's, wide with a strange poignancy. "Be good to him, Catherine," she said very softly, "that man loves you so very much."

Ariel lowered her lashes instantly, as if regretting her words. When her eyes rose once again, the strange look was gone. She laughed. "I'm holding up dinner! Peter! Why don't you come over and lend us your gourmet tastebuds?" Ariel took a sip of the broth herself, blowing carefully at the liquid in the spoon.

Her husband appeared next to the girls, smiling at each as he took the spoon. "More pepper?" Ariel queried.

"*Nein, nein!*" Peter replied, shaking his head and touching his wife's cheek with a gentle finger. "Garlic. We need a pinch more garlic!"

"You'd think he was Italian!" Ariel laughed. "He loves garlic in everything."

Clay made his appearance at that moment, casually dressed in form-hugging jeans and an open-necked short-sleeved cotton shirt. Cat found herself staring at her husband and thinking that he had a marvelous inborn talent for looking ruggedly and casually sexy, dressed and undressed. Clay was a fastidious person, she knew, yet other than that, he gave little thought to appearance. Part of his charm was that total self-assurance that had nothing to do with ego.

"Just make sure you keep eating the garlic right along with him, Ariel!" Clay laughed, approaching their threesome. "That way neither one of you will ever notice!"

Cat noted that tender light in Clay's deep eyes as he addressed Ariel, but she had little time to think about it because his arms slipped around her waist and he rested his chin on her shoulder, looking into the pot as his fingers laced over her abdomen. "Smells good," he murmured, then nuzzled the bare flesh of her shoulder, sending her little chills with the warmth of his breath and the velvet of his voice as he added, "but then, you smell delicious. . . ."

"Maybe we should have had this party tomorrow night!" Peter laughed, slipping his broad hands over his own wife's shoulders as he and Ariel both gave Cat and Clay benignly understanding smiles.

"Maybe all four of you had better break it up!" Sam called from the salon. "Mon," he complained with mock seriousness. "I'm not taking off with any of you anymore until I have me a wife to bring along too!"

General laughter followed his comment, and Clay announced that they would eat immediately.

The champagne seemed incredibly effervescent that night, the food amazingly delectable. It was a very wonderful time, Cat thought, even as she occasionally mulled over Ariel's strange words and behavior. What was it that puzzled her so? Cat wondered. Ariel and Peter were very very happy; just very good friends to Clay. It was natural that Ariel should worry about a man she knew like a brother. It's a pity that I don't really think that, she thought to herself, then forced herself to take her mind off her pinpricks of unease. It wasn't so terribly hard. She sat beside her husband, enjoying his casual touch, that of a long-attuned lover.

We're friends tonight, she thought, and that awareness made her very happy. Usually, tension was static between them, but tonight she could appreciate being with him, the masculine clean scent that was his, the crisp feel of his shirt, the comfortable hardness of his thigh beside hers, the clean look of his freshly shaved jawline. And when she was tempted to reach out and touch his bronzed skin, she felt freely able to do so.

It was interesting to listen to the conversation that flowed around the table. For the first time Cat felt that she was receiving an insight into her husband's life—the years that were lost to her. Peter talked about the trials of turning to salvaging from smuggling—legitimate

166

piracy, as he called his new vocation, and told of Clay's patience and exasperation as he attempted to set them all straight. His crew loved Clay, Cat thought, they were a free breed, driven by nothing but the wind, yet they gave him their love and loyalty.

She also learned that the actual crew was much larger. When the barges and cranes were brought out to begin bringing up the *Santa Anita*'s treasures, she would meet another group of ten.

Cat was surprised to learn that Ariel was a Bahamian national by birth. "I'm surprised that you of all people are surprised!" Ariel laughed. "I was born on Eleuthera. A community of German descent has been thriving there for several centuries. You know as well as I do, Cat, that many Europeans made the islands their homes years ago!"

Thinking of her own tiny cay with its mixed nationalities, Cat had to agree.

When the meal was completed, they moved languorously above deck. Cat noticed that a Bahamian patrol boat was anchored near them, and she glanced at Clay. He gave her a grim nod, but said nothing. She understood that they were now under the government's protection.

But she didn't have long to think or ponder. The mood had been set for the evening, and that mood was celebration. Cat was to learn where Clay had learned his prowess with the guitar when Peter retrieved his own instrument from his cabin and insisted on doing harmonies with Clay. Ariel, who informed Cat that both men had taken lessons from Luke, had taken a few lessons herself on flute from Billy. Before long the sea air rang with a freewheeling calypso beat, and Sam and Cat were left to be the hysterical audience as the threesome sang old tunes with their own brand of new, delightfully bawdy lyrics.

The moon was high in the Bahamian sky before Cat realized she had laughed so hard that she hurt. The music died down, and the conversation turned to instructions from Clay to Sam about the following day. Cat yawned as she listened to Clay talk, hardly able to keep her eyes open as she rested lazily against his shoulder, her feelings those of complete well-being.

167

She was almost asleep, her eyes closing dreamily, when she felt him shake her shoulder. "Go on in to bed," Clay told her gently.

Cat started, to see that they were alone on deck. Clay smiled with tender patience. "Peter and Ariel have already gone in. Are you awake enough to walk?"

Cat nodded drowsily and managed to stand, looking at him with confused hesitancy. "Aren't you coming?"

Clay shook his head. "I'm first watch. I'll be with you in a few hours."

"First watch?" Cat murmured. "But we're protected—"

His eyes were very dark and fathomless as he interrupted her. "In circumstances like these, we always hold watch on our boats. Now go in to bed. I'll join you shortly."

Cat nodded mutely and turned to go, feeling a certain misery, as she was sure their possible difficulties were her fault. Clay caught her hand and spun her around, easing the terseness of his curt explanation with a gentle kiss upon her brow. "It's just a safety precaution, Cat," he said softly. "Now go and get some sleep."

Cat gave him a rueful smile, then moved to obey him. In the cabin, she stripped off her clothing to scrounge through her things for a negligee, but then her eyes lit upon the navy velour robe of Clay's she had worn previously. If she couldn't sleep beside him on their still-rumpled bed, she would feel a bit more secure wearing his soft and comfortable robe.

Without Clay, Cat suddenly discovered that she wasn't quite so drowsy. She was, in fact, a little high-strung. Pacing the small cabin, she stuck her hands into the pockets and walked to the porthole window to look out upon the darkness of the night, the silver play of the pale moon upon the water.

She was reaching happiness, she thought, if not thorough contentment. But then, contentment and the security they both needed would take time to come.

She frowned suddenly as her fingers curled around something they had been idly touching in the pocket of the robe. It was a paper of some sort, yet did not have the actual feel of paper. Cat clutched her fingers and brought it out. Her heart seemed to take an immediate leap to her throat. It didn't feel exactly like paper because it was a picture, the type taken by an Instamatic camera. It was folded and frayed, as if it had perhaps been in the pocket of the robe through several washings. But the subjects of the picture were still clear—painfully clear.

As Cat stared at it, she felt the rise of hot moisture in her eyes. She had guessed all along, so she shouldn't be shocked. But she had never really wanted to know.

The picture showed Clay, standing on the deck of a boat. His hair was long and wind-tossed; he wore his full beard. He was dressed in his customary cutoffs, and as usual his strong lean body looked damp and salty from the sea. He faced the camera, and he was laughing ruefully, as if he had objected to the picture being taken and then resigned himself to its inevitability.

He wasn't alone. His arm was protectively and tenderly around a woman, a tiny, very pretty woman who looked up at him with adoration in her eyes. The woman was Ariel.

I've known that they were together at some time, Cat thought sickly, so what difference does proof make? It must be over, long over. But why had it ended, Cat wondered. With pain clawing viciously at her stomach, she thought of the gentle tenderness with which Clay always treated Ariel. And then her question changed to one that hurt even worse. Had it really ended? Did a special kind of love remain despite Peter, despite herself?

It was a long time before Cat could force herself to lie in bed. She couldn't confront Clay with the picture, not when she remembered his words when she asked about Ariel. Ariel is Peter's wife, had been his firm reply.

Haunted by doubt, Cat lay awake for hours, until she heard the knob of the door twist with Clay's return to the cabin. Then she closed her eyes and curled far to her side of the bed, feigning a deep sleep as her heart pounded.

She heard Clay disrobe in the darkness, felt him as his weight lowered next to hers. And she couldn't control a flinch as he reached out to touch her. A silence followed. Then he muttered, "What's the matter with you?"

Cat attempted to ignore his question, but it was repeated with his muttering rumbling to a hushed roar.

"Nothing!" she hissed.

"Then why are you pulling away from me? There's something wrong, damn it," he said, rolling her by the midriff to face him in the dim moonlight.

"No, there isn't," Cat lied stubbornly.

He stared at her intently, his taut expression unreadable in the darkness. "Talk to me, Cat, or straighten out. I won't sleep with a distance of two feet between us."

She said nothing, but saw his anger as he tightened his jaw. His head bent low and his lips claimed hers, his tongue probing a firm entrance to the fullness of her mouth; she knew there would be no turning away from her husband this time. His hands raked a rough exploratory course over the curves of her body, and she knew it made no difference that he refused to allow her to turn away. She couldn't force herself to turn away anyway.

CHAPTER TEN

It was dark in the bowels of the *Santa Anita*, dark in an eerie green way that even now, after four days of continual exploration, still sent goose bumps rising over Cat's arms. She could control the instinctive fear the ghost ship called from her spirit, but she never lost the haunted feeling. And sometimes, although they had already brought numerous priceless artifacts to the surface with the very delicate and tedious use of air hoses and gentle fingers—fine porcelain, silver- and goldware, crystal that had miraculously survived the ages—Cat felt as if her victory were also a lesson in humility and sadness. Tears would ridiculously singe her eyes as she wondered if she should have left her ghost ship alone, buried with poignant memories of lost lives beneath the erosion of the sand and sea.

Soon the barges and cranes would move in. Encrusted cannons would be raised, the huge and heavy anchor with its iron fittings. The ocean would become a vortex as she was forced to release her suction upon the treasures she had claimed. And still they hadn't found the Aztec crown jewels. Cat was sure they were here, deep within the lower decks. The true treasure was always carried deep.

The tobacco the ship had carried had long since disintegrated, as had the llama wool prized in Portugal and Spain. But the ship's manifest had also listed a cargo of gold and silver, all yet to be found.

They were in a counting room, Cat decided, surveying the bracketing on the walls and the remains of a heavy desk and chair, almost entirely eroded. Her light flared upon darting sea life, tiny fish that clung to the green darkness for safety and secrecy. For an instant her light caught upon her husband's mask, and she saw Clay's eyes, deep and pensive as they always seemed to be when he looked at her now. His stare caught hers for a just a second, questioningly. Then the question was gone, the fathomless and businesslike jet returned. He signaled to the right; Cat shrugged.

His glance was icy, but there was also pain in his eyes. Cat was well aware that he didn't know what truly haunted her; she couldn't bring herself to try to talk about Ariel. She had simply retreated, and although she couldn't deny his touch, and made no attempt to prove other than that she was perfectly content to share his bed, it was now she who was holding back.

Clay didn't know why she had retreated, and strangely, at this absurd point, she had stumbled upon the answer to totally frustrate and dismay him. In his terms, she had finally beaten him at his own game. He could hold, take, and claim her time and time again, and although they were both rewarded with sweet ecstasy, he knew he was reaching for something elusive. It couldn't be caught with the power of his strong hands.

I have to talk to him, Cat thought now. She knew that the foundations for anything they might have, had to be laid with honesty. But she was so afraid to be honest. She had wanted to discuss Jules, air her feelings first of guilt, then of pain, disillusionment, and disgust. But she couldn't even put those things into words

171

with Clay. He was possessive and jealous, and her own heartsick worry caused her to want him to continue to feel that way. Because she was jealous, and it wasn't a simple emotion. She could have accepted that women had drifted through his life. What she was finding so unbearably hard was that he hadn't had meaningless affairs. He had engaged in an affair that had meant very, very much. . . .

Cat abruptly ceased her mental wandering as she noticed a sheaf of half-rotted planking that appeared out of place. A sixth sense suddenly seemed to tug at her and Cat swam slowly to the softened timbers. She tugged at the ragged end, feeling dizzy and giddy as it gave immediately and revealed a hatchway they had previously overlooked. A hole that appeared black as night beckoned to her, compellingly. Cat tugged at her cord, waiting with impatience for Clay to come to her. She felt his touch, possessive and proprietary even in the water, yet so strangely comforting because she wanted to be possessed and possess in return—and then, together, they flared their lights below.

The decking beneath them was almost entirely destroyed. Offshoots of coral tore through the hull like strange stalagmites, creating a scene that might be the work of a modern, impressionistic artist. Nature and man merged together in a crazy scramble.

Clay moved cautiously downward, then waited for Cat to follow. Carefully they floated through age-old litter and wreckage, exploring dark crevices with caution. Cat fluttered backward in panic as one of their first forays revealed an evil and terrifying moray eel. She was sure she stopped breathing, as did Clay, when the startled creature lunged with lightning assurance for his hand, luckily catching only the thick glove that shielded it. And of course they hadn't quit breathing. The bubbles that were their lives continued to rise.

Then Clay was waving at her madly, a brilliant smile radiating beneath his mask. Cat saw what exhilarated him so, a three-by-five-foot casket so encrusted and tarnished she would have thought it part of the ocean floor. He beckoned her to keep her light steady, signaling that he wished to raise the object before opening it. But it was heavy, too heavy for even Clay's considerable strength. Cat was sent to the deck above to retrieve Peter, and then she and Ariel were following the men in a slow ascent to the surface, going half crazy with their anticipation as they forced themselves to take the proper decompression time. But eventually they reached the surface, and Sam was able to use hooks and leverage to bring the casket aboard the *Sea Witch II.*

"It's been corked somehow," Clay said excitedly as he carelessly tore away his equipment. "We need to go carefully . . . very carefully. We may find whatever this holds in perfect condition."

Cat and Ariel were left to stare as the men slowly and cautiously wedged with their knives at the seal of the metal, painstakingly careful so as not to damage any precious relic inside. It looked rather like the opening of a clam, Cat thought, and then she realized she was about to keel over because she had been holding her breath so long. She forced herself to breathe, taking great gulping breaths, her body trembling, her heart pounding tumultuously. Now! she kept thinking, ready to scream. Surely they had it. Open it! Open it!

But her husband's eyes suddenly turned to her, a soft light hazing their glitter as he lifted a hand toward her. "It's to you, Mrs. Miller," he murmured.

Dry-mouthed and weak-kneed, Cat made her way to the casket. Everyone aboard had stopped breathing, she thought ridiculously. She couldn't hear a sound, just the sensation of air and breeze.

Her fingers trembled convulsively as she touched the black, encrusted metal. The men's efforts were applaudable. With a ferocious screech, the rusty hinges gave. Cat lifted the top. . . .

Not even the ravages of time could mar the intricate beauty of the Aztec crown jewels. Their light, beneath the warm Bahamian sun, was so dazzling as to blind. Brilliant rainbow hues created a kaleidoscope of unearthly enchantment: blood-red rubies, skyburst sapphires, amethysts, diamonds, emeralds. . . .

"Oh, my God!" Cat breathed, and then she was touching the gems, trailing their blackened gold chains, gaping at the exquisite settings.

She felt the others as they knelt beside her, felt the awe each of them experienced as their fingers touched, trembling, upon the treasure.

173

Clay rose first. Cat lifted her eyes to her husband's and saw a soft query in them. "Well?"

Her breath caught in her throat. Instinctively she knew what he asked. "Oh, Clay," she murmured. His smile broadened, and then he was reaching for one of the signal flags.

Moments later the Bahamian patrol boat was alongside them. Cat saw the men aboard were grim and heavily armed. Her heart took another flutter.

It had all been prearranged. Clay knew she believed the pieces belonged in the museums of the country of their origin. And that's where they were going, before a gold or gem fever could insert itself in any of them.

Cat glanced uneasily at the crew, but all wore a secret smile of satisfaction. They had found the jewels; that was enough.

Cat lowered her lashes. "Thank you," she said huskily, and it wasn't until later, much later, when she and Clay were confined in their cabin, that she asked the question plaguing her.

"Clay, you run a salvage business. These people work with you for the profits—"

"Cat!" he interrupted her, laughing as he gently cradled her head to his chest. "The *Santa Anita* will still bring plenty in rewards. We will all profit. But we're not straight pirates, you know. The sea and her treasures are ours because we also love and respect them. The Aztec crown jewels belong to those whose ancestors broke their backs and lost their lives in pursuit of their creation. And they belong to the world. In the museum, they do belong to all men."

"Thank you, Clay," Cat said thickly. For the first time in days she realized she was being open with him. "I can't tell you how much I appreciate this. . . ."

"Then how about showing me?"

"Pardon?" she murmured. His fingers, light upon her shoulders, tightened. Cat tilted her head back and stared into his eyes. A flame of intensity flared in the deep jet recesses that obliterated all but the edges of deepest brown. His facial muscles were taut; his lips were a thin line that barely twisted into a grim, bittersweet smile of poignancy.

"You won't talk to me, Cat," he said huskily. "And the one thing

174

I can't force is your mind. I reach for you, and I hold you, but you're not really there. You keep so much in, Cat. We should have talked about DeVante. I don't know what you were feeling, I don't know how deeply you cared, whether his betrayal cut like a knife, whether he keeps you from me now more than before—"

"No," Cat protested with a strangling sound. "I'm over Jules. I told you that."

"Then talk to me."

"I can't."

"Then come to me, Cat." His fingers tangled into her hair, his voice, deep and rich and husky as night, caressed and tantalized and demanded as it whispered with soft heat close to her lips. "When I reach for you, you are not really there. And you haven't reached for me. Come to me now, Cat. Come to me, you make love to me. . . ." For a moment his fingers clenched so tightly into her hair that her throat was forced into an arch that held her face not an inch from his. Dark eyes held hers, searching with that strange poignant heat that curled just the edges of his lips.

Cat closed her eyes. She felt so weak, her will sapped, taken by his strength, by the desire to still her own fears, to envelop herself in the heavenly security of the magic world that obliterated all else, the magic of his touch.

She never opened her eyes. Her lips crossed the infinitesimal space to his, parted and touched, and then she was sliding against him, mouth, teeth, and tongue beginning a slow torment that would cover his length as she melded against him, into his arms, and the sleek cushion of his body and the bed. . . .

Magic had done its trick nicely. Cat slept deeply, exhausted from the considerable exertions of the workday, and cocooned in a marvelous feeling of comfort and well-being, her husband's body heat keeping her warm and secure as she curled against him.

He had been muttering groggily a long, long time before the sound permeated her consciousness, bringing her slowly from the inner web of that deep, deep comfort.

She was rudely jostled as he began to toss, and she awakened

175

fully, realizing that he was in the throes of a bad dream, gutturally protesting . . . fighting.

Cat frowned and touched his shoulder, shaking it lightly and whispering his name over and over. Her words had no effect; he didn't hear her. He shook off her touch and his tossing became more fevered, as did his incomprehensible ramblings. As she watched him in the moonlight with growing alarm, she saw a sheen of sweat break out across his shoulders and chest, drip in tiny rivulets down the rugged lines of his profile.

"Clay!" she exclaimed, attempting to catch his flailing arms as her concern began to rise to a bewildered panic.

His muscles tensed, balling into tight knots. She could clearly see the cords in his strong neck stand out. His flailings became more and more vehement and erratic. She began to comprehend one of the words he whispered louder and louder with increasing fervor, and the word that he shouted was *no!*

"Clay!" Cat exclaimed again, desperate now to awaken him. He was such a large man, and with his muscles powerfully tensed against whatever it was that he fought, her own strength was inadequate. Avoiding his unaimed blows, Cat rolled against his body until she could straddle him, then attempted to get a steady grip on both his shoulders so that she could give him a good shake as she gasped out his name and all the inane assurances she could think of.

"Clay—"

A stunning blow caught the side of her head and she was sent flying from his form with a force that took her reeling frame all the way to the floor. Truly panicked, Cat stumbled to her feet, shaking her head to clear the stars that blinded her vision from the impact. She could do nothing for him, she realized, with tears stinging her eyes. He was simply too strong for her, too swamped in the awful clamp of the dream, but she had to wake him, she had to make it end. There was no help but for her to call in Sam.

Fumbling and half crying with haste and confusion, Cat slipped into Clay's robe and tossed the sheets over his naked form, sure his thrashing would kick them off again but too concerned to worry about the possibility. She barely had her belt secured before she was pulling open the cabin door in quest of Sam, her mouth open to shout.

Her words never left her throat. Sam, Peter, and Ariel all stood in the short hallway, staring at her with eyes that clearly mirrored her state of concern and alarm.

Cat finally spoke. "Sam, I need you."

Her mammoth friend hesitated a second, his eyes darting to Peter and back. It was Peter who took the first action. He came for Cat, securing an arm around her as he nodded to his wife, who slipped past them both into Clay's cabin, pain deep in her beautiful powder-blue eyes. Cat frowned in tense bewilderment, thinking only to wrest herself from Peter's arm. She didn't need the help of the tiny blonde, she needed to be with her husband herself with a burly man to give assistance.

"Peter—" was as far as Cat got with her protestations.

He interrupted her immediately and soothingly. "Come on, Cat, let's go out on deck. Sam will make you a cup of tea and we'll talk where it's cool."

Cat couldn't move away from Peter. He was a man built like her own husband, a man of the same breed, equipped with the same quiet strength. "I don't want tea," she choked out as she was half led, half dragged through the hallway, salon, and galley to the deck doors. "Clay . . . Ariel . . ."

"Ariel will handle Clay," Peter said softly. "And maybe you don't need tea. Sam—" Peter called over his shoulder. "I think Cat might need a brandy instead."

Peter didn't release her until she was seated in a deck chair, and even then he stood over her, a knee bent over the rail preventing her escape. A second later Sam was handing her a brandy, and holding it with her until she had taken the first swallow. Then he took a silent stance behind her, trying to offer support and comfort in his silent way. Peter met Cat's stricken eyes and began to talk.

"I wasn't with Clay and Luke and the rest when they were picked up," he said softly. "I met them all later on Eleuthera. But from the time they were arrested until they did escape, Clay was the one who kept them together, living with hope. He was determined to get away, so determined that he made several attempts to escape before

177

he finally did. They had an isolation cell—a hot pit where a man had only room to sit hunched over with his arms hugging his knees, for punishment. Clay was kept in one for a week once when the guards they bribed failed to come through with the boats."

Peter hesitated a moment as Cat stared at him in shock. She had always wondered how Clay had survived his exploits unscarred, and now she was understanding the form of the torture he had endured.

Cat licked dry lips. "So now he has nightmares." It wasn't a question but a statement. "And Ariel knows how to handle my husband's nightmares."

Peter hesitated a second time. "Clay came with Luke to his home on Eleuthera when they succeeded with their escape. He met Ariel there. They lived together for several months."

Cat wondered how, as numb as she was feeling, that knowledge could riddle her insides with such acute, stabbing pain. Yet, in a way, she did know what hurt so devastatingly. Ariel was beautiful, gentle, sweet, and very wonderful. She wasn't another woman one could rationally hate or despise.

Her voice was toneless, so toneless. "Is Ariel really your wife, Peter?"

Peter smiled very gently and reached down to take Cat's hand. "Of course she is my wife. Everything ended between the two of them long ago. She is a very special creature, my Ariel. She always knew that something haunted Clay. That something was you, Cat. We have all known about you for years. Clay always spoke of you. That is why we feel so intimate, as if we have known you all that time too."

Peter was trying, Cat knew, really trying. But she could feel nothing. She loved her husband, ached for him until she felt her insides cry, but all she could feel on the outside was numbness.

"Why didn't he come back then, Peter? Why didn't he return long ago? Why did he leave me thinking him dead?"

"Because it had been years, Cat. He heard that you were doing very well, that you were happy, content with your life. He was never sure if you would be pleased to see him or not, and he didn't want you taking him back out of pity. He was plagued very badly by the nightmares at first. He never wanted you seeing him like that. But

178

then when he heard that you were getting serious with DeVante, he started to get worried. We'd heard things about DeVante in our various business dealings, and that's when Clay started checking him out and . . . well . . . you know. Jules was up to his teeth in debt. Clay couldn't stand the thought of your possibly being used or hurt. So he knew then that he had to come back—no matter how you received him."

"Oh, God," Cat murmured. His every action had been for her, and yet Ariel could soothe her husband; Clay could put his faith in the tiny blonde but not in her.

It was then that Ariel appeared on deck, slipping her arm around her own husband and trying to smile easily as she faced Cat. "He's sleeping soundly again, Cat. Go to him now."

Cat felt silent tears stinging her eyes, but she didn't cry. She shook her head. "I can't, not right now."

Ariel lowered her lashes and bit into her lip miserably. She glanced at Peter, then back to Cat.

"Please, Cat," she murmured, "he is your husband. He always was. I—I always knew. You see, he loved you so deeply. . . ."

"Cat," Peter interrupted his wife. "Ariel is *my* wife. We love *each other* very much. Clay is a very good friend—the best of friends—to both of us. The past is over; we all accept that."

Cat nodded vaguely. They were right, of course they were right, yet she felt nothing but this numbness.

"Please," Ariel whispered. "Go, be with Clay."

But she couldn't; she simply couldn't.

"Thank you both," she managed to say. "It would have helped if Clay would have told me himself."

"He was afraid," Ariel said. "Things were so unsettled between you to begin with. He wants you so badly, Cat. He didn't want you further upset by the past and things that didn't matter."

Cat nodded again. "Please," she said, forcing a smile for both the Gruutens and Sam—quiet and yet there in the background. "Please, you all go back to bed. I want to be alone for a while."

They began to protest, but Cat assured them she was fine, that she would go in shortly. Unhappily, they finally left her.

But she had no intention of going in to Clay, not tonight. She had to think, to feel the breeze of the sea, to seek her answers within the night ocean air. To pray that the terrible numbness would go away.

Cat didn't sleep at all. She stared out at the endless dark ocean until dawn broke to create colors of gold and blue and magenta from the black of night.

Funny, but she could easily, so easily, close her eyes to her own past. Jules had proved himself to be a corrupt fortune-seeker, ruthless in his methods. His face was already hazy in her memory. She had never really loved him, she had never allowed herself to do so.

Nothing disparaging could be said about Ariel. And the Gruutens were not only Clay's employees, but his very good friends. They could not disappear from their lives as Jules had.

Ariel wanted Cat to have her husband. In the gentlest of terms, she had always given and did now give Clay to Cat.

Because Clay loved Cat.

And Cat loved Clay, so very much. He had once more become her life. But despite herself, despite logic, despite love, Cat just wasn't sure she could reach out and take the gifts offered her.

He woke with a peculiar feeling of dread, aware that something was very wrong before he even opened his eyes. Reaching a hand across the white expanse of the sheet, he found that she was gone.

Clay hopped quickly from the bed, fumbling hastily into a pair of swim shorts.

He always awakened before Cat. During the day she was walking energy, vitality filled her every movement. It was only natural that she should be a very deep and sound sleeper, taking long to awaken, eyes usually heavy-lidded and sensually endearing with lazy reproach when she was brought from the depths of her sleepy world.

Clay moved like a windstorm from his cabin into the salon, barely glancing at Sam, Peter, and Ariel at the table before rushing through for the deck. A quick and astute gaze informed him immediately that Cat was nowhere to be seen.

He returned to the salon, his feeling of dread finalizing as he found his friends staring at him unhappily and somewhat guiltily.

"What happened?" Clay demanded tensely, hoping against sick hope that he didn't already know.

Peter didn't look directly at him. "You were dreaming again. Cat couldn't snap you out of it. The best Ariel could do was get you back into a sound sleep."

"Oh, Jesus," Clay moaned. "Then Cat knows . . ."

"Everything," Ariel supplied miserably. "But, Clay, I think she already knew . . . or guessed."

"Where is she?"

It was Sam's turn to look up. "She took a thermos of coffee and lit out in the dinghy at about six."

Clay turned to leave the salon. Ariel called him back. "I think she's okay, Clay, she wanted time alone, time to think about things."

Clay smiled ruefully. "I just want to make sure she's thinking about the right things."

It wasn't difficult to locate Cat. The dinghy wasn't more than three hundred yards from the *Sea Witch II*. Without taking time to actually plan out all he wanted to say, Clay dove into the water, stroking furiously for the small dinghy. Ridiculous, but it seemed as if time was of the essence. Every second that passed seemed to increase the gulf forming between them. If he didn't reach her, he would lose her.

She didn't seem particularly surprised to see him as his head surfaced from the water, nor did she seem particularly pleased. Feeling absurdly like an awkward teen-ager, Clay smiled and murmured a hello as he trod water beside the dinghy, watching her eyes as she quietly sipped coffee from the thermos top and thoughtfully returned his stare, her gaze seeming to reflect the sea.

"May I come aboard?" he asked.

She shrugged, and waved a hand. Clay hefted himself over the edge, and faced her across the two planked seats.

"Are you willing to share that coffee?" he asked softly.

Cat poured more coffee into the cup and handed it to Clay. She finally spoke. "How are you feeling this morning?"

Clay ruefully shrugged his brows. "Fine, thanks." He fell silent for a second and then caught her eyes. "I love you, Cat."

Cat lowered her lashes and accepted the coffee back from him. "I believe you, Clay," she murmured in return, raising her eyes once

181

more to his. She smiled a little sadly. "I just wonder why . . . and how. You didn't love me, you and I both know that, not when we were first married."

Clay took a deep breath. "I don't think I knew what love was at first, Cat. And I'm not sure that you did either. But I didn't marry you because of your father, Cat." He paused for a moment, and when he spoke again, his voice had grown very husky. "I only knew after that first night aboard the *Sea Witch* that I had to have you; I wanted you to be my wife. But I think I had a lot of preconceived notions about role-playing in a marriage. I thought it was okay for me to be the wanderer. I was the provider—I expected you to be the homemaker. Always there. Then I found out that I was insanely jealous. I did a lot of things to hurt you because I thought I was going to go crazy when I came home that time and found you flirting. I think that was when I discovered how very much I did love you—as soon as I cooled down from wanting to commit murder. The day I went down, Cat, I was thinking about you, about us, how I wanted to come home and tell you all those things, admit that I was insanely jealous, admit that I needed you. I was dreaming of how we could begin to mend all the patches. Oh, Cat," he murmured with a deep sound that was between a groan and a sigh. "When I knew nothing else, I knew that you existed, somewhere."

"But you had an affair with Ariel," Cat interrupted softly.

"Yes," Clay admitted, deciding that, make it or break it, it was time for complete honesty, time to lay foundations if there was to be anything for them now. "I had several affairs over the years, Cat, but I broke with Ariel when my memory returned, because she is a very kind and gentle lady. Neither of us would use the other when we both knew that my dreams were real. I had a wife, one that I loved very much."

Cat didn't reply, she was staring out at the water.

"Cat," Clay continued very quietly, very gently, "that was long, long ago. Forgotten by all of us. Ariel and Peter are very happy."

Cat nodded vaguely.

"Damn it!" Fear suddenly caused Clay to lose control. He had to clench his fists to his sides to keep from gripping her shoulders

182

and demanding that she acknowledge him. "Talk to me, Cat, say something!"

She brought her eyes to his and smiled sadly. "I'm sorry, Clay, and I don't really know what to say. I knew, not as fact, of course, but I did know before last night about Ariel. And I know it's over. Peter is very comfortable and assured with his marriage. It just hurts, Clay. When you needed someone, it wasn't me. It was Ariel. And I can't help it. When I look at her, I imagine you holding her."

Clay started to speak, but Cat lifted a hand, halting him. "Do you know, Clay, I sat there all those years, unable to let someone else touch me. It was amazing that Jules—for what he was worth—tolerated such an arrangement. And you made me admit that, Clay. You were so pleased to hear that I hadn't been with anyone else—"

"Cat," Clay managed to interrupt. "I love you, and yes, I've admitted I'm very jealous and possessive. It's one of those so-called male traits that I'm afraid I can't help. But no matter what has been, I love you. I would have wanted you still, I would have accepted anything, if I could just be sure that he didn't hold your heart. I suppose my methods were rather poor, but I didn't want you taken by DeVante, Cat, and once I was with you again, all my better reasoning went out the window. I had to have you back, no matter what it meant using, force or trickery. Or the *Santa Anita.*" He fell silent for a second. "Please don't hate me for being glad I've been your only lover, Catherine. It's like a very special and very sweet present."

"I don't hate you, Clay," Cat murmured, glancing at him with wide eyes. "I love you," she added huskily, "you know that. It was pathetically easy for us both to discover that fact. I just . . . oh, Clay, you don't share anything with me. My lord, I have only a vague notion of what went on all those years, of all that you suffered. It takes you away, Clay. And it leaves little for the future. What do I do? How do I handle the nightmares that plague you? I don't think I can handle your always needing another woman. . . ."

He was losing her, Clay thought; he could feel his hands growing clammy with his fear. He wanted to reach out and hold her, to force her into his arms, to remain there. But there was no force for that which was elusive, yours only when given freely. He had to let her come to him. She alone could give them a future, the love he needed, the home he craved.

"There are things we both need to learn, Cat. We've started by working together. We need to learn to build a home—together. To love and trust openly, to talk when things need to be said. I very rarely dream anymore, and a bucket of water over my face will wake me up—although I would just as soon you use such a drastic measure as a last resort. If being around Ariel bothers you, we needn't see her or Peter again. I'm sure they'll both understand if I ask them to find employment elsewhere." He suddenly broke; his fingers were trembling as he clenched them together, a quiver took hold of his entire system. Suddenly he found himself reaching out, taking hold of her shoulders, burning her lips with a fevered and passionate kiss, demanding that she open to his hunger while also imprinting a sweet, giving poignancy that was the depth of his own need. His hands trailed over her shoulders, lovingly feathered her breasts, the sleek line of her shapely spine to the small of her back. He tore from her then, his tongue flaming a final moist trail of wistful need with erotic lightness over the sweet swell of her slightly bruised lips. He stared at her again, holding his grip firm on her shoulders as he felt the trembling assail him anew. "I love you, Cat. You're my wife, and I need you. I want a home together, a family when we're both ready. We have problems, but I don't believe any are insurmountable. If we both love one another and need one another—and it is you I need, Cat, no other woman—we work at those problems. I think we can make it. And I'm more than willing to put in way above fifty percent of the effort because you're everything I want out of life, you are my life, a part of me, the woman I love who shares a love for the sea and sky and sun we both crave. It's all up to you now, Cat. If you think you can make it with a man who is admittedly a shade on the domineering side, definitely possessive, and an ex-con of sorts, who is nine out of ten times dripping with seawater, that man will be waiting to take you home. But remember this about him—he loves you. You're in my blood, I never knew just how much."

He released her suddenly, and grinned ruefully. "That's where it stands, witch. You think about it."

Cat watched in stunned surprise as Clay hefted his frame in a smooth leap back into the water. She brought a finger to her still-tingling lips, thinking of all he had said, assimilating his words and fevered touch.

Suddenly she realized the numbness was gone, his touch had reawakened her. She was warm and trembling, her flesh burned at every spot he had tenderly coursed.

It hit her with an aching tremor that she was being a tremendous fool. The world was hers, all the world that *she* desired, all the world she would ever need. And like an absolute idiot, she was allowing him, her world, to slip through her fingers.

Cat stood in the dinghy, heedless as it rocked beneath her jolted movement. "Clay!" she shouted, stopping his smooth crawl through the water. Forgetting the dinghy entirely, Cat dove after him, surfacing to a swim that sheared the water, not pausing until she reached him, threw her arms around him, and brought them both spiraling into the depths. She didn't care. As long as he was with her, she wasn't even sure she needed to breathe.

Near the crystal surface, her lips caught his, returning with a thirst all that he had given her. Clay gave a powerful kick, catapulting them both back above the sun-dazzled sheet of the water's surface where they laughed as they trod water, both gulping in air.

"Oh, Clay," Cat gasped, "I do want you, I do love you, I do need you! I'm ready to put in my own hundred percent, more, much more, than that. But Clay, you're going to have to be prepared. I don't think I'll ever be able to watch you leave again. I wouldn't be able to stand it! So you will always be with me, my love, just like the song, and you're going to have to really talk to me, too, because I'm going to want to know all about those lost years . . . all the things that bother you, because if you dream again, the only woman you'll have there is going to be me. . . ."

Once again they spiraled below the surface as Clay shut off Cat's monologue with a deepening kiss that consumed her, his tongue plunging deeply, filling her with a warmth that radiated from her body within the crystal cool of the ocean. Once more they surfaced, gasping but still clinging together, only the efforts of seaworthy legs keeping them afloat.

"It's a damned good thing we're both strong swimmers," Clay chuckled, his voice low and hoarse, "since you only seem to be able to find your voice in the sea!"

Cat grinned in return. "No more, Mr. Miller. I'm afraid you may find me very vocal in the future!"

Clay smiled and arched his brows. "Really?"

"What else can one do with a domineering, dripping-wet man?"

"Lots of things," Clay replied, raised brows hiking up a shade further. "Want to find out? Except I do think we should leave the water. If I'm going to drown, I would prefer to do it metaphorically in ecstasy, rather than in water."

Cat smiled wickedly and began to swim toward the *Sea Witch II*. A second boat, she thought with a deep and loving poignancy, and a second chance. She would never let either go.

As they reached the aft ladder, Cat turned to Clay. "By the way, you won't be asking Peter or Ariel to find employment elsewhere."

Clay frowned. "But Cat, if being near Ariel bothers you . . ."

"It will bother me, sometimes, Clay, but I think I'm mature enough to handle it. And I'm grateful to her, too, Clay. She must have done a great deal for you at a time when I was unable to. I think I love you enough to live with that . . . no, I'm positive I love you enough. In fact . . ." Her tone lost its serious note and the sun that dazzled the water lit a tantalizing enchantment into her eyes, "I love you so much, that at this moment, at this precise moment, I don't give a damn who's aboard our boat. I'm going to sail right through to *our* cabin and happily, very, very happily, try to show just how much I do love you."

Clay chuckled, planting a nipping kiss on her shoulder as he propelled her up the ladder. "I don't think anyone will notice," he said, his voice a husky velvet. "Sam will be keeping an eye out while Ariel and Peter dive. We found the treasure chambers, they'll be ready to find and bring up the gold and silver ingots."

"Oh!" Cat exclaimed, pausing halfway up. "Oh, Clay, I forgot! Don't you want to be there to find the gold?"

"No." Cat was stunned as he planted a hand on her derriere and pushed her over the edge into *Sea Witch II*. Before she could protest or pick herself up from the decking, he had come behind her and swept her dripping form into his equally dripping but marvelously strong and heated arms. "I came searching for a treasure, my love, but all the treasure that I sought is here, here in my arms." Whimsically he kissed her eyes. "Emeralds far more dazzling than those of the Aztec jewels, and"—he began a delightful patter of moist, feathered kisses along her shoulder to the sensitive flesh of her throat and added huskily—"here I have a found a gold more beautiful and volatile than that even of the sun."

Cat circled her arms around his neck. "Do go on," she murmured, every bit as aware as he that, indeed, they had both truly found treasure.

Clay smiled and began to stride with her in his arms across the deck. "My love," he murmured, "I intend to do just that."

EPILOGUE

In the heat of the night he was running, running.

A low-lying ground fog shielded him, putting him on another plane of reality, as if he were racing on a treadmill through endless clouds. He could hear the sound of his breathing. It was a good sound, as was the feel of his run, long legs stretching, muscles released, each slap of his feet carrying him onward over the coolness of damp sand.

He ran for the joy of running, for the delicious feel of the air filling his lungs, the energy and vitality that soared throughout his body. And because ahead of him, he could see her. . . .

An ethereal figure in the mist, she was clothed in a cloak of deepest sable hair; it draped her slender figure like velvet, drifted in a fan of silk, framed the fine features of her face . . . a slow-curving, enticing smile . . . emerald eyes that lured with challenge and promise. . . .

He knew her, he knew the smile, he knew the eyes that glittered their beguilement. Oh, so well he knew the stunning sea witch who haunted his dreams day and night.

She laughed, a sound that was melody on air, the delightful tinkle of water, breathy and light. And she turned to run, that cloak of luxurious hair spinning behind her, long lean legs agile as she padded swiftly across the sand.

He increased his own pace. Laughter filled his own chest, and the sound was good. It, too, was breathy and light.

He reached out for her. And his fingers tangled into that cloak of richest night velvet.

Her laughter became a tiny exclamation, and then they were no longer running. They were tumbling to the sand, laughing as they rolled along its delectable dampness. His hands were touching silk, that of her hair, that of her sleek, golden flesh.

He leaned over her, smiling as his fingers curled gently over her shoulders. Her emerald eyes met his, brilliant with love and laughter. . . .

He awoke in a cold sweat, and it took him several seconds to assimilate his surroundings. Then a smile curved his lips. Dawn was breaking, yet the remainder of their nighttime fire still flickered in the sand. He reached a hand beside him, then his smile became a frown as he touched nothing but sand.

He looked up, toward the shore, and his smile tenderly returned as he lifted a brow in appreciative query. She was coming to him, from the sea, golden skin damp and shimmering, her lips ever so slightly parted, her eyes a glistening seduction of the enigmatic sea itself. She moved to him slowly, her walk steady and lithe, her slender form at radiant perfection with the gentle sway of her bare hips.

Her smile deepened as she stood before him; a smile of deepest beguilement and sweetest ultimate promise.

He reached out to touch her. His hands encountered silk and velvet, vibrant and alive, pulsing with warmth and heat.

She was in his arms and they were rolling in the sand . . . emerald and jet eyes meeting in a dazzling flame to challenge that of the crimson burst of the morning sun.

He reached for her, and she was there.

It was summer again.

The season of the sea witch.

And he was home.

LOOK FOR NEXT MONTH'S
CANDLELIGHT ECSTASY ROMANCES ®

Candlelight
Ecstasy Romances™

$1.95 each